Devil in A Suit

GEORGIA LE CARRE

Chapter One

IVAN

"Here you are, Mr. Ivanovich. I've narrowed the list down to five of the best properties in the market right now." Greta, my uber-efficient PA, hands me her iPad. "Each one offers everything you've specified for. Please press play when you are ready and the first video will start."

I tap the screen and a property advert comes on. A woman in her early twenties smiles in front of an open doorway. She has an American smile, big and full of optimism. I call it the US-Dollar smile. No Russian woman would ever smile like that. Russian women are too pragmatic. They know there are bears in the woods, the winters always come early, and the Government is not your friend.

"Sorry, that's not the property. That's just an advert," Greta apologizes. Her voice sounds slightly annoyed. Her whole life is an orderly, well-oiled machine and she hates it when even the littlest thing goes wrong.

"We are subscribed to the no advertisements premium

subscription," she continues. "This must be a glitch. I am sorry to waste your time, Mr. Ivanovich. Please click the skip button."

The button comes on the screen, but I don't click it. I am too mesmerized by the woman on the screen. My eyes eat her up as she walks down the narrow corridor of a cheap apartment.

"And here we have a spacious living room with a fantastic view," she lies shamelessly to the camera as she walks into a ridiculously small room. Only a cockroach would find that room spacious. She passes by the window she had claimed had a fantastic view and the outlook is literally a brick wall. Undeterred by the tawdry reality around her she sails through her sales pitch. Stylish, modern, well-appointed, central... The ease with which she lies through her teeth is impressive.

"Just press that little button on the right-hand corner that says skip," Greta urges, her voice flustered.

But I don't touch the button. The girl has entered a tiny brown kitchen where she starts to wax lyrical about how wonderful and cozy it is. Apparently, the prospective buyer can have breakfast in that cramped space while the sun shines in through the east facing window. She passes by said window and I nearly laugh. Even a jail cell would have a bigger opening.

"Here, let me press skip for you, Mr. Ivanovich," Greta says anxiously as she reaches for her iPad.

I look up. "I know how to press skip, Greta."

Her eyes widen and she straightens her spine. "Oh, okay."

I return my attention to the woman on the screen.

Something about her.

Something about her.

She leads the viewers to the bedroom and sits on the bed. Words are falling out of her sexy mouth, but I have stopped listening. My cock is rock hard. I freeze the advert and look up. "That will be all, Greta."

"Oh!"

For a few unguarded seconds, she looks at me with a confused expression. Then she takes a step backwards. "Okay. You can call me when you have finished viewing all five short-listed properties."

I nod and she turns away.

I stare at the woman in the video. "Who are you?"

I watch the advert all over again. Something powerful, deep in the pits of my guts starts uncoiling, waking up. It has been asleep for a long time, so it moves slowly, but it will not be denied. It will stop at nothing to get what it wants.

And it wants her.

I have never had such a visceral and instant reaction to a woman. What is even stranger is that she is not my type at all. Generally, I gravitate towards long-legged models with nomadic lifestyles. Having a woman willing to fly out to different locations in the world at a moment's notice is important to me.

I take a screenshot of her agency's name when it appears, then I watch the rest of the video. The second property is the only one that appeals to me. I press the button that brings Greta into my room, and she appears at the door almost instantly.

"Are you ready for me to arrange appointments for you to view the properties, Mr. Ivanovich?"

I hold the iPad out to her. "I want to view the second property on your list, but first I want you to contact the woman in this advert. She is to handle the entire purchase transaction."

She pauses momentarily, a strange expression on her face. If I didn't know better, I would think she is jealous. But I do know better. Then she moves forward, takes the iPad from me and looks at the screen where the name of the agency is displayed.

"Fitzpatrick &Co is not one of the better agencies in the city," she says stiffly.

I pick up my coffee mug. "The agency is small?"

"Tiny," she replies with a touch of disdain.

"So they could use the exposure and commission…"

"The property you are looking to acquire is worth more than a hundred million dollars. Her agency would not have the experience to handle such a sale."

"What is there to handle? I am the buyer. I know exactly how much I am willing to spend."

To this, Greta remains silent, contemplating my words.

"Two birds, one stone. The girl and the property."

Greta's eyes widen with shock. "You mean. Oh!" Then her face becomes blank and cold. "When would you like me to contact her?"

"As soon as we land. Schedule a showing with her before the week is out."

"Yes, Mr. Ivanovich," she responds promptly.

A couple of attendants in the lounge approach to inform us that my plane is ready. They take our bags and lead the way onto the tarmac towards my sleek dark plane.

I look forward to falling asleep on the flight. I'm exhausted after a week-long trip in Shanghai, so for once, I actually welcome the long flight back to New York.

Chapter Two

LARA

"Fuck. Fuck, fuck, fuck, fuck, fuck, fuck, fuck."

All of these are uttered quietly under my breath because it irks me to hear them out loud. Yet, as I stare at my ringing phone on the extended tripod hanging from the top of the ceiling, there is no other way to express my frustration.

I forgot to put my phone on airplane mode and now instead of recording me, it's ringing and interrupting me every single time I start the timer. Maybe if advertising on YouTube works out, I'll be able to buy some proper recording equipment. The call rings until it disconnects, and once again I reach up as best as I can, stretching my arm to its limit, holding tightly onto the stair railing so I won't fall, and press the record button.

I need this shot. It will make the house look so magical. I will stroll down, and the overhead shot will capture the beauty of this apartment. Yes, it's old and some people will think it is shabby, but for me, its charm is undeniable. It is my hope that I will be able to close the sale this month. My month so far has been rough, but with this listing, things are starting to look up.

The recording starts, and with a big smile, I begin to walk down the stairs, the steps creaking softly under my feet. But once again, my phone starts ringing, piercing the quiet.

"For fuck's sake," I scream.

There is no one to hear so I let rip. I wait for the phone to stop, leaving me with my frustrated image and the glaring red record button. I'm pretty sure it's only Derek from the office. The phone stops and ten seconds pass before it starts ringing again. Surely he won't call more than three times. Silence descends and I am sure that he has given up on me, but as I try to reach for the phone once again to start recording, yet another call comes in. My frustration boils over and I rip off the duct tape and answer the call.

"Are you freaking kidding me?" It is so noisy in the background, and I can't understand why.

"Derek! Stop freaking calling me; you're going to make me lose my mind."

"Why aren't you picking up?" he asks. "I've been trying to reach you."

"I'm working," I reply. "I'm freaking recording, and I need my phone, and you've been interrupting me for the past thirty minutes."

"I'm sorry, but this is a hundred times more important."

"What is it?" I ask, realizing for the first time how noisy the background on Derek's end is.

"Well, something big, really big has just happened at the agency, and your dad wants you back right now."

I frown. "What's happened?"

"I can't tell you why. It's a surprise."

"Look. Stop playing games with me, Derek, and just tell me. I want to finish this video before I get back to the office."

"Lara, I'm not kidding," he says. "This is serious and huge. You won't believe it even if I told you over the phone, but regardless, you need to get down here within the next thirty minutes tops. Plus, we've ordered pizza—the good kind, not the cheap stuff from around the corner. If you're not here, I promise you it will be gone."

"Derek, I don't care about—"

"Oh my God, just get here now," he snaps. "You can go back to your videos or whatever afterwards. Hurry up."

He hangs up then, leaving me staring at the phone in disbelief. He wants me to leave the video unfinished and go back to the office without even knowing why. The thought of wasting time commuting back and forth is stupid so I call my dad.

"Hey, Dad. Why is your office manager insisting that I get back to the office right now?"

"It's huge," he says excitedly, and once again I notice the ruckus going on in the background.

"What's happening?" I ask curiously.

"Just get over here right now. How far away are you?" he asks.

"Half an hour."

"Take a cab."

"Uh, we can afford cabs?"

"We can afford it!" he booms.

My eyebrows rise. "Really? Since when?"

"Lara, take a cab," he says and hangs up the phone.

My hand falls to the side. Wow! Something big must be happening. I leave my things as they are since I will have to come back anyway, lock the apartment, and head out. It doesn't take me long to find a cab, thankfully, but with the little late morning traffic, it takes me nearly twenty minutes to arrive back at our office.

Through the shop window, I see everybody gathered around the coffee table. My steps quicken because even though I've racked my brains during the whole journey here to imagine what this big mystery could be about, or why I couldn't just be told over the phone, I came up with nothing. Maybe someone closed a deal, a huge deal, but even that is no reason to be so dramatic.

I stand at the door, bemused. The atmosphere is wild. Everyone is smiling and chatting away with plastic flutes of what seems to be champagne in hand, though it's probably just cider or apple juice because we most certainly can't afford real champagne. Anna spots me. Waving, she hurries over and grabs me by the hand, pulling me in.

"The pizza's almost gone, but your dad saved you a couple of slices. They're in the fridge with your name on it. There's cake too."

This makes me smile. It's a small gesture, but it warms my heart because it is not often that my father is loving.

"Sasha's done it again," she says as we reach the fridge, "but for real this time."

Sasha is the lead agent in my father's company. While I am always struggling to even get a deal, she finds and closes them effortlessly.

"What do you mean for real?" I ask as I dig my fork into the slice of cake.

"She just scored a huge client. When I say huge. I mean ginormous, mahoosive... humongous."

My eyes pop open. "She sold a house? Where?"

"No, she hasn't sold it yet," Anna replies.

Now I'm confused. "Then why the celebration?"

"A Russian billionaire wants our agency to represent

him. The property in question is a seafront mansion in Southampton and it has a price tag of a hundred and twenty million. We couldn't even dream of landing a listing like this," she almost screams. "Do you understand now why we're all so happy and excited? Just think of the commission. That's like ten million shared between us and the seller's agency."

"Wow! That's fantastic," I cry. I'm impressed, happy and relieved, all at once. It means our agency can finally get into profit again. It was touch and go for a while there. No wonder Dad asked me to take a cab.

"Yes, it's wonderful. Just wonderful," Anna cries happily. "And we have Sasha to thank."

I glance around at Sasha. She is flicking her long shiny blonde hair back and laughing. Her face is flushed with happiness. A part of me wishes I could bring home the sale like her. She makes it look so easy. "I didn't know Sasha knew any billionaires."

"Apparently, she doesn't know the billionaire."

My head snaps back. "What?"

Anna shrugs. "Why else would they ask our agency to handle that kind of property? It's completely out of our league... unless it was a direct recommendation from one of Sasha's high-end clients, or even from one of her friends in the bigger agencies. It makes sense. She's Russian, he's Russian."

I reach for the plate of pizza. "Who cares why the job came to our agency? We really need this."

"Yes, we do. It's not going to be easy. I hear billionaires are a pain to deal with. I just hope and pray she'll be able to pull it off."

"She will," I reply. "We'll all help her as much as we can."

"Lara!" I hear a call from across the room and see my father. He looks even more giddy than everyone present. It has been months since I have seen him look anything even remotely close to happy, let alone this almost unhinged joy. Just earlier that morning, I had been concerned he wouldn't even come to work because he looked so blue and dejected. Now he is positively beaming and who can blame him? This is the light at the end of the tunnel for us. I run over to him and accept his bear hug.

"Oh, Dad," I whisper.

"You've heard?" he asks.

I nod and grin at him. "Yes, Dad, I've heard. I've heard."

"Okay, we're about to make the call now. To find out more details." He turns to the other staff. "Everyone, gather round and quiet down. Sasha, are you ready to make the call?"

"Yes, Mr. Fitzpatrick," Sasha replies.

I send her a happy smile.

Everyone gathers around and quiets down, and Sasha takes her seat with Joshua behind her shoulders for moral support. She says a quick, quiet prayer and then puts the phone on speaker.

It instantly begins to ring. It occurs to me suddenly that we have celebrated even before the negotiation call has even been made, but it is endearing nonetheless.

"Greta Schmidt speaking?" a woman answers. She has a cool professional voice and a strong German accent.

"Hello, this is Sasha Kuznetsov. I am from Fitzpatrick & Co. We were contacted earlier about a Park Avenue listing and given your number as a contact..."

"Ah, yes... I am Mr. Ivanovich's PA, and you will be dealing with me on this matter. He would like to schedule an appointment to view the property in question in the next two days."

"Next two days?" Sasha repeats and winces because she

knows it will take time to connect with the seller's agent and stage the house properly to show it at its best.

At this response, the lady goes briefly silent, and my heart jumps. As I look around, I can see the nervousness in everyone's eyes. Sasha most definitely doesn't miss this either.

"Is that not possible?" Greta Schmidt's voice is cold and disapproving.

"Of course, it is possible," Sasha says quickly. "It will be ready. I'm at your service. When would Mr. Ivanovich like to see it? Anytime at all. Even now."

Greta allows herself a small almost mocking laugh. "There are two spaces in Mr. Ivanovich's calendar. How does tomorrow sound?"

Sasha's eyes glitter with excitement. "Tomorrow is wonderful."

"What time?"

"3.00 p.m. sharp. Please do not keep Mr. Ivanovich waiting."

"We'll be ready."

"Good."

"Thank you," she says, and just like that, the call comes to an end. For a long minute, no one speaks or even moves, and then once again the entire office erupts into chaos—smiles, celebrations, and congratulations. I rush headlong into my father's chest.

Suddenly the phone begins to ring again. We almost miss it, but Derek is alert enough to yell for us to be quiet. Sasha scrambles for her phone and picks it up, clearly out of breath with excitement.

"Hello," she says.

"The girl," Greta Schmidt's voice says crisply, "the one that makes your advertisements and social media posts?" she says, and all eyes turn to me. I wasn't ready for all that attention because I'm doing what I never do at work. I'm leaning in a very unprofessional way against my father. I quickly step away from him and stand on my own.

"What about her?" Sasha asks as she picks up the receiver and takes the call off the speakers. I watch the light die from her eyes.

"What's happening?" my father whispers, but no one has any response.

"Holy shit," I whisper hoarsely. Maybe they saw my unprofessional, cheaply made videos, and decided we were a joke. "Have I just cost us this listing?"

"That can't be," my father whispers back, but his entire demeanor has changed. He even looks a bit white around the mouth.

Sasha ends the call.

"What did she say?" everyone asks breathlessly.

Sasha manages a smile, but I can see the terrible disappointment in her lovely eyes as she turns to face me.

"They want you to do the viewing, Lara. Not me," she says softly.

Chapter Three

LARA

t first, I'm sure I must have misheard her, but the shocked murmurings all around convinces me I couldn't have.

"That can't be," I laugh nervously.

My father smiles at me, and there is pride in his eyes. "They said they want the girl posting on our social media page and on our adverts. That would be you."

Well, of course, it would be me, I think. No one else wanted to be involved in my tomfoolery, even though I had constantly tried with every fiber of my being to persuade them that it was one of the best ways to expand our agency. Sasha actually thought it made our agency look less professional.

"You've got to go close the sale," Dad says with a big happy smile.

I let out a deep breath as the magnitude of what has just been dropped on my shoulders finally sinks in and I can't help but feel overwhelmed and scared. The fate of the agency and all the staff depends on this. I look at all the faces gathered around me with expectant hopeful expressions and then I look at Sasha. There is a frozen smile on her face, and I know instantly. She is expecting me to fail.

I turn to my father anxiously. "But, Dad, I can't do it. I'll screw it up."

"You won't screw it up. Sasha will help you," my father says firmly.

I shake my head. "Dad, I know you love me and you can't help but see the best in me, but the reason I do social media and the adverts is because I'm a terrible salesperson."

"No, you're not," he says loyally.

"Remember the Anderson family? They were ready to sign on the dotted line. What did I do? I started mentioning leases and stuff I shouldn't and they walked away from the deal."

"You were new then. You know better than to do that now."

"Dad, the showing is tomorrow," I wail. "Even if I was experienced enough, I know nothing about the property or how to stage such a high-end listing, let alone sell it to a billionaire."

My father frowns. The enormity of the problem is finally becoming clear to him.

"Maybe we can handle the sale together," Sasha suggests softly. She knows what I know. She deserves this listing, not me.

The light returns to my father's eyes. "Yes, yes," he says eagerly, "that would be the best solution. Both of you can work it together. Sasha can do the selling and you can smile a lot and offer to pour him a glass of champagne or something."

DEVIL IN A SUIT

I almost collapse with relief. "Yeah, that would work for me."

"Good. Good. There's a lot of preparation work to be done so, Sasha, make contact with the seller's agency straight away and arrange a meeting. I want to be present for the negotiation. And the rest of you, tie up everything you're doing and get ready to help get this show on the road. We need to get the keys of the property and make it look amazing."

I turn to Sasha and smile gratefully at her. She smiles back, but for a second it is the smile of a stranger, then her smile widens and the old Sasha is back.

"We'll split your commission in half. Fifty percent for me, fifty percent for you. Okay?"

"Okay." I nod enthusiastically. To be honest, I would have been perfectly happy even with a ninety percent ten percent split.

"The seller's agency is Astor and I know the top salesperson there very well, he is Russian too, so setting up a meeting for your father and me today will be no problem, but before I call them, I hope you don't mind if I give you a little advice."

"Of course. Please do."

"It would be really good if you can go out and buy or rent a nice professional-looking suit for the meeting tomorrow. Black or red."

I look down at the skirt and jacket I'm wearing and then back at her. If she thinks a suit could magically make me look like her, she's driving in the wrong lane. Also, my credit card is maxed out and my savings are meagre, to say the least.

"Here," Sasha says, writing something down on a Post-it note. "My friend owns this boutique. I will phone her and ask her to help you find a good suit. If we get the deal, you will buy it off her and if we don't, you will return it and pay her a small rental fee." She holds the note. "Is that okay with you?"

I take the note. "Yeah, that would be great. Thank you."

"Maybe you should visit the hairdresser too. I'll call my hairdresser. He'll give you a good discount."

"Oh... okay."

"And get a new pair of shoes to go with your smart suit. It's got to be high heels."

"Of course," I agree quietly. She is right. All my shoes are scuffed from running in and out of subways.

"Also wear some make-up. At the very least, lipstick, mascara, and blusher. Eyeliner would be a bonus."

I take a deep breath. "Sure. Anything else."

She smiles. "Perfume. Get something fresh and light."

I nod obediently.

"Oh, and I'll make an appointment for you to have a session with my nail lady tonight. She's Filipino and she does house calls. You need a manicure, and if your shoes have open toes, then a pedicure too. Would eight o'clock be alright?"

My head is spinning at the way Sasha has completely taken control of my appearance. "Yeah, I guess so."

She reaches for the phone. "Good. Have fun shopping."

I stare at her with surprise. "Uh, don't you need me here to help at all?"

"Nope. Everything here is under control. You have to transform yourself into a high-end estate agent by tomorrow and you don't have that much time." She begins to dial. I stand there stupidly for a few seconds more.

"Ivan, my darling," she coos. "You won't believe what has just happened."

She launches into rapid Russian and I turn away and head towards the door.

If I must transform myself to help close this sale, then transform myself, I will.

Chapter Four

IVAN

https://www.youtube.com/watch?v=QzXnz0pIbsE
-Vivaldi – four seasons - winter

Today, for some inexplicable reason, a memory from the time before I fell out with my father comes to me. It is more than a decade old, but time has not decayed or dimmed it in any way. It is crystal clear as if it happened yesterday. Everything; the sights, the sounds, the smells, the colors, and the emotions are still intensely vivid.

On my sixteenth birthday my father gifted me twenty percent of his stock portfolio to manage. Legally, I couldn't drink or drive, so it was an incredible show of trust and I was determined not to disappoint him. I studied the market carefully for six months, then I moved the entire twenty percent into five unconventional tech stocks. It was a risk, but a calculated one. In one and a half years I had tripled the portion I controlled while my father's main portfolio, managed by experts in London, showed a six and a half percent increase.

He called me to his study.

It was seven in the evening so there were dinner guests gathered in the music room. A pianist was playing Rachmaninoff as I passed by. The world outside my father's palace was covered in deep snow as it was in the dead of winter, but his study was warm and smelled of burning wood and sweet tobacco. I opened my mouth to greet him, but he raised a finger to motion for me to wait. He rose from behind his desk and filled two glasses from a bottle of vodka that was specially distilled for him in Bavaria. I could hear the logs crackling and spitting in the big fireplace as he raised his glass.

"Congratulations, my son," my father said and his voice shook. In the firelight his eyes shone with so much pride and love, my heart swelled in my chest.

Even though I was only eighteen, he let me keep the entire profit. It was that million and a half that became the foundation stone of my wealth. The castle in Scotland, the chateau in Nice, the one-hundred-and-thirty-foot yacht parked in Monaco, the planes, the garages full of flashy cars, the priceless art collection, the watches, even the Saville Row tailored suits on my back... everything can be traced back to my father's decision to not only trust me with so much his wealth but to then let me keep that first profit.

I wonder what my life would have been if he had not done that for me.

Now, as I stand before the floor-length mirror in my closet, I feel hollow and unsatisfied. Almost disappointed. Is this it? Where did the pride and love of that winter evening go? Never since that evening, have I felt the wonderful pure emotion my father and I shared. Infected by the lure of easy wealth, I have become a creature of the stock market; a pitiless, merciless money-making machine.

My heart is frozen.

There is no one I can trust not to betray me if the price is right. There is no one I love. And no one who loves me. There are no children to tuck into a warm bed. What I have are acquaintances and mutually beneficial relationships. They do something for me and I pay them for their service. As such they care nothing for me. And neither would I expect them to.

The hard cold truth is: I am alone with my money. And that is fine. My money will buy me any little compulsive liar I desire for as long as I want. Lara Fitzpatrick's image appears in my head. She is an unsophisticated nobody working for a failed estate agency, but something about her compels me to have her.

I've gone over it many times in my head.

Why her?

What is so special about her?

Her Irish heritage is clear from her milky skin, blazing blue eyes, and thick dark hair that she tames into a ponytail high on her head, but there is something fierce and tempestuous about her beauty. As if she belongs on a windswept moor, her hair running loose and wild behind her. And yet she wears her feral beauty carelessly. The way that a lone leopard sitting on a bare tree branch with a glorious sunset behind it does. So beautiful it wins its photographer a prestigious award, but it is totally unaware of its own exquisiteness.

To be honest, the craving for her astonishes me. My life is littered with beautiful available women, but there has never been one I simply had to have. Every one of them I could have easily turned away from and found an equally acceptable substitute for.

Not her.

There is no acceptable substitute for Lara Fitzpatrick. She is like a storm brewing in the sky. You can rage and rail against it, but there is no way to stop it. Already, I can feel my skin crackling with electricity. It is exciting and thrilling, but only a fool will not recognize that such a relentless hunger must be quickly attended to and completely purged or everything else will become meaningless.

I select a blue striped tie and begin to knot it.

In the mirror, my eyes glitter with excitement. I am really looking forward to this... negotiation. More than I have looked forward to anything for a very, very long time. Miss Fitzpatrick doesn't know it yet, but there is a service she can provide for me and in return, she will get what everyone wants from me. A nice chunk of money. A fair exchange. I will keep her until I get bored of her... a month should be more than sufficient. Then we will part ways and never meet again. That is my way. The way of a lone wolf.

I run a brush through my hair, grab my jacket, and head downstairs.

"Good morning, Sir. Breakfast is ready. Shall I serve it?" Muriel, my English housekeeper asks from the bottom of the stairs. She is wearing her customary black dress, and not a hair of her short iron-gray hair is out of place. Her face is, as always, stoic and expressionless. She is nearly four feet nine inches tall, but she is irreplaceable in my household. No matter where in the world I go, if I'm staying more than two weeks, she comes with me.

"Not today, Muriel," I throw over my shoulder as I stride towards the front door.

I hear the sound of her hard black shoes hurrying after me. "Will you be home for lunch then, Sir?" she asks just as the door is pulled open by one of my two bodyguards.

"No, but tell the Chefs to put a little more effort into dinner. I have a feeling I'll be particularly famished by then."

"Very well, Sir," she replies and steps back with a solemn nod.

I slip into the faintly perfumed backseat of my Rolls Royce. Vivaldi's Winter is playing softly in the background.

"Turn it up," I say to Nikolai and he meets my gaze in the mirror and turns up the volume. "More," I say until the whole car is vibrating with the sound of violins.

I have to admit that it feels good, really good, to be exhilarated about something. I haven't felt this alive for years. And so, I allow myself to look forward to meeting Miss Fitzpatrick. Perhaps she will be completely underwhelming to meet, and all of this time and effort would have been for nothing. If so, I will go back to wanting Muriel's breakfasts and expanding my blood, sweat, and tears to making money I don't need.

Chapter Five

LARA

"Let's look at you, then," Sasha says from the doorway.

I turn from the box of canapes that I'm carefully transferring onto a black lacquer tray and find Sasha looking breathtakingly beautiful. But when she comes forward, a slight frown is on her forehead. Her eyes critically inspect me from top to bottom.

"What's wrong?" I ask, touching my new bangs uncertainly. The hairdresser said I have the perfect heart-shaped face for bangs, but I'm not used to having a bunch of hair on my forehead.

Sasha takes a deep breath. "I didn't expect to see you in such a revealing outfit. I thought you were going for clean and presentable."

My eyes widen with surprise. Sasha is dressed in a red dress that can only be described as sexy, with a plunging neckline and most of her long slim legs on show too. She actually looks like she is on her way to a party or a club. I choose my words carefully. "Olga, the shop assistant at the boutique you recommended, helped me choose this suit. She seemed to know you well and she told me this outfit is what you yourself would have chosen for an important showing."

"Well, it looks a bit different on you," she says cattily. "Never mind. Perhaps you can button up your jacket."

I don't agree that my top is too revealing and I'm not at all happy about the condescending way she is looking at me, but I bite back the sarcastic retort bubbling in my throat and silently button my jacket. This deal is too important to poison the air with a petty argument.

But Sasha is not finished. She comes closer and plucks a single strand of dog hair off my jacket. Shaking her head with disapproval, she puts it into my hand. I force a smile and let my fingers close over the offending hair, before stuffing it into my jacket pocket. I couldn't resist taking Mrs. Winterman's impossibly cute German Shepherd puppy into my arms when we shared the elevator earlier, and I really thought I'd brushed myself until I was fur free, but apparently, I hadn't been successful.

"You'll be serving the hors d'œuvres. Show me your nails," she demands bossily.

I hold out my hands obediently, and she nods. "That's fine." Her eyes move upwards to meet mine. "Are you nervous?"

"Enough to shit my pants."

A small smirk tugs at her lovely mouth. "Don't worry you'll be fine. All you have to do is smile sweetly and let me do all the talking."

"Yup, I can definitely do that. Aren't you even a bit nervous?" I ask curiously.

"Not at all." She shrugs carelessly. "High-profile clients are usually the easiest to deal with. No fussy demands or protracted price negotiations. Ivan Ivanovich will probably spend ten to thirty minutes before deciding. His staff have already given him a rundown of why a property like this would be a good asset to acquire. Basically, he's just here to check out the aesthetic element and give the final stamp of approval."

I nod. "I put the champagne on ice an hour ago so it's ready to drink as soon as he comes in. After that, I'll get busy with serving the refreshments and stay out of the way so you can focus on doing what you do best."

Her gaze runs down my body. "Sure."

Sasha is deliberately being rude and I don't know why, but now is not the time to air grievances. "Right. I better return to my canapes."

"Ah... to be so rich that you could afford to buy a place like this," she murmurs and begins to elegantly twirl around the opulent room.

I watch the pretty picture she makes and say nothing.

She stops and looks at me with a wistful expression. "Do you ever dream of owning a place like this, Lara?"

I stare at her with astonishment. "No. Never. What would I do with 24000 square feet and three floors?" I shake my head. "I dream of old houses with cozy rooms full of charm and character."

"Really? I do. I've been seriously considering retiring from real estate altogether and just wooing one of my clients. I've just never been able to catch anyone at this level... yet."

I cock my head at her words. "Does this mean?"

She smiles a secret, rapt smile. "Darling, I didn't wake up at 6 a.m. to get my hair and makeup done and squeeze into this dress just to sell a house. Neither am I—"

She stops abruptly when a black SUV appears in the parking court outside, followed by a gleaming Rolls Royce.

Behind it, is another black SUV still on the driveway. My eyes widen. I had expected some show of money, of course, but jeez.

This is more like a James Bond entrance.

For a few seconds, we are both frozen, and then Sasha wriggles her shoulders before straightening her spine. "Showtime," she says with a hard smile and heads towards the front door. I too straighten my back, even though I know he can't see me. We have to be on out very best. I hang around next to the champagne bucket, wondering if I should pop the cork now.

From the tall windows, I see no movement from the Rolls Royce, but two big burly men in black suits jump out of the first SUV. They have Bluetooth buds in their ears and wear mirrored sunglasses. Their bodies are alert and look all around them warily as if they are trained special forces soldiers. Good lord! Two more large men get out of the second SUV. They split and start walking into the grounds. The first two come up to the front door.

Sasha opens the front door and I hear her speaking with them. I can't make out what they are saying from where I am standing, but the conversation seems curt and cold. A few minutes later Sasha starts walking in my direction, a sullen expression on her face. I know she is looking for me, but I can't understand why.

"Lara?" she calls impatiently.

I come out of the shadows and head over to the grand foyer of the house. Sasha smiles, but it is so painfully forced I almost want to ask her if she is having a stroke.

"No phones are allowed," she says flatly.

I can't help frowning. This is prime social media content. What a sly bastard. Still, I control myself and with a smile at the two bodyguards, nod in agreement. They do not smile

DEVIL IN A SUIT

back. They have not removed their sunglasses and their eerily expressionless faces remind me of the characters from the *Men in Black* movie. One of them holds his hand out, and under my bangs both my eyebrows nearly reach my hairline.

"Oh!"

"Yeah. Mr. Ivanovich insists on privacy," Sasha mutters.

It is then I notice her phone is in his hand. I switch mine off and hand it over. The MIB drops both into a plastic bag, seals it, and slips the bag into his jacket pocket.

"Should we go over to welcome Mr. Ivanovich?" Sasha asks and starts to walk towards the entrance, but one of the MIBs raises his palm to stop her.

"No, please," he says coldly. "Which of you is Lara Fitzpatrick?"

"I am," I reply.

He turns to Sasha. "The showing must be done by Miss. Fitzpatrick alone. Your services will not be required."

Hell freezes over in Sasha's eyes. "What?" she explodes.

I shouldn't be shocked, but I am. I know they did ask specifically for me, but we all thought it wouldn't matter if there were two of us doing the showing. It shouldn't matter. I don't understand what is going on. She is Russian, and he is Russian. Wouldn't he prefer to have the viewing done while speaking in his mother tongue? What reason could this man have for insisting I do the showing myself?

I can feel my stomach cramping with panic. The plan was for me to do as little talking as possible so I spent no time learning about the history of the property or the important and interesting architectural stuff connected to the house. Only bits and pieces of what I'd heard Sasha say hangs around in my head. If he asks me for any details at all, I'm going to look unprofessional and sloppy. Besides, who will pour the champagne and serve the canapes?

"I am not the lead estate agent," I blurt out.

"This is not a negotiable request," the man replies indifferently.

If it's not negotiable, then it's not a request, is it, I think sourly, but obviously, I don't say my thoughts out aloud. I make a face at Sasha.

"He's watching from the car," Sasha mutters fiercely under her breath, her expression and demeanor are now as hard as stone. "Control your expressions, be polite. Knock this out of the park. Remember, half of the commission is mine."

"Yes." I swallow. "Yes, of course."

"I'll walk down to the beach and wait for you there." She gives me one last flinty look before she walks away. I watch her stiff back disappear from sight and it doesn't feel real. Nothing feels real. My hand flutters to my stomach. I am shaken, nervous, and stressed all at once.

One of the men says something in Russian. Instinctively, I know that he is signaling to someone in the car that the coast is clear.

Slowly, I turn around and look out of the windows. The chauffeur is pulling open the passenger door of the Rolls Royce, and my gaze is riveted on the client as he is revealed in pieces.

First, sleek dark shoes attached to a tailored charcoal trouser leg. Then a head of dark unbelievably lustrous hair. A side profile of a clean-shaven man. Already I can make out he is beautiful and broad-shouldered. And supremely confident. Suddenly, he unfurls fully and I catch my breath.

No way!

This must be a prank. Billionaires are supposed to look like Warren Buffet and George Soros. Fat, old, money-obsessed workaholics. This man is ripped like freaking Tarzan. His green gaze meets my staring eyes through the glass window.

And our eyes lock. I can't move a muscle. I find myself struggling to breathe. I watch him the way I imagine a rabbit paralyzed by sheer terror watches a python slither quietly towards it. It knows it's going to be crushed and swallowed whole, but there is not a thing it can do about it. It can only shiver helplessly as death comes.

His eyes never leave mine as his long legs stride forward relentlessly. It's like watching a movie in slow motion. The wind catches his glorious hair, lifts it, and drops it. Wow! God sure gave him plenty. His gaze never leaves mine. I don't move forward. I can't. For a moment my view is obscured by a column, and I am able to blink. Still, I can't move. It is only when I catch the unimaginably expensive whiff of his cologne that I know I've nearly fucked up this sale.

Needing to rectify this, I take a deep breath and lift my foot intending to take a step forward, my hand extended. Then he comes back into view. Bigger and bolder than before. And I don't know how or why, but my foot catches on nothing and my knees give way. I collapse to a crouching position on the floor. Shit. I stare at the granite floor. So highly polished I can see the reflection of my horrified face on it.

As I stare at my face with dismay, a sleek dark shoe comes into view a foot away from me. The python has arrived. I close my eyes. Oh shit.

Don't fuck this up, Lara. It's not broken. Just start again and everything will be fine.

The whole agency is depending on me. My father is depending on me. I have to persevere. I'll just offer him a glass of champagne and take it from there. Everything is always better with champagne. I open my eyes and raise my head slowly, my gaze travelling the long length of him. And that slow journey becomes my first mistake of the morning.

I reach his eyes and my heart... stops.

Chapter Six

IVAN

It is true that I have played a few scenarios in my head of how our first interaction will go, but never could I have dreamed of this. Her, prostrate at my feet. This is perfect. Her face is upturned, her eyes are enormous. They are exactly how I imagined them to be. Full of stormy passion. Her mouth is so full it is like a ripe-red fruit.

Begging me to take it.

I know then: she is not the girl with flowing hair wandering alone on the moors, she is the wild and unpredictable moors itself. Her cover of beautiful purple flowers hides the countless men she has blinded in thick fog and buried in watery graves on her marshes.

She is dangerous, but I'm not afraid. I want to be one of those men. Buried inside her.

I stare at my find almost in disbelief. God, she is beautiful. Much more beautiful in person. To think I entertained the thought she might be underwhelming. The breathing living Lara Fitzpatrick is more sexy, more mesmerizing, and more

DEVIL IN A SUIT

delicious. I want to reach out and stroke her head. I want her lips to be wrapped around my cock.

But instinct tells me we are natural-born enemies. Ice and fire, black and white, predator and prey, and never the twain shall meet. She knows it too. I see it in her sapphire eyes. She is not going to come easily to me. It will be a fight, but I enjoy a good hunt. An elusive prey. I will have her. No matter what.

"Hello," she whispers.

"Are you planning on staying down there for the rest of the viewing?"

She jumps up with an embarrassed smile. "I am really sorry about that. There are marbles on these floors. I swear. Invisible marbles."

In real time I watch it click in her head that she is supposed to be selling me the house, not turning me off it. She freezes like a cartoon character. It is an indescribably fuckable little quirk.

"No. Wait," she says quickly. "I didn't mean the floor is slippery or anything like that. It is a perfectly good floor. Perfect... mid-century stone. One of a kind." She snaps her mouth shut suddenly and takes a deep breath. "The thing is, Mr. Ivanovich, I'm not as knowledgeable about this house as my colleague Sasha. And the best part is she's Russian too so I'm sure you'll be more comfortable with her. She's waiting on the beach for me so if you'll just wait one minute I can get her and we'll do this viewing with the both of us."

"I can understand and speak English, Miss Fitzpatrick," I say dryly.

She swallows hard. "Yes, Mr. Ivanovich. Of course, I didn't mean to suggest you couldn't I, uh... It's just that I wanted you to be as comfortable as possible."

"I'm comfortable in six languages, Miss Fitzpatrick," I say, turning away from her to look around the house. I find I have very little interest in it. The subject of my interest is behind me.

"Six? Wow! My apologies. I just wanted to give you our best."

I turn around to look at her. "And you're not it?"

She blinks. "Can I get you a glass of champagne, Mr. Ivanovich?"

"No, Miss Fitzpatrick. I don't usually start drinking until later in the day."

"Right."

She has obviously been caught unawares. Clearly, she was expecting to be a supporting role and not the one taking center stage. I wonder what she would say if she knew that I don't care whether she utters a single word about the house or not. I am going to buy it as long as she gives me what I want.

What would Miss Fitzpatrick say if she knew what I am really here for?

Chapter Seven

LARA

He folds his arms across his chest and waits for my answer, but I am too gobsmacked to respond. Unable even to think straight. Everything about him stuns and disturbs me.

If only I had gone online last night when I got home and researched his name. Found out what he looked like. I will have been somewhat prepared. I will not be standing here gaping at him like a small-brained goldfish. But I was so tired yesterday after running around all day helping to stage this property, and it was well past midnight by the time I got home.

Now as I stand before him tongue-tied and awkward, I remember Sasha talking to someone on the phone about a green-eyed eye candy. No wonder she got all dressed up for this hunk. It explains why she looked at me this morning as if I was not her colleague but the competition.

Start again, Lara. Just start again.

I clear my throat and work up a bright happy smile on my

face, but instead of smiling back his dazzling mossy-gold eyes watch me intently.

"Uh..." I shake my head to clear it, almost sure by now that I have already lost the sale, but I am determined to try. Even though I cannot for the life of me imagine selling anything to this man. I take a deep breath and step forward, holding out my hand.

"Let's start again."

He takes my hand, but a jolt of electricity sparks between us as soon as our hands touch and I pull away quickly in surprise. His eyes narrow and my heart sinks. I am making a total mess of this viewing. Everything has gone wrong. I've even messed up the handshake. I take a deep breath to calm myself and my nostrils fill with the scent of his cologne or aftershave.

It is a complicated sophisticated smell. The smell of great wealth. My mind files the spicy scent under Distracting And Poisonous because my brain starts malfunctioning. To my horror, my mouth starts sprouting complete nonsense.

"The foyer makes for a grand entrance, doesn't it? And just look at this beautiful flower arrangement. I got it from the flower shop around the corner from our agency. They make amazing arrangements. I can give you their address and they can come and change the flowers weekly, and it'll be the first thing you see when you come down the stairs. Flowers are an instant mood brightener."

His eyes widen slightly and I snap my mouth shut. Oh my God. What a disaster. Now I know for sure I am completely done. My job is to show the house, not the damn flowers, but even though I have glanced through Sasha's notes about the property, not a single piece of information about the many special attributes of the house comes to mind.

With a frown, I look at the stairs then, trying to remember

what I can say about it beyond grand and gorgeous and tall... really tall, just like you, I want to climb you and...

I turn away from him, shut my eyes and wonder if this is a result of the bang to my head I took last week when I fell off a ladder while trying to film a video. It must be a delayed reaction. I almost want to cry. I swallow hard. Very soon he is going to lose interest and walk away. I can't do this to my agency and to my father. I can't fail this monumental task. I would never be able to forgive myself. Even if I had to go on my knees to beg him to buy the house, I would, but I sincerely doubt kneeling down to get someone to buy a 120-million-dollar house has the potential effectiveness of minus zero. At that moment I hear Sasha's voice in my head. Half the commission is mine. And just like that, I snap out of whatever disease has caught hold of me.

I turn to him then and force myself to look directly into his eyes. I am so close I can see the gold flecks in them.

"The stairs are one of the most beautiful aspects of this house. Made with black Caracalla marble slabs and hand-carved rosewood with a daring backdrop of salmon pink and European art. The magnificent chandelier up above is one of a kind. Fifteen thousand pieces of crystals and the main lamp was specially blown in Italy. Murano to be exact. Have you ever been there?"

"I have," he replies quietly. "Have you?"

"No, Mr. Ivanovich. I'm a Brooklyn girl and I usually don't venture further than Manhattan." The second the words come out of my mouth I realize how unsophisticated I sound. And it makes me realize how strange it is that he has chosen our small and struggling agency when there are bigger agents in the city who can probably give him a much better service. Why did he want us? And why me specifically?

"Murano is overrated, Miss Fitzpatrick," he says. "You're not missing out on much."

"Oh!" A nervous laugh erupts from me. "Their craftsmanship though, with this chandelier and the other lighting fixtures in the house, is breathtaking. I'm not saying they were all made in Italy, but they're all very unique and specially crafted."

"So you've said," he mocks, and I want to bury my head in the granite.

"Let's move on to the living rooms." My cheeks are hot as I turn and start walking away from him. "There are four, but this one is the loveliest. You have a fine view of the sea, and the glass walls almost make you feel like you're outdoors. The sea is calm now, but in winter you could curl up here all cozy and warm with a glass of whiskey and watch the lightning and thunder break all around you. Wouldn't that be wonderful?"

He doesn't respond.

I choose to take that as a blessing. If he doesn't speak, I can pretend that he is not behind me and I am the only one in the house. That is the only way I will be able to form coherent thoughts and get through this nightmare of a viewing.

And so I keep talking, and as my focus returns, I am able to remember more details about the house.

He remains silent and I become even more intrigued by him. I have no choice then but to look frequently at him, needing to check if he is bored by my chatter. But it seems as if I am the main focus of his attention.

Chapter Eight

IVAN

I don't give a rat's ass about the house.
And if she is clever, she must already know that. If I had no interest in her, I'd have walked out by now. Nothing she has said so far has made the house more appealing to me. She is a terrible salesperson. I have a day of meetings ahead of me, so I get right to the point.

"Show me the master bedroom, Miss Fitzpatrick."

She whirls around with surprise, and something shifts in my chest. I ignore it and hold her gaze, but I have to admit I have never met a man or a woman who affects me the way she does.

"Master bedroom? That's on the first floor, Mr Ivanovich." She tries not to frown, but she knows skipping the rest of the tour to go straight to the master has to be a very clear indication that I don't care for her presentation.

"Yes. That's what I want to see, Miss Fitzpatrick."

She nods. "Of course." I watch the sway of her hips as we head up the 'black Caracalla marble and hand-carved rosewood staircase with its daring backdrop of salmon pink and European art'. Her hands tightly grip the bannister. She opens a pair of double doors, walks in, and stands in the middle of a spacious bright room. Her body faces away from me.

We are finally completely alone. No bodyguards, no prying colleagues. Just the two of us—my desire and her nerves.

I look around me. It's a good bedroom with a stunning view of the sea, but I have no interest in anything but the painting over the bed. It is so appropriate it almost makes me laugh. I turn my attention back to her. She is staring at the floor silently. No doubt, she believes the sale is lost.

"The painting over the bed. Tell me about it," I invite.

Her drooping head snaps up. She looks at the painting and I see the dismay on her face.

"I'm sorry, I... I don't know anything about it, but I can find out for you. I'll just make a quick call to Sasha. I'll just be two minutes. If you—"

"It's from the legend of Leda and the Swan," I interrupt. "When the Olympian god Zeus coveted a Spartan queen called Leda, he took the form of a swan and... ravished her." I move closer to her. I can hear her shallow breathing. I can smell the fresh fruity scent of her perfume. "Do you see her soft white nape caught in his bill, Miss Fitzpatrick?"

She exhales slowly and nods.

"Look at those puny terrified fingers pushing at the feathered glory of a God in swan form, but mastered by the great wings, caught up by the brute blood in the air, she is helpless. He caresses her widening thighs and enters her violently... by the time his indifferent beak drops her he has impregnated her with twins."

She turns to me, her eyes wide, her mouth parted. "Why did you ask me about the painting if you knew all about it?"

"That is not the question you should be asking?" I ask.

"What is the question I should be asking?"

"Why did you end up here alone with me in this bedroom?"

"Why?" Her voice is hoarse, but she doesn't cower away.

"Because I covet you."

Her mouth falls open with shock. "I think I misheard you."

"You didn't," I say, slipping my hands into my pockets.

"Oh." Her eyes widen. "Oh," she says again in disbelief. "That is why you specifically asked for me?"

"Yes," I reply.

"Um..." She begins to pull at her collar as though it is suddenly too tight. "I'm sorry, Mr. Ivanovich," she begins. "I mean, I'm not sorry. I'm incredibly flattered, but I'm just. This is just so—"

"You're not interested?" I ask softly.

"I..." She is so shocked and astonished it is quite entertaining to watch. "I think I'm going to need some time to... er... process your...er... interest."

"That's fair. There's no rush. You know how to reach me when you have processed my... er... interest." I turn around to leave, but she stops me with a shout.

"Wait!"

I turn around, one eyebrow raised.

"I'm sorry," she says, frowning. "For yelling... But I just need to clarify something. You don't actually want to buy this house, do you?"

I smile. "I do."

"Oh." She stares at me with confusion.

Chapter Nine

LARA

Being this close to him is mind-bending. I feel off-balance. Almost dizzy. The whole situation is surreal, to say the least. Like a dream. Everything is outrageous. And nothing makes sense. My gaze won't leave his lips. I can't believe how soft and flushed they look. They are the perfect shape—not too thin and not too big—just enough for me to wonder what it would feel like if I just leaned in and tasted them, felt their softness against mine.

Jesus! What is wrong with me?

"I just want to get this straight, Mr. Ivanovich," I say, trying to keep my voice steady. "What you're really saying is that if I agree, pardon me if I'm wrong or mistaken, and if I am, I apologize profusely, but are you trying to say that if I get involved with you, you will buy the house?"

I wait for his response with bated breath.

I don't think I have ever waited for anything this intensely or nervously before, except maybe when I was checking my emails repeatedly for my SATs and college entrance acceptance letters. I was convinced my entire life hung on those results, and it feels the same way now, as though my entire life henceforth hangs on whatever his answer will be.

"Yes, Miss Fitzpatrick," he replies sardonically.

The shock is unbelievable. Can he really be serious? Heat rushes through my whole body and then I am suddenly afraid because I have to suspect then that he is insane. Who spends that kind of money because he fancies a girl? Maybe this is what all billionaires do.

"You're willing to spend one hundred and twenty million on a house based on a whim?" I croak in disbelief.

He takes a step closer and I start to tremble like a leaf in a storm. I think of Leda. Her puny pale fingers pushing helplessly against the glory of the swan and its great wings. I can't help it. My eyes swivel towards the painting and he laughs darkly.

"I'll let you in on a secret, my Spartan Queen. To a very rich man money is meaningless. If everything has a price and money is worthless, it means everything is essentially free."

I stare at him, speechless. How did I come to be here? This is not my world. In my world money is in short supply. All the people I know scrounge around every day just to pay the bills and put food on the table. But this man is turning my world to ashes. He is willing to spend the GDP of a small country to sleep with me of all people. Why me? I am not glamorous, sophisticated, or insanely beautiful like Sasha. He reaches a hand out and rubs his thumb along my lower lip. The skin of his thumb is soft. He has never done a day's hard work in his life. Something I have never felt stirs deep in my belly. It is like a clawed hand. Moving, gasping, strong. Its strength astonishes me. It starts a fire inside me that no one else has ever ignited.

I want him!

With every fiber in my body. I want my body to entangle with his. I want him inside me. The world outside ceases to exist. I forget that Sasha is waiting on the beach. I forget that what is happening should be classed as crazy. All I know is the rush inside me and the emptiness in my body that only he can fill. My mouth opens and seeks his.

I don't know what would have happened if a lone seagull flying close by the floor-to-ceiling windows had not made its high-pitched cry. The shrill screech jolts me out of my hypnotized daze and I jump back with a shriek. My hand slaps over my horrified mouth.

"I'm sorry," I mumble, but I don't know what I am apologizing for.

"Sorry? Don't be. I want you and I'm willing to pay a hefty price for you."

His words are like a bucket of cold water over my head. The strange desire for him disappears and I feel only fury. How dare he? Who does he think he is? I have never in my life met someone so presumptuous and arrogant. He is beautiful and rich on the outside, but his soul is so ugly and poor. I'm not for sale.

"No offence, Mr. Ivanovich, but I'm not attracted to you," I say coldly.

Chapter Ten

IVAN

Good. She is offended, but I want to offend her more. I want to push all her buttons and see what comes forth.

"Why are all estate agents such liars?" I goad softly.

"What the hell is that supposed to mean?" she growls, throwing her head back proudly. Her eyes flash and she transforms from the meek little assistant, falling over, and babbling nonsense to a splendid tigress. If I thought her beautiful before, now I think of her as absolutely riveting. I can't take my eyes off her. In fact, for the first time in my life, I can barely hold myself back. I'm losing control.

My hand curves around her waist. She catches my wrist and tries to push me away, but it is impossible to budge me unless I want to be moved. She realizes how futile it is to struggle and stops.

"Poor Leda," I murmur.

"How dare you?" she spits furiously.

"Don't you want a taste of what you are rejecting, Lara?" I ask.

Her mouth opens in shock. "No. Let me make myself crystal clear. I wouldn't sell myself to you if you were the last man on earth."

I laugh. "Very original, but purely out of interest, what is your price, Lara?"

She flushes. "I don't have a price."

"Every woman has a price. Anything from the price of a few drinks all the way to a ring on her finger. I expect you have a very high sense of propriety. And this is why I am prepared to spend such a hefty sum to ensure that you know I am not propositioning you because I think you're cheap. On the contrary, I understand your value, and I want to indulge in it"

"I don't have a price," she says frostily. "Are you planning to force me?"

I smile. "No. Even though I know you will enjoy it."

"You're insane," she shoots back, eyes glittering, but I notice she has forgotten to fight back. Her hands are almost caressing my chest. I wonder if she can feel just how hard it is racing because of her.

"I notice you didn't call me a liar though."

She says nothing. Just stares up at me with those amazing sparkling eyes. They burn with blue fire and tell me a whole different story than her tongue is.

"Your colleague is just about to come into view. We don't want her thinking you have a price, do we?" I let her go.

She has to sit on the bed to be able to catch her balance again, and it quite pleases me, I have to admit, to see her so flustered... so undone. I will see her naked and flushed on my bed. Sooner rather than later.

"I'm sure you have an impossibly busy day ahead, but perhaps tonight when you are lying in your bed alone you will put aside your bruised ego and reconsider my offer. There is much to gain and nothing to lose. It will be a brief liaison, but you will enjoy every minute of it. See it as a reprieve away from your current life. Everyone needs one from time to time. This is your opportunity. You have my secretary's number."

I stroll out of the room. All I have is her scowl and shock and fury, but that fills my lost soul with satisfaction.

As I reach the bottom of the stairs through the main open-plan living room, I see her colleague waiting on the patio. She smiles at me. Beautiful woman and she understands the game. How easy it would have been if it was her I wanted and not the spitfire upstairs. I nod at her and head out towards my car. My phone begins to ring, and I ignore it because I don't want to spoil the delicious high I'm feeling.

Alexei pulls the front doors open for me as soon as he sees me approaching. Not until I am in the car and well on my way to the office do I pull my phone out of my pocket to see who called. I see Greta's name on the screen and frown. Before I call her back, she calls again.

"What is it, Greta?"

"I'm really sorry, Mr Ivanovich. You did inform me that you were taking the morning off, but a very urgent matter has just been brought to my attention and I thought I should inform you immediately."

"I'm listening."

"I just heard from Liam in the Paris office and Solov in Moscow has confirmed this information as well. It seems the National Crime Agency in London has asked the United States government to participate in their investigation into your affairs. Looks like your case is already on the table of the KleptoCapture Task Force."

My mood instantly plunges from fantastic to annoyed. The desire of Western governments to harass innocent but wealthy Russians in order to show Putin who is boss is getting tiresome. I'm not an oligarch, my wealth is not from ill-gotten gains, I have no political connections with the ruling power structure in Russia, nor have I dealings with her criminal underworld and yet I am being investigated like a common criminal.

"Why?" I ask, irritated.

"I don't know what damning information they think they have on you or where they are getting it from, but it seems whoever has been feeding it to them is also promising them that there are financial links to politicians in the U.S. It's been confirmed as of this morning that a new investigation has been opened against you by the Department of Justice."

I look out of the window, unseeing. Damn them to hell. I am certain this witch hunt is linked to my family. I'm not them, but the inquisitions just keep coming. They will never find evidence for any of these wild accusations. They won't because I have never bribed a politician in my life. Why would I? I've never needed the help of those corrupt creatures to make a buck. So they will never find anything, but perhaps they don't really need to—they just want to make a splash, drive fear into the other Russians who do have something to hide and frustrate me in the process. Bastards.

"Do you know who is dealing with it?" I ask

"David Madley from the US Attorney General's office," she replies.

I can't help but scoff. "Madley from the Southern District?"

"That's the one. Solov thinks it might be a good idea to set up a meeting with him, but I wonder if perhaps it would do us good to pretend to not know about their probing for the moment. This way it wouldn't seem as though we are on our guard."

I consider her words. "I'm going to go with Solov on this one. Arrange a meeting with him for later tonight. At the club perhaps? I have a feeling he'll like it there."

"What reason shall I give him?"

"Just tell him that it is high time we catch up."

"Alright, I will."

"About Miss Fitzpatrick..."

"We're still looking into her and her family, but something rather interesting has come up with regards to her father that you might be able to use as leverage. I will send you a report this evening."

"Good," I reply and end the call.

Chapter Eleven

LARA

I feel like I've just survived an explosion, and yet somehow, despite the chaos, in the dead silence, I am still alive and breathing. I haven't moved from the spot he left me in, and where his skin has touched mine still tingles. In a daze, I turn to look at the painting and I see it from a completely different light. Leda's pale naked body half hidden by the swan's great wings. Her fair thighs open... Oh God!

I jump when I hear Sasha's voice calling me. In the silence, the sound is loud and jarring causing me to spring into action. I really don't want to think of any of this because truly I need time to process what has happened to me in silence, but she has taken the opportunity of this away from me.

I scramble up and walk quickly towards a mirror. I look strange. I can't have Sasha seeing me looking so flustered. Taking a couple of deep breaths I calm myself down. Then I head for the stairs. Sasha is standing at the bottom of the stairs looking at me with a strange expression.

"Hello," I say as coolly as I can.

"I saw him leaving. It's a huge house so I expected him to have stayed longer. What happened?" she asks, her voice filled with surprise and curiosity.

I reach the bottom of the stairs and start moving towards the kitchen. "Yeah. He uh... left."

She follows me closely. "Yes, I can see he is gone, but that was awfully fast. Did everything go well?" She knows perfectly well that everything didn't go well.

"I didn't think so."

Next to the champagne bucket, I see our phones still in the plastic bag. As Sasha retries her phone, I grab the champagne bottle and pull it out. It drips water on the expensive marble surface.

"Why? Didn't he have any questions?"

I pop the cork. "Not really."

"Is all lost?" she asks impatiently. I can't blame her one bit for being irritated or annoyed with me after all the effort we put into this viewing, but I really don't know what to tell her. In order to save my ass, of course, I'm tempted to mention the real reason why everything went south, but I really don't want to. Not until my dad hears from me first.

I fill two flutes and hold one out to her.

"What are you doing?" she asks with a scowl. "It's clear we're not celebrating."

"We're drowning our sorrows," I say grimly.

She can no longer hide her disappointment and her voice is full of blame and accusation. "What did you do wrong?"

I take a big mouthful of freezing-cold bubbles. "Everything, Sasha. I got it all wrong. From the start to the finish. I'm really sorry."

She puts her glass of untouched champagne down. "Why are you behaving so strangely? Can't you just tell me how the whole viewing went? I just want to know where we went wrong."

Where we went wrong? That's one hell of a story. I drain my glass. Wow, champagne hits hard on an empty stomach. I already feel a little drunk. And already Mr. Ivanovich seems like a dream that never happened.

"There's nothing to tell. I don't think he wants to buy this house. He had a busy day ahead of him and he had to leave suddenly." I reach for a canape and pop it into my mouth. It is supposed to be lobster moose on a savory saffron biscuit, but it tastes like mud on my tongue. I reach for another and Sasha pulls the whole platter out of my reach. I look up at her.

"You don't think? So he hasn't actually said no to the property?" she asks hopefully.

I sigh. "No, he hasn't said no outright, but I'm pretty sure he's not interested. Sorry, Sasha. I know you worked at this."

"Stop fucking apologizing," she explodes. "And just fucking tell me what happened from start to finish. Because if he hasn't said no, then we're still in the game. Men like him have an impossible schedule. Look how early he requested this showing. It shows he probably has an impossible day ahead of him and this is the one moment he could find to come and see the house. Of course, you shouldn't have let him go without agreeing on a fixed date for another appointment, but that's okay. You're inexperienced at this. We Russians are quite stoic as a people. We don't show much emotion on our faces. It is possible he's still interested in the property, but since, as you say, he didn't show much interest, he probably just wants it as an investment and not a residence."

There are a lot of probablys in her line of thinking, but I say nothing. What can I say? What I have told her is sort of the truth. Knowing her and what she had hoped would happen between her and the billionaire the truth will be even more unpalatable.

"Let's follow up with his secretary tomorrow. She did say that I could contact her when and as needed."

"Alright," I say, and for some reason this makes me feel childishly relieved even though I am very well aware that it is pointless for Sasha to call his secretary. He has told me in very explicit terms exactly what he wants—me in exchange for purchasing the house. I shouldn't have considered his offer for even one second, but for a few revealing seconds I did entertain it, and as we head back to the office it is clear to me why.

Because for those few seconds, every fiber in me wanted to say yes. I have never wanted to say yes more in my life. If I had met him in a club I would have gone home with him without a second thought. If he had not made sex a condition, it would have been an easy yes. A very easy yes.

Sighing, I stare out at the skyline and the beautiful city and can't help but feel even sadder despite the fact that the sun is out. Everyone will be expecting good news and now they will get the news that Sasha wasn't allowed to do the viewing and I had fucked up, but because I am the boss's daughter, they will be forced to hide their feelings and only be able to gossip amongst themselves about my incompetency. I hate the idea, but there is nothing I can do. Just as we arrive, I turn to Sasha.

"Please tell the others what's happened. I have to go to my father."

"Um..." she replies. "I'm not sure I know exactly what the story is."

"It's just like I told you. He had a busy day and had to hurry out and it is unlikely that he will buy the house."

She looks irritated. "Why do you have to give up so fast?

He hasn't said no, so as far as I am concerned, there is still hope and that is what I'll be telling everybody."

My phone rings suddenly and as I retrieve it from my pocket, an errant thought flashes into my brain: is it him? The instinctive thought and surge of excitement that comes with it bothers and maddens me. I hate to admit to entertaining even the slightest twinge of hope that he is on the other end. He is an insolent, presumptuous, misogynist brute with money to burn and there is no walking back from that. Wanting anything to do with him would be insane.

I tell myself that I am just checking in order to be on guard and once again communicate that any further insistence on his part will be met with legal action. That I'll sue him for sexual harassment. I have no idea how I would go about doing such a thing, but the idea seems apt and plausible. That will teach him to go around trying to buy unwilling women. A little voice in my head laughs at the idea that I was unwilling, but I banish the irritating voice. I see my dentist's name on the screen and the forbidden thrill inside me deflates instantly.

I confirm my appointment for later in the week, then head over to my father's office, but just as I knock on the door he pulls it open.

"Hey," he says with the biggest smile on his face. "I heard you guys were on your way back. I was about to come out to meet you."

His eyes are sparkling and alive in a way that they haven't in a very long time. I know about his difficulties and how worried he has been about keeping this place open, and my heart plunges at the thought of giving him the bad news. Behind me, I can hear Sasha giving everyone the less than enthusiastic news and I can feel the excitement in the air drop.

"Hey, Dad."

With his hand on my arm, he pulls me into his office.

"Don't do that," I say. "You know I don't want you to treat me differently than everyone else."

"Fuck them," he replies and looks at me intently. "Have you been drinking?"

"I had a glass of champagne."

"At this time of the morning?" He frowns. "What's wrong? You look like a smacked puppy."

I stare into his anxious eyes. What do I tell him? The truth so I can take the blame off my shoulders right now? Or the same story I told Sasha so I can have a little more time to think about what to do next? It isn't that I am considering the offer, it's just that I don't want to let everyone down. Especially my father. Even the thought of seeing the light go out of his eyes fills me with dread.

I swallow hard. "Nothing is wrong. Mr. Ivanovich had to leave midway through the viewing. Sasha's going to contact his secretary."

"Well," my father says, relief in his voice. "That's not too bad. Things happen and he's a busy man, but more importantly, what impression did you get? Did he seem to like the house? Was he bummed to have to leave without finishing the tour?"

I hate lying to my father and desperately want to tell him the truth, but I just can't. Crossing my fingers, I give him a version of the truth.

"I got the impression he liked what he was looking at," I reply slowly.

"So why does everyone out there look like someone just died?"

"I guess they expected Sasha to close the deal today, but I was doing the viewing and I couldn't—"

He frowns. "You were doing the viewing? The plan was for Sasha to lead. What happened? Why didn't she?"

I shrug. "He wanted the viewing done with only one person. Me."

My father raises his eyebrows and looks at me speculatively. "How strange. I would have thought given that they're both Russian he would have been more comfortable with her. How was he in person? I did a bit of research about him last night."

"Oh! I wish I had."

"Well, he comes from Russian nobility, old money. Apparently, his father is an acquaintance with Putin and at some point, he has ties with the Russian Mafia, but to all intents and purposes, his son is legitimate. He made his fortune as a celebrated trader extraordinaire. So young yet so accomplished." He grins. "I've been seething with envy all night."

"As if," I reply.

"No, really," he says with a laugh. "The man is quite amazing. What did you think of him?"

"I uh... I'm not sure what to make of him yet. I think I'm going to get back to work. I have some videos that I filmed for some apartments and I'd like to edit those and get them out."

"Sweetheart, about those videos—"

"Not sweetheart," I correct. "We're in the office and we talked about this. You have to stop seeing me as your daughter."

"You have no idea how impossible that is, but okay, Miss Fitzpatrick."

I give him a look, and he smiles.

"What about the videos?" I ask.

"Instead of spending so much time on them perhaps it's time for you to go along with the other more experienced salespeople. You need more hours under your belt of closing sales. You've done a good job so far but experience in sales is matchless, and you're getting very little of that if you're focusing mostly on media."

"Media is crucial too, Dad. Otherwise, we can never really grow. Plus, I think it is high time we stopped pretending that I can ever be an accomplished salesperson. Let me do the media for you and let Sasha and the others do the selling, okay?"

He raises his hands. "Sure, honey. No pressure. Just do your best, okay? Doesn't matter what happens, we'll be okay. Let's talk about it this evening when we go out to celebrate."

I stare at him unhappily. By not telling the truth I'm just leading him on. Giving him false hope. I feel almost on the verge of tears. "The deal isn't done yet. There's nothing to celebrate. And to be really honest, Dad, I am pretty sure there's no deal to be had there. It's a lost cause."

He studies me, the hope replaced by doom, then smiles a forlorn twist of his lips. "You're right. It's always a bad idea to count your chickens before they are laid, but let's not lose all hope."

For the rest of the morning, I avoid everyone and pretend to be too busy editing a video to be able to stop and talk. At lunchtime, I go for a walk alone. As I become one with the bustling crowd of people around me, it is impossible to believe that this morning a Russian billionaire had made sleeping with me a condition before he would spend a hundred and twenty million on a house.

But it happened.

An hour later without having had anything to eat, I go back to my desk. There is a black box tied up with a broad cream ribbon. Even the box looks expensive. There is no card attached, but I know instantly it is from him.

"A courier dropped it off," someone says.

My hands are shaking as I tug at the silky ribbon. I open the box and deep in tissue my hand encloses around something hard and cold. Grasping the thing gently, I pull my hand out and look at it.

A swan. A beautiful exquisitely blown glass swan.

"Wow, that's gorgeous. Who sent that?" Tessa asks.

"An old friend," I say and put the swan back into the box. When Tessa turns away I throw the box into the bin next to my desk. Then I pick up my bags and run to the subway as fast as I can. I need to get home for some peace and quiet and, of course, the only sounding board I trust not to be biased in helping me try to figure this out.

I am two stops away from home when I get off the train and hop on one going in the opposite direction back to the office. No matter how hard I tried, I couldn't bear the thought of the cleaners throwing away that beautiful work of art.

That swan is mine.

Chapter Twelve

IVAN

"*We're joining with European Allies to find and seize their yachts, their luxury apartments, their private jets. We're coming for your ill-begotten gains.*"

U.S. President Joe Biden, 2022

I walk into the exclusive Crocodile Club right on time, 10.pm. sharp. It definitely was a genius idea to meet at the club, because the Southern District Attorney wasn't exactly reluctant to meet when he heard where it was to be held. You have to be a billionaire to be a member and this will probably be his only chance to see the interior of the Crocodile Club.

My conversation with him is important. It won't decide whether I lose all my assets and end up behind bars, but I'm hoping it will shed some light on why I'm being investigated.

"Good evening, Mr. Ivanovich," one of the provocatively dressed hostesses, slinks over to me with a smile. "Your guest has not arrived yet. Would you like me to take you directly to your private room or would you prefer a drink at the bar first?"

"Private room," I say.

"This way please." She walks ahead of me. Her outfit has the high neckline of a Chinese Cheongsam, but suddenly stops halfway down her round ass. It is pure bait and while I appreciate the lure, I know I have it bad for Lara because I am not the least moved by the sight. Not even a twinge.

Turns out Lara's rejection of my advances only makes me want her more. I'm not really surprised by that. Nothing gives me a raging hard-on like a difficult challenge, but what does surprise me is to learn the lengths I will go to, to get what I want. Lara has just brought out the monster that has been living quietly inside me. For the moment it seems as if there are no lengths I will not go to have her. Perhaps, if I had not held her in my arms and felt her heart flutter like a caught bird. Perhaps, if her eyes had betrayed her...

Under the chandelier the crystal glasses and gold cutlery on the table glitter and shine. The hostess pours me a glass of my usual Scotch and slinks out. The good thing about this club is the way the staff are discouraged from engaging the clientele in banal conversation. I look at my watch. I have read Greta's file on David Madley. He is young, ambitious, hardworking, and unfortunately too idealistic. Probably why he hasn't been selected by the right money connections yet. He is also always on time. The fact that he is three minutes late sends a very clear message that I am more than able to interpret.

He is the one in power and he would like me to squirm in my seat.

I take a sip of my drink. That's one thing I'll never do. Squirm for him. The only person who has ever made me squirm is Lara Fitzpatrick. Like mustard on a worm, I'm twisting hard. There is a knock on the door and I look at my watch again. Only five minutes late. He has already lost the power struggle.

"Enter," I call.

"Mr. Ivanovich," he greets quietly as he heads in.

He expects me to stand, but when I remain seated, he smiles and takes his seat as well.

"My apologies for being late," he says. "I don't usually come to this part of town, but I do appreciate your invitation. Hopefully, we'll be able to put the opportunity to good use and get some progress out of our meeting."

"A drink?" I ask.

He looks towards the hostess, his eyes roaming her curves. "I'll have whatever Mr. Ivanovich is drinking. If it's good enough for a billionaire it's good enough for me."

The hostess pours him a drink and walks away. His eyes watch her ass as she leaves. He turns towards me when the door closes. "Nice girl."

"There are more like her upstairs. I will take you up when we are done here if you want," I say casually.

His eyes become sharp with interest. He hides it by looking down into his whiskey. "Thank you. I will take up your offer, Mr. Ivanovich."

"Call me Ivan," I invite.

"I've read up on your impressive success story, and always thought we could be friends, but of course, we move in different circles."

"And yet here we are in the same room having a drink together."

He takes a sip of his drink. "Yes, but only because you believe I'm about to dislodge you from your exalted circle."

I smile. "No one can dislodge me. Not even the Department of Justice of the United States of America. Even if they succeed in unjustly stealing everything from me, in a few years, I will be again sitting in this club, in this room, and you, the representative of the unfair monster, will still only be a guest here because of my benevolence. And that is because this is where I belong, David."

"What a shame for you then, that your real problem is your roots. Which means you will always be fighting the monster."

I know exactly what he is referring to. "You're referring to the assumed ties I have with my family?"

"Exactly. You're from a royal lineage, from a dynasty spanning all the way back to the last emperor of Russia. While you claim that your illustrious family has nothing to do with your businesses or your source of wealth, I find this hard to believe."

"Is that why you're investigating me?" I ask. "Because my family is rich and you don't believe that I'm a self-made man?"

He laughs. "This is the land of opportunities and capitalism, so I will not say you had absolutely nothing to do with your immense success. In fact, I don't care whether your family contributed or not. Hell, I wish I was from a bloodline like yours; being poor is not all that it's cracked up to be."

I take a sip of my drink. "Poor? You're the DA of New York."

He watches me keenly. "True. Some days I feel like a king, and other days, well... more like a bug that can be crushed by people with raw power in higher places than me."

I lift my gaze once again to hold his. "What of now? How do you feel?"

He smiles slowly. "I feel like a king, Ivan, and I will feel even more like one once I get upstairs."

I smile back. "In that case, I'll not make you wait much longer. Let's get straight to my case. What excuse are they using to look into my affairs?"

"The same reason the French and British are coming after you."

"Because I am Russian and I am rich?"

He has the grace to look uncomfortable at the truth. He clears his throat. "Unfortunately, you invested in Chinese steel. Your steel, Mr. Ivanovich, builds our bridges and buildings. We can't have them being subpar. That's an unthinkable loss coming our way even if it's two hundred years from now."

As if anybody in the political sphere gives a damn what happens in two hundred years. All of them only care about what happens during their tenure, but I don't voice my thoughts. "Yes, I'm one of the investors in those steel companies, but you know as well as I do, that the US can't embargo me because of a problem of quality control."

"As you yourself said, it is their excuse. But a head's up. This is just the beginning. The real problem is the persistent rumors. Rumors of political intrigue in high places..."

"Who is purporting these rumors?"

"You surely don't expect me to reveal my sources."

I study the man. "I have done nothing wrong and you know it. Not only that you have absolutely nothing on me, but I have something on you."

"What do you mean?" he asks warily.

"You dream of being the higher power, or running for higher office, don't you? What is it? Governor? Mayor? You'll need backing and funds. Lots and lots. But no one will back you because you are principled and refuse to be corrupted. I am very open to being your ally. All you have to do is ask."

He stares at me, and then he smiles. "You wouldn't be trying to bribe me, would you?"

I chuckle. "You are smarter than that, David. We can be friends or enemies. I do not have reason at this very moment to consider you an enemy, but the ball is in your court."

"This meeting started out friendly and I'd like to conclude it in the same manner. As long as I find nothing untoward in my due process, I will owe you one courtesy call to warn you ahead of time if the bureaucrats decide to move against you."

"For that, you will never again have to feel like a bug," I promise.

"And they will never beat you. You are where you rightly belong. I see that now," he says softly.

Chapter Thirteen

IVAN

Closing the PDF Greta sends me, I delete it from my phone. I lean back against my car seat and stare out of the window. What I am going to do is cruel. Very cruel. I have never done anything like this before. And if I do it there is no going back. She will hate me violently, but... I will get what I want. Is it worth it? The answer flashes into my head, clear and definite.

Yes.

Yes, it is worth it.

I think of Lara's fingers unwittingly caressing my chest while her mouth says no. Yes, I can live with her hate. I want only her passion and that instinctive, animalistic need I saw briefly in her eyes. I know she wants me. The only thing standing between us is her pride and a stupid sense of propriety.

In the background, Violetta, the tragic fallen woman in *La Triavata* is singing, 'Nothing in the world matters except pleasure. Let's enjoy ourselves. Love is a flower that blooms, dies, and is gone forever'.

The car comes to a stop outside a shop in a rundown area in Brooklyn. There is graffiti on the half-closed roller metal shutters. A hooded man jumps out of nowhere and comes forward. Alexei and Igor do their thing and he finds himself suddenly trapped between them. I get out of the car and walk towards them. The man turns out to be very young, no more than nineteen, but his eyes are shifty. He has spent his whole life in the slums and knows only to cheat, lie, and steal.

"You here for the game?" he asks.

I nod.

"This way, bro," he says. He seems nervous, but that is on account of the intimidating size of Alexei and Igor.

I follow the youth down a narrow steep concrete staircase into a dingy basement where an illegal gambling club has been set up. Dice in the front, blackjack and poker at the back. I walk towards the back. There are already five men seated at the table. Everyone looks up at my arrival. They are waiting for me. I am the whale, the mark. They think they are going to skin me for anywhere between sixty to a hundred thousand dollars. Alexei and Igor stand at the door. They face outwards because the danger is not from the gamblers, but from the masked robbers who come in with guns. I take a seat at the table with the men. Three I can see are the degenerate gamblers, the losers, and the other two are the sharp professionals. They nod at me, but their eyes give nothing away.

A heavily made-up woman in a tight dress comes up to offer me a drink.

"Scotch on the rocks," I say, even though I have no intention of drinking anything in this establishment.

"Are we all ready to start?" the dealer asks.

I put my first thick wad of cash on the table. The only

person who blinks with greedy surprise is Lara Fitzgerald's father.

We start to play. The professionals make sure that three degenerates and I win for the first few rounds. They are carefully persuading us to be careless and overconfident. Lara's father's face is flushed, his eyes are glittering, and there is a sheen of sweat on his skin. He is exactly as Greta described in her report: gambling addict by night, doting father and real estate company director by day. He asks for another glass of whiskey and leans forward eagerly. He thinks he is on a winning streak.

And he is. He wins the next game. "Excuse me, lads. I need a bathroom break."

"Me too," I say and stand.

As he walks to the urinal, I watch him dispassionately. He seems lost and disconnected. A flawed man drowning under the weight of his own addictions. As unbelievable as it seems, his coping mechanism is to double down on his compulsions and hope they will get him out of the very troubles they got him into.

Some part of me feels sorry for him and for what I am going to do to him tonight. A trusted inner voice that I've always listened to, cautions that I've never played so dirty before and once I walk down this twisted sinful corridor, the door will close behind me, and I will never be the same again. But even that warning doesn't deter me. The need to have her is greater than the fear of damage to my soul. I tell myself that should all go according to plan, they will both come much better off than they are now.

"You can do this," her father mumbles to himself as he pisses. "Don't screw this up. This is your last chance."

"Good game?" I ask.

"What?" he asks, looking in my direction. His face is pitiful. A mixture of pain and desperation. I realize he holds his drink well, but he is actually already quite drunk.

"Lady Luck is smiling on you tonight, huh?"

"Yeah," he replies, but strangely shakes his head as if even he can't believe his own assertion.

"Then why so glum?"

"Because I'm bad with numbers," he mutters. "I messed up and now I'm trapped, in too deep, lost too much, owe too much. Can't pay my debts. I can't get out of this sinking world."

"Why are you gambling even more?" I ask.

"Don't know what else to do. This is my last hope. I have to get myself out of this crushing debt. And I need to do it fast, or else I will start losing everything by the end of next week. The house, the car, the agency, everything... so many lives are going to be affected, especially—especially my baby girl's." He shakes his head. "It's bad. It's bad."

"Maybe you'll win it all back tonight."

He zips up and heads over to the sinks. "God knows I want to believe that, but the stakes are too small and my winning streak won't last. I need a few big wins and then I'm out of here forever. I'll never look back, I swear it. This is it for me."

"I'm happy to increase the stakes," I say, "but are you sure you can handle it?"

"Are you serious?" His head has snapped around, and his beady eyes are suddenly full of fire. That he is an incurable, degenerate gambler is finally undeniable. Unless he gets some serious help, this man will never stop gambling. The door to the forbidden corridor creaks open and I step into the velvety darkness. It doesn't feel wrong. On the other side is Lara and her hate and her beautiful passion.

"Yes," I reply. "How much do you owe?"

Suddenly his eyes narrow. "You look familiar. Have we met before?"

No doubt he's seen photos of me in a suit and in his befuddled state doesn't recognize me with a basketball hat on. "No, we've never met."

He looks at me challengingly. "Are you good for a quarter of a million?"

I nod. "Stanley will vouch for me." Stanley is the guy running this scam.

"That's good enough for me."

"One game. We'll play for your debts. If you win, I'll pay off all your debts, if you lose you owe me a quarter of a million."

The fog and desolation clears, as if by magic from his eyes as they nearly pop out of their sockets. He is suddenly alert, excited, and supremely confident. To him, there is nothing like the rush of playing for everything with someone he has seen lose the previous few games.

"Well then, let's go play," he says eagerly and starts walking ahead of me.

I look around at the other gamblers in the room. They are nothing but little fish—an eyesore. I send a message to my guys guarding from outside the room. A few seconds later, they appear at the door, huge and intimidating, and in an instant, the room feels claustrophobic and cramped.

"Excuse us, gentlemen, but this table is now closed. Please leave the room," I say calmly.

The two professional gamblers stand instantly. They are here for easy money, not trouble, but one of the degenerates who has had too much to drink looks at my men, and starts to puff up. He still has money in his pocket and he wants to carry on playing. He starts to protest, but I don't have the time or the patience to engage with him. Alexei steps forward and glares down at him. When the man starts to stand, Alexei clamps down hard on his shoulder. The man flinches and cries out in pain.

Alexei steps back.

The man massages his shoulder and looks confused. Everyone grumbles, a few curse words slipping through, but they all rise reluctantly to their feet. The room empties and a heavy silence settles.

"I'm ready when you are," Lara's father says.

Chapter Fourteen

LARA

The doorbell rings and I hurry out of the kitchen, spatula and apron in hand. I open my front door to Leila. She has a bottle of wine in one hand and a covered dish in the other.

"You said you wanted to talk, so I assumed we'd be staying up late. I brought my famous sweet potato pie and a bottle of Italy's finest. At least that's what the guy minding the shelves at the store told me. One bottle is probably not enough, but we both have to go to work tomorrow, so I had to, very sadly, force myself to only stick to one."

Smiling, I move out of the way as she sweeps in.

"Oh my God! What is that wonderful smell?" she asks heading towards the kitchen.

"It's just me. I've been baking scones," I reply as I shut the door behind her and hurry back towards the pot simmering on the stove.

She looks at the spread of food on the kitchen table. "Have you been cooking all evening?"

"Yeah."

"Why? There's enough here to feed a whole country. Wait! Good God, are you pregnant?"

I scrunch my face. "What? Why would your mind even go there? You know I always cook when I'm tense."

"Holy shit, this must be serious stress then," she says, trying to find a space on the crammed table to put her pie on. She goes to the drawer and retrieves a corkscrew. "I guess we better start drinking."

"Alcoholic," I tease.

"At this point, I can't even argue. I'm so harassed at work, last week I considered replacing my coffee with neat vodka."

"What?"

"I'm kidding, calm down."

"You better be," I reply.

She starts to pour the wine into two glasses while I put the lid back on the pot and head over to sit next to her. She pushes over one of the glasses, and then she instantly downs more than half of hers.

"Wow! Is your work that stressful?" I ask.

"How stressful could managing a store be?" she asks. "It's not, it's just... I don't know, I think I'm bored. I want a change. I'm looking for other options, but nothing really appeals to me, but not to worry, I'll figure it out. Maybe I'll become a wine connoisseur or something."

"I think those jobs are mostly for people who have an interest in wine but aren't addicted to it."

"Very funny. Still, we're here to talk about you, not me. Tell me what's wrong."

I take a small sip. The man stacking shelves was not wrong, the wine is good. "You'll find this hard to believe. I don't think I quite believe it myself, but I had to show a billionaire client a house today."

Her eyebrows fly upwards. "A billionaire client instructed your agency? Wow!"

"Yeah, I know, but that's not the unbelievable part."

"What do you mean?" she asks, leaning closer.

I tell her everything, every detail. From start to finish. Afterwards, she stares at me, her mouth wide open. I point towards the swan. "And that's the swan."

She walks towards the crystal piece and stands looking at it. "Fuck me. That is some expensive shit," she says in an awed voice.

"I did warn you it was hard to believe," I joke weakly.

She holds up her hand to silence me and for a few moments, neither of us speaks while she processes my situation. When she finds her voice again, she is shooting from all cylinders. "On a scale of one to ten, how ugly is he?"

I pick up my glass of wine and take another sip. "Actually, he's quite... dishy."

She walks back to the table and looks sideways at me. "What's his name?"

"Ivan Ivanovich."

Wordlessly, she pulls out her phone and googles him. I wait for it. A few seconds later her scream nearly tears down the walls of my tiny apartment.

"Holy fucking shit!" she yells. "This guy! This guy wants to pay you to sleep with him. That's fucking amazing."

"Leila, I can't believe you! That's not amazing at all. He wants me to prostitute myself to him—"

She looks at me like I'm crazy. "Are you kidding? I'd sell both of us for a hundred and twenty million dollars."

"That money doesn't go to us. It's for the owner," I correct dryly.

"What percentage does the agency get?" she asks crisply.

"I don't know. I haven't calculated it, but it'll be more than I've ever earned in my whole life."

She laughs incredulously. "Seriously. What are you thinking of? What's the problem here? We've both dated guys who weren't even one percent of the man this guy is, and we gave it up for them. I mean, I love you, you're my best friend and everything, but honestly, you're stark raving mad if you don't take him up on his offer. Jesus, Lara. This is like a once-in-a-lifetime thing. Nobody else is going to come along and make this offer again. If you don't take it, you'll always regret it."

I stare at her with surprise. "Wow, I really thought you'd—"

"That I'd have some reservations about sleeping with Russia's version of freaking Adonis?" she cuts me off impatiently. "Hell, I'd be jumping in there with both feet. What you need to find out is why you have any reservations about going for it. I know I'd do it even if there was no money involved."

I consider her question and don't get a clear answer even though I have not been able to get the intriguing and infuriating man out of my mind successfully for even a few minutes since he made his offer.

"Look. Be honest. If we'd met this guy on one of our girl's night and he came up to you and asked you to go home with him, what would you have said?"

"Yes," I admit readily.

"There you go," she cries triumphantly. "It's just sex, Lara. Both of you are going to have a great time, but this time around, you also get to help your father get out of debt."

"Can you not just casually say that," I say. "He doesn't know I know anything about his debt. I found out by mistake when I was trying to pay one of his bills. It's not really all that much, but if he knows I know, he'll be ashamed and devastated, and I don't want to do that to him."

"He's not here, is he?" she mocks. "Anyway, I think the problem is bigger than you know. The last time I saw him, it didn't look like it wasn't really all that much, your dad looked like he had the weight of the world on his shoulders. You shouldn't pretend with him, Lara. It's getting to be a serious problem."

"It's just a bit of gambling," I say defensively.

She raises one eyebrow. "And the drinking?"

"He doesn't do it during the day," I say feebly. "And I will intervene, but just not yet. He's going through a hard time right now, with the business being the way it is. It'll be better once this period is over."

She looks at me, and then she sighs. "People hide just how bad things are from others—you do know this, right?"

I pick up my glass once again and drain it. "Yes, I do. It's always been a problem. I can remember one time when I was eight years old and my father had gambled away his whole salary and my mom was so furious she refused to cook any food for him for a whole month. The problem has got worse since mom passed away. I will tackle it, but I just don't want to go in there all guns blazing, I want to do it right, Leila, and not make it worse."

"Okay, I trust you. Now, let's get back to the rich, drop-dead gorgeous asshole. Jeez, I love the idea of him. Can I have him?"

I grin at her. "Yes, if you're willing to share the money…"

"Oooo yes. You know I will." She stops and becomes serious suddenly. "Listen, Lara, I know I'm giving you a hard time about saying yes, but you don't have to. You've always been more proper and careful than me, and you've never just given yourself to anyone. And I've always respected that. It's an admirable quality. And right now, you're only considering this offer because of the weight it will lift off your dad's shoulders, but I don't think he would want you to do that for him. Especially, if it will mean you will lose something important to you."

I nod slowly as her words grind into my head.

"Maybe, the debts are not as bad as I think and if you keep working hard with your videos and ads soon enough, you'll be rewarded and the money will come pouring in."

"Oh God, if only."

"Why not? You know me, always looking for the quick, easy fix to my problems, but you're not like me. You're always wary about the easy way out. That's probably why you feel so unsettled about this."

"Yeah," I reply. "Maybe."

She pours us both another glass, then she clinks hers against mine. "Let's just chalk this up to some cool story we'll talk about in the future when he dies of an incurable STD and ends up in the news."

At her words, something twists inside of me. I stand and walk to the oven. Opening it I take the scones out. "I don't want him to die. He was—he wasn't rude or horrible."

"I'm hungry." She gets up and heads over to the stove. "Mmmm, beef stew. You make the best stews."

I finally make my decision. I put the tray of scones down. "I won't do it," I blurt out.

At my bold announcement, she turns around a piece of beef in her fingers and nods her approval. "Good. That's awesome. You stuck to your principles. Now let's eat Irish stew and be poor together."

Laughing, I join her by the stove, but halfway around the

counter, my phone starts ringing and I freeze. My heart starts pounding. I meet Leila's gaze. She too is frozen in the act of taking cutlery out of the drawer.

"That's him, isn't it?" she whispers, her eyes wide with intrigue.

"He doesn't have my number," I whisper back.

"Well, answer it then," she orders.

I feel incredibly stupid as I scramble around frantically looking for my ringing phone in amongst all the food, but as soon as I note that the caller is not one of my contacts, my heart is in my mouth.

"Hello."

"Lara." The way he calls my name... smooth, commanding, unmistakable. And my mind goes blank. I cannot believe he is actually calling me. I thought, no, scratch that, I almost believed it was all an improbable dream. That I would never see him again or even hear from him for that matter.

Leila is making faces so I turn away from her and try to put myself in order. My skin is already prickling with anticipation and excitement, which is mad because I've already decided I want absolutely nothing to do with him.

"I'm in an illegal gambling club in Brooklyn," he says.

I wonder why he is telling me this, but I am glad he is, because I can add it to the things I find unattractive about him. I want nothing to do with anything illegal. "Well, uh, good for you. Enjoy yourself. Good night, Mr. Ivanovich," I say, prepared to hang up, but his next words shock me into fearful stillness.

"And I've got your father with me."

"What?"

"I'll send you the address. I believe you're not far away. This is not my kind of place so don't be long."

The call gets disconnected abruptly and seconds later my

phone pings with an address in Brooklyn. I look up at Leila and I feel my world is spinning out of control.

"You'll have to eat by yourself, Leila."

Chapter Fifteen

IVAN

"Was that my daughter on the phone?" Lara's father asks incredulously.

"Yes," I agree calmly.

"How do you know her number? I do know you, don't I?" he asks, his voice sharp with accusation and new fear.

I look at the man before me, and can't help but feel a twinge of pity for his sorry ass. At how low he has come. He would never believe it now, but my unwelcome intervention in his affairs may be a blessing in disguise.

"Who are you? You didn't randomly pick me, did you? You know who I am and you did this on purpose," he shouts furiously, his voice rising higher with every new allegation.

"I didn't make you lose it all away. You did that all on your own," I tell him, keeping my tone flat and emotionless. The point is to make him believe there is no point in attempting to appeal to my better nature because I have none. What I want from them, they will never willingly give, even if I pretend to be the nicest person in the world. So there is no point in being cordial. It will only make them think they can defy me, that perhaps it's a good idea to try and test their luck.

"You bastard!" he shouts, slamming his hand down on the table. The sound echoes around the bare walls of the room, but it doesn't affect me at all. He stares at me with hatred as if I've stolen his entire world. Even though it was already lost to him. He doesn't know I am the only one who can give it all back to him.

"Mr. Fitzpatrick," I say, exasperated. "I never pegged you for a sore loser."

"You sent for my daughter," he says, his voice cracking with impotent fury. "How dare you?"

He is getting tiresome. I glance down at my watch. Lara should be here soon.

""Why the hell are you bringing my daughter into this?" he roars.

"Because," I reply, keeping my tone calm and even. "This situation has nothing to do with you. It's all about her and you are just someone standing in the way."

He looks completely confused, his expression one of astonishment. "What do you mean? What are you talking about?"

"Let's just wait for Lara to get here. I'm sure she'll explain everything to you."

He shakes his head. "No. No. The game was between the two of us. If you want things to remain cordial between us, you better rectify it now and tell her not to come."

I cock my head, watching him closely, truly astonished by his naivety. It's like he's unable to comprehend what's happening right in front of him. "Mr. Fitzpatrick," I say calmly, my voice as steady as ever. "Given the losses you've suffered, I don't think you should be giving me any orders. It amazes me that you are. Where is this confidence coming from? Tell me. Please."

I watch the man closely, noting every shift in his expression. He's trying to keep his composure, but he's barely managing it. He stares at me, unable to speak further, masking the fact that he is close to tears with that rigid, furious face.

"You lost everything tonight," I continue relentlessly, my tone blunt. "I even warned you to stop, but you didn't listen. Your house, your business, even your car. You should have stopped when you realized just how good I am, or after you confirmed it the second time. Instead, you bet even bigger, putting not just your life, but your daughter's, and all those who work for you in jeopardy. You put yourself in this mess with your addiction, and now you're about to drag everyone else down with you."

The man sits there, seething, but unable to refute a single thing I've said.

"I'm not your enemy. I'm just a man who wants to help."

"Help? What do you want in return?" he asks, glaring at me, his face flushed red, a mix of fear and near panic etched into his expression.

I lean back, settling comfortably into my chair, a smile on my face. "Your daughter knows what I want. Only she has the power to save you now."

Before he can respond, there is a knock on the door. I nod and Alexei steps forward to open it. It's the waitress from earlier. Behind her is Lara. She looks both worried and furious, her hair is disheveled. I can already see it on a pillow flowing underneath her as she writhes under me.

"Dad!" she calls as she hurries into the room. She throws a glare in my direction before turning her focus back to her father, clearly demanding an explanation, unsure whether to be alarmed or relieved.

"You're fine?" she asks him.

This makes me laugh softly. "What did you think I was going to do to him?"

She checks her father's face and his arms, her worry evident. There's something about the concern in her eyes that makes me stare, a flicker of recognition. There is real love there. They are both struggling, but the deep bond between them is clear. I envy that. I know I will never have it. I learned a long time ago that people in my position will never know if the people around them are there for love or for the benefits.

It was a hard lesson to learn, but it has served me well.

"What's going on here?" she asks, straightening. She glances at the men in the room before her gaze locks back onto mine, her eyes sharp and unyielding. "This has now entered the territory of harassment, Mr. Ivanovich, and I swear to God, I will not let it go. I don't care how rich you are."

I stare at her. Her face is scrubbed clean, and the slip of white lace she's wearing underneath is probably from a nightgown tucked into joggers. She threw on a denim jacket on top in her rush to get here.

"What is happening?" she demands. "Why are you harassing my father?"

I turn to the man and give him a pointed look. "Do you want to explain, or should I?"

He glowers at me once again before shifting his full attention to his daughter.

Chapter Sixteen

LARA

"Sweetheart," my father begins. "I might have gone a bit overboard tonight with the gambling."

The suspicion that has been brewing and forming in the corner of my mind finally bubbles to the surface. I stare at him, blinking hard, my voice is barely audible. "How much have you lost?"

He hangs his head.

I have never seen my father hang his head, no matter how bad things have gotten for us, and the fact that he's doing it now breaks my heart. It's as if everything is crumbling around us, and I can't catch the falling pieces.

"I'm in debt," he mumbles, his voice so low I almost can't hear him. "The market's been slow and hard, and I've had to borrow to keep things going... to keep everyone paid."

His voice drops further, almost to a whisper, and I lean even closer, placing my hand on his shoulder. He stares at my hand for a long time before he can continue. I turn my back on the bastard behind me. I won't give him the satisfaction of seeing how low my father has fallen. No matter what he will not get what he wants from me, even if I have to fight tooth and nail to ensure it.

I go close to his ear and ask, "Was he cheating?"

He whispers back in my ear. "No, to be fair, he wasn't cheating, he was just completely unpredictable. He folded when I expected aggression, and he bet when I least expected it. He made moves that defied traditional strategy. When I thought he was losing he went all in." He shakes his head as if in a daze of disbelief. "Was it intuition over mere mathematical calculations or just pure magic? I don't know. I don't even know where this guy comes from?"

"I'm sorry. I'm so sorry… I ran out of places and people to borrow from. So… this was the route I tried. It was the only way. I won, I lost, I drank, and I came back… after the loss today, I just… we won't make it until next month, sweetheart," he sighs, the weight of his words pressing on both of us.

I look into his eyes and nod. "It's all right, Dad. We'll figure it out."

He shakes his head sadly, brokenly. "No, we won't. Not now. The payments on everything have been late now for months, but it still might have been okay… if I hadn't run into him… it's all his now, Lara. All gone. All of it… gone."

Suddenly, I feel unable to stand the smell coming from my father, the reek of alcohol mixing with his total defeat. I straighten and look down at him. He is broken. Totally. My heart feels heavy with sadness. I know it is partly my fault. I knew there was a problem, but I buried my head in the sand and hoped it would sort itself out. Well, it didn't.

"The two of you are quite audacious," the man behind me interjects with breathtaking arrogance.

"What?" I snap, feeling the sadness evaporate and fury take its place.

"You are both acting like I committed a crime when all I did was win at poker. Why exactly am I the villain here?"

"Because you've taken everything, you bastard," my father yells, his voice cracking with emotion. "You've taken every single thing I own."

"No," he replies coldly. "You'd already lost everything before you sat in front of me. You really thought you could just win a quarter of a million at a gambling table?"

My head is spinning. Jesus! This guy is talking about a quarter of a million dollars! What's really going on here? Is that what Dad owes him? My first reaction to the enormity of the problem is instinctive and irrational. To flee: run: never come back.

"Dad, we need to leave," I say urgently.

"Good idea," the Russian taunts. "Leave and I'll sell your debt on to the Russian mob. They're very good at collecting from the unwilling."

"That is illegal," I flare back.

"So is not paying your debts."

"We'll figure it out somehow. Just leave us be."

He looks at me curiously. "You have no idea how much trouble your father is in, do you?"

I swallow. "We don't need your help."

"All you have to do is say yes, and I will make all of this and even more, go away."

"You can't just go around buying people."

"I can't?" All traces of amusement disappear from his face.

I clench my hands into fists as I stare at him, my pulse quickening. "No. That's not how the world works. Nobody gets everything they want."

"That is exactly how my world operates. I see what I want, and I am willing to pay the price."

I start to respond but stop myself and try to hold my temper back.

"You didn't tell him, did you?" he asks, his eyes boring into mine.

"I don't know what you mean," I say, glancing at my Dad and feeling the tension build inside my chest.

He leans back, crossing his arms. "If you're too ashamed to tell him, I'm willing to keep it a secret as a courtesy to you."

I glare at him as my dad touches my arm, demanding my attention. I can feel my face heating up as I turn towards him.

"What is he talking about?" my father asks, frowning deeply.

"One word from your lips," Ivan Ivanovich persuades silkily, "just one word and you'll have everything you want and more. Think of the peace of mind you'll be giving your father. This can't be good for his health, can it? The constant worrying, the drinking to numb his anxiety—it must be a living hell."

I can't look at him, not for even a second. Because if I do, I will fall apart again. I won't be able to think and manage this situation. But if I ignore his presence, I can focus solely on the facts, and if I coldly focus on the facts, then I know I can make a logical decision. A quarter of a million. Dad owes a quarter of a million and this man can make it all go away forever.

"What the fuck is going on here?" my dad growls.

I shut my eyes briefly. "Dad, can we have the room, please? I need to talk to him."

"Absolutely not," my father refuses belligerently. "Why the hell would I leave you alone with him? Lara, I'm really sorry he dragged you into this, but I'm fine. He's not threatening me physically. No matter what, I will find a way to resolve this. I'll call the police. There is no way for him to force me to pay him anything. This whole place is illegal to start with. It's a terrible position and I put myself in it, but I'm still the one in charge here, and I will take care of it."

"Actually, she, and not you, is in charge here," a cold voice taunts from behind me.

I turn and glare at him, wanting nothing more than to punch him square in his handsome face.

"What?" my father's astonishment and anger echo through the room. "What does any of this have to do with my daughter?"

I turn around to block my tormentor's mocking face, and standing firm, face my father, and lie to him.

"Dad, this is Ivan Ivanovich and he's my ex."

My father freezes, the color draining from his face. "What?" he gasps incredulously. Then his eyes start shining with new fury. "I knew I knew him. This man is your ex?"

I continue to lie through my teeth. "Yes, he's my ex-boyfriend, and... this is just a sick game he's playing to get back at me."

I expect my tormentor to jump in and ruin everything, but to my surprise, he stays silent.

"I'm sorry, Dad. He's been trying to talk to me, but I wouldn't give him the time of day, so he set up the showing today. I didn't find out who he was until this morning, and when I did it was too late, we had all already wasted our time and effort."

My father's eyes darken as he stares at me with a mixture of shock, astonishment, and disappointment. "You didn't tell me any of this this morning."

"I know, I'm sorry. It's just... the whole agency was depending on this, and when I saw him this morning, I didn't know how to explain to everyone that he had been playing us all."

"I am not playing anyone," Ivan says. "I intend to buy that house.""

I turn to face him directly. "Do it," I challenge.

"Do what?" he asks.

"Write the check. You talk a lot, but can you actually back your words? Write the check right now and sign it, or there will be no further discussions."

He smiles mockingly at my challenge, then nods at one of his two goons.

With that single signal, one of them leaves while the other remains standing still and wary. I can hardly believe he's actually going to go through with it, but when a few minutes later the man returns with a checkbook in hand, my jaw nearly drops to the floor.

He scribbles across the page, signs it, rips the check out, and hands it over to me. I stare down at the sheet and see the words and figures written clearly in black ink.

"One hundred and twenty million dollars," he says, watching my reaction closely.

I stare at the check and can't help but feel amused. "You really think this means anything? Anyone can write a check."

"Why don't you wait and find out tomorrow if I'm good for it," he says. "Take it to the bank and let me know."

He rises to his feet and I panic, feeling my control over the situation slip away.

"Wait!" I call out, louder than I intended.

He turns, his face blank.

"Dad," I say, turning back to my father, but he shakes his head emphatically. "No, I'm not leaving. We will resolve this here, together. This is all my doing and I'd rather go to prison than have you suffer the consequences."

"For God's sake, Dad, please just leave," I plead, unable to hold back my temper any longer. "I told you... he and I have this unfinished thing. We will resolve this together, and you will get back everything you've lost to him."

But he shakes his head obstinately like a child making a final useless stand against a parent. "No."

"Please, Dad."

Suddenly, he looks small and defeated. His eyes start to swim as he stares at me with guilt and regret. My heart aches at the sight. Rising to his feet, he shuffles out of the room. I watch his sad figure until the door shuts, and then I turn around to see that the Russian has once again taken his seat.

He plays with the gold ring on his little finger, turning and twisting it. Then he looks up at me from under his lashes and it makes my heart skip a beat. The sensation is so unfamiliar my legs feel like jelly. I have to look away and quickly sit. Obviously, these strange sensations have nothing to do with sexual attraction for there is no one else I hate more in this world than him. It must be the intensity of hate.

I hate feeling so powerless. From the glint in his eyes, I know this is going to be a bargain with the devil.

My voice is barely above a whisper. "At this point, seeing the kind of man that you are, I'd rather die than sleep with you. But I don't want to die, and I don't want my father and his business to die either. He has run that agency for the past ten years. It's his baby, his last big dream and he won't survive its loss."

He responds calmly, his tone light as if he is discussing the weather, and it puts me on edge. "Let's not sugarcoat the situation. Your father is an addict, in an endless black hole. That baby and that last dream you speak of, it will be lost again right in this room, or in another sordid place just like this. No matter how many times you throw money at him, he will piss it all up. He needs help and fast."

I stare at him, flabbergasted, realizing a total stranger has seen what I didn't. Or rather what I didn't want to see, but I can see now the enormity of the problem that needs to be faced and faced urgently. I take a deep breath. Hopefully, I am not too late.

"You are right. I will get him the help he needs. If you will be kind enough to turn this debt into a loan? We'll pay you back. Every last cent. I promise. It might take a little while, but—"

He raises his hand, cutting me off mid-sentence.

Chapter Seventeen

IVAN

"I don't do instalment payments," I tell her with amusement. "It's not a policy of mine, and even if I were to agree, what are we talking about here? Twenty years? Thirty? Do you want to be in debt to me for that long?"

She stares at me with consternation, and I notice a fascinating twitch in the corner of her left eye. I like that little quirk a lot and I realize that it's actually wonderful she hates me. I don't want her to be soft and foolish; instead, I want her fiery, arrogant, and full of fight. It's exactly what I need to set me on fire.

"So what's your plan?" she asks. Ice drips from her words.

"My proposal is for you to pay off the entire debt in a month," I say. "Maybe even less. I am neither willing nor able to deal with you or any other woman for longer than that. A month of your time, and all of your problems, as well as your father's, disappear."

"Mr. Ivanovich," she replies disdainfully. "You don't seem to grasp what the problem is here. I can't even bear to be with you for one minute, and you want me to be with you for a month?"

I expel my breath. We're getting nowhere. Never have I been engaged in a negotiation so ineffective considering I am the one with all the bargaining chips in hand, literally. I rise to my feet, and instantly, she does the same, panicking and preparing herself for my next move.

"You can't bear to be with me for one minute? Yet, here you are for the past ten minutes wasting my time."

"I'm wasting your time? May I remind you, I'm not here by choice. You called me. I'm enduring you because my father has become entangled with you and I'm trying to solve the problem at hand in a way that is satisfactory to all parties," she throws at me, even as she takes a fearful step back.

"I know you're attached to your pride," I say quietly as I close the gap between us. "It's as big as a man's, and probably even bigger. I don't blame you. You've made your own way in life and you don't want to be considered a damsel in distress, but sweetheart—"

"I'm not your sweetheart" she grates through gritted teeth.

I smile at the fire in her voice. "Sweetheart," I repeat, savoring the way a vein in her temple pulses with irritation. God, she fascinates me. "As much as you detest the idea, you are currently a damsel in distress. It's no consolation to you, but your dad put you there so be mad at him, not me. I'm the white, or you might prefer, dark knight, swooping in to save you."

By this time, I'm a mere step away from closing the distance between us and she is already pressed up against the door and trying to melt into it as if it could hide her from me. Her chest rises and falls rapidly, the tension between us almost tangible.

"If—if you come any closer, I will hit you," she threatens,

her voice shaking. Her warning charms me. She is so small, barely reaching my shoulder, yet she talks like she has weapons of mass destruction strapped to her waist.

More than anything, I need to feel her waist. To feel just how small it is in my grasp, and to feel the warmth radiating from her. But I don't touch her. Not yet. I move just close enough that my scent and my presence envelop her completely.

She shuts her eyes, and I know she feels it too. The electric pull between us is more than enough to set the entire room ablaze. I lean in, intending to breathe her in, and I am instantly hit with that whiff of her perfume. It's cheap, basic, but on her, it is a potent aphrodisiac—like savoring aged fine whiskey, the kind you remember years later.

I feel her movement before I see it, and my eyes open just in time to catch her hand coming for my face. I seize her wrist, gripping it firmly. Her wrist is tiny, nearly disappearing in my grip, and the softness of her skin contrasts sharply with the force she tries to exert.

"Really?" I ask, my tone mocking. "You've decided to add a lawsuit for assault to what you already owe me?"

I let go of her hand and she raises it again, but this time I deliberately don't stop her. I feel the sting across my cheek. She doesn't move. She waits, fierce eyes locked on me. She knows she has crossed the line and she doesn't care. The audacity. It's an incredible turn-on, an irresistible challenge. Blind lust rages inside me. Like a fire. It's uncontrollable.

Taking a deep breath, I shut my eyes and school my features. She mustn't know how little control I have when I am around her. How much power she holds over me. Only when I have wiped all expression from my face do I open my eyes to look at her again.

My tone is so cold and steely she would never for an

instant suspect or even believe that what I really want to do is throw her on the filthy table behind me and fuck her until she screams. "I think," I inform her. "You are mistaken about the kind of man I am. I want you, but not that badly. Not enough to tolerate disrespect."

She glares at me, but I've seen this look too many times in the eyes of too many people not to recognize it. The glint of fear. She cannot hide it, no matter how hard she tries to mask it with bravado.

Still, she responds, and my interest is sparked once again despite myself. "Well then stop freaking calling me 'sweetheart. My name is Lara, but you can call me Miss Fitzpatrick."

I stare into her eyes, my gaze unyielding. "Do you know why I'm so adamant about having you?" I ask.

Her brows furrow at the question, and I see the confusion flash in her eyes.

"It's because I trust myself. All my life, I have believed in myself—had faith in my desires and trusted my instincts. I have pursued them relentlessly and that is why I am where I am today. When you caught my eye in such a spectacular way, I knew there was something different about you."

"Then you should have expected the slap—"

"Shut the fuck up," I growl, my hand slipping around the back of her milky neck. I cannot control my fingers, they have taken on a life of their own, they caress her soft skin. I feel my breath catch.

"And now you want to kill me," she hisses, working up a sneer, and I think I fall in love with her fight right there. She is so flushed with anger, so gorgeous, her eyes burning with pointless defiance.

"Let's play a game," I say. "In order to move forward with this conversation you can choose one of two things to do to appease me. It has to be one or the other, or I will end all possibilities for negotiations with you. I'll sell your father's miserable debt on and you'll never hear from me again."

"I choose not to play this game," she bites out, her voice sharp. Once again, I am pleased.

"Why the haste, sweetheart?" I ask. "Shouldn't you hear what I have to say first? I guarantee they are interesting options—perhaps you'll even want both and not know which to choose."

She looks at me skeptically, but she's listening. What other choice does she have?

"A)." I start as my eyes trace her delectably angry features. Her huge eyes, her long lashes, and the slight dusting of freckles across her nose that have become more visible under the harsh lighting of the room.

"You get on your knees right now and suck me off," I say.

All the color drains from her face. It's fascinating to watch, and I almost smile, but I manage to hold back. "This is payback for thinking you can just hit me like I'm nothing."

I can almost feel the chill running through her entire body. It is clear she has never slapped anybody in her life. Only me. Because I drove her mad.

"Ask me what the second option is," I murmur, holding her shocked gaze.

She trembles despite her attempt to mask it. "What's the second option?" Her voice quivers, but there is still some defiance there. She is a natural-born fighter, but I always knew that.

I lean in even closer, ensuring she feels every bit of my presence. "I'm sorry, what did you say? I couldn't quite hear you."

Her eyes flash. "What is the second option?" she repeats, louder and more ferociously.

"That's more like it. You sound so adorable when you're

compliant." I move my hand from the back of her neck, brushing it down her skin upwards towards her face. She flinches, of course, but I know it's just a show. She's always so fucking dramatic. "The second option," I tell her as my thumb presses against her full bottom lip, feeling its softness. For a moment, I'm tempted to taste it, but I restrain myself. For legal purposes—both now and in the future—it's better that she chooses what I do to her.

"The second option is... I want you to spill into my hands."

Her eyes widen with astonishment, and she stares at me with disbelief. "What?"

"It's exactly what you think," I reply, watching her reaction carefully.

"I want to slide my fingers into you and fuck you until you're spilling down my hands, and then..."

"What?" she whispers, scandalized... and excited.

"Then you're going to lick your juices off my fingers. I want you to see how you look when you are turned on, when you climax, and when you taste yourself."

Her eyes nearly pop out of their sockets. "You're joking, right?" she asks, her voice cracking as she tries to hold onto some semblance of propriety.

I bring my hand back to her cheek, stroking it gently. "Why?" I ask softly, my thumb brushing over her soft, pillowy lips again. "Do I look or sound like I'm joking?"

Chapter Eighteen

LARA

Okay, that's it. The man is certifiably insane. I am dealing with a sick individual with twisted perversions. That is the only explanation I can think of. How can he even think of asking what he just did from someone who is almost a total stranger? I want to scream, but I know my father will most definitely hear and come bursting through the door. I don't want to make matters worse than they already are. My situation is already far too precarious.

"No," I say, my voice firm.

The madman smiles. "No to which option? Number one or number two?"

I gather my strength and, with both hands, shove against his chest, trying to push him away, but he doesn't budge in the slightest. He's like a big rock in the way of the rest of my life.

"Fuck off," I cry.

To my great surprise, he backs away. He lets me go, and finally, for what seems like the first time in forever, I am able to catch my breath, my chest rising and falling as I fight to steady myself.

"Okay," he says, his tone surprisingly calm. "If that's what you really want, then I'll leave."

I am shocked as I watch him turn around, picking up his phone and checkbook from the table. With another look at me, he begins to walk towards the door. Just as he reaches the door, I find myself unable to move out of his way, my body refusing to let him pass.

He watches me without a word, and then he smiles. I absolutely loathe that infuriating smile of his. Everything would be so much better if he just didn't smile. It feels like he's mocking me, enjoying every moment of this, and it makes my skin crawl.

"What's the matter?" he asks, "Don't you want me to leave."

I don't budge. Summoning all the strength I have left, I manage to look up and meet his eyes, my own blazing with a determination I didn't know I had.

"My father's debt," I remind tightly.

"You'll both have to figure out a way to settle that," he responds, his tone so detached and callous it makes me shiver.

Desperation claws at me as I consider my options once again, my mind racing as I weigh the consequences of each choice. There's no easy way out of this, and no matter which choice I take, it's going to be painful. But I have to choose. I have to take control of the situation in whatever way I can. For the first time in my life, I consider something I never thought I would. I square my shoulders, and taking a deep breath, I make my choice. The words escape my lips before I can stop them.

"I'll go with option two, but can I kiss you first?"

His eyebrows lift with surprise, probably feigned. But he's

mocking me, for sure, enjoying every single bit of my abject humiliation, and I hate him so much that it feels like my entire body is trembling with the intensity of my loathing. I shut my eyes for a moment, gathering myself before reopening them to look directly into his.

His eyes are a rare bright green, mesmerizing, but by approaching me this way, by manipulating me in such a cruel manner, there will never be any space in my heart for him. I will hate him until the day I die, and even beyond that.

"Why?" he asks.

"Allowing someone I just met to do such an intimate thing to me is not normal." I bite out, my voice sharp and filled with disgust.

"But hitting them across the face is?" he counters.

I cast my eyes to the grimy concrete floor. Shit. I did do that. I lost my head and just reacted instinctively. At that moment, I suddenly feel the full weight of my situation. It's not good, but I have to admit, at least to myself, that I did escalate things. The situation was already tricky, but I went ahead and made it a hundred times worse.

"Sorry about that," I say, hearing the resignation creep into my tone.

He frowns, and for the first time, seems genuinely angry with me. "Platitudes and apologies? From you? No thanks."

Chapter Nineteen

IVAN

"Just fucking do what you want and get it over with," she flares up.

That's better. I don't want a pitiful heroine in a tragedy. I want a fighting, kicking Irish spitfire. Part of me wants to just take her right there and show her that all of her high and mighty protestations are blatant lies. She wants it as much as I do, but she just wants the raw lust hidden behind romantic nonsense, bouquets of red roses, boxes of chocolates, and kisses. She is a pain in the ass, but I will play her little games for now. Eventually, I will lay bare her hypocrisy. I will show her the torrent of lust raging deep inside me and her. I don't want to kiss her, I want to fucking devour her.

A kiss she wants. A kiss she will get.

My hand curves around the back of her tiny waist as I swoop down on her mouth. Softly... because she wants romance. But as I register the taste of her, a frisson of pure desire, like a bolt of electricity, runs through my whole body. The intensity shocks me. I freeze and pull away, but as I do, I see the same shock mirrored in her eyes, I understand that whatever this is, it's one hundred percent mutual.

For a few seconds, neither of us moves. Strange thoughts enter my mind. It's just a kiss. She's beautiful. Her father is outside. She has been baking. I can smell vanilla. This place is too dirty for her. Then my brain short circuits... and I wrap my arms around her body and crush it against mine. Her soft warmth seeps into me.

I kiss her again, truly kiss her. Tasting her lips, sucking on them.

She is sweet... so fucking sweet it makes me feel lightheaded. I slide my tongue against hers, and her tongue begins a delicate and sensual dance with mine. I can feel my excitement building, so I keep going, hooking her tongue and pulling it into my mouth, sucking hard, taking what I want.

She pulls away suddenly, gasping for air, her eyes enormous, her pupils dilated.

I straighten my jacket. I didn't expect the chemistry between us to last even a month, but I can confirm now that I might have been wrong. Something about her is different...

Her hand closes around my wrist. "I'm ready now."

I shake my head. "Not here."

"What's the deal? What will be expected of me?"

"Available whenever I need you. Attend social functions with me. Leave the country at a moment's notice."

"For one month?"

I nod.

"Okay. We have a deal."

"Good. A contract will be sent to you. You can discuss whatever you need to with my lawyer or request clarifications."

"So you pay off his debts... and still buy the house?"

"Where has all your shame gone?" I mock.

She has the grace to look shamefaced.

"I never go back on my word. Yes, I will buy the house, but all your father's debts will be only covered if the deeds for the house, car, and business are transferred to your name."

She frowns. "Why is that a stipulation?"

"You have one chance to make sure he never loses the roof over his head again. I'd take it if I were you."

"Thank you," she whispers.

"And if you truly impress me, I may even throw in the two hundred and fifty thousand your father lost to me. You have an hour to consider my proposal," I tell her.

"What?" she asks, eyes widening. "Why can't the contract start tomorrow."

"Lara," I say firmly, "if you're not in my bed tonight, with your legs spread wide, giving me everything I want, this offer is dead. I want what I want when I want it, and I do not tolerate delays."

"Understood," she says tightly.

Chapter Twenty

LARA

Finally, I understand. I am going to have to sleep with him.

Not just because my father is probably out there contemplating suicide, or everybody at the agency including me will be out of a job by the morning if I don't say yes, but because I really, really want to. I can pretend to him and everyone else that I'm doing it for altruistic reasons, but I can't cheat myself. I know I'm doing it because I desperately want to.

The kiss was good.

In fact, good is a wild understatement. The kiss blew my freaking socks off. It's the way I'd imagined how two bald eagles locking talons and performing their death spiral courtship must feel as the dare devils cartwheel at full speed towards the ground.

My head is still spinning.

I wanted him from the first moment I looked up and met his emerald eyes, but as Leila said, the only thing holding me back was my pride. His approach had been supercilious, callous, and arrogant. No wine, no flowers, no chocolates... That is not the way I prefer to transact with a man, but all that was before *that* kiss.

I have something he wants, he has something I want and if he is also willing to get my father out of the terrible mess he has got himself into, why not? This is a solution to all of our problems.

Thankfully, I believe this fire in my gut will burn out fast and since the basis of our relationship is purely physical it will then fizzle out without too much fuss. On his part he has so many women to choose from I am pretty certain this is a thing that will probably not even last a full month.

"So..." I say, "I have to make my decision within the hour."

"Yes," he replies. "Let me know your address and someone will come to pick you up."

My heart nearly stops at his haughty tone, but it's impossible to argue with him further because he turns and shuts the door behind him. It must have been pure adrenaline that kept me standing, but now that it's just me in this filthy room, all my bravado and strength vanishes. All the strength completely leaves my legs and I stumble towards a chair and sit down.

Am I really going to do this? I ask myself, somewhat in shock. At that moment it all seemed reasonable, but now, in the silence of my own thoughts, it sounds insane. He is insane. We are both insane. I know my dad will be coming in like a rampaging bull soon, so I compose myself as best as I can.

There is a knock on the door. My heart jumps and I press my hand against my chest and watch as the door is pushed open, and my dad lurches in. He looks huge and blurry. There is a pitiful sadness in his eyes. Not at all like a bull. And just like that, what I had agreed to do, makes sense again. It will all be worth it if I can save my dad and get him back on the right path.

He takes his seat beside me and mutters, "I just saw that bastard leave."

I nod in response.

"Are you okay?" he asks, his gaze piercing through me.

"I am," I reply, trying my best to work up a smile, even though I know it will be nearly impossible to convince my father that it's genuine.

"I don't even know where to start apologizing," he mumbles. "I am so sorry for putting you in this position. To see me like this...to..."

"Dad." I reach out, catching his hand, "Don't. Don't think that way. Please sit down, let's talk."

He does so, and for a moment, both of our gazes land on the check on the table.

"Is that valid?" he asks.

I stare at it as well. "I don't know."

"Maybe we could just cash it tomorrow and disappear forever."

I smile dryly at him before looking away. I need time to properly map out my next steps. I have to be especially careful with my father because I know he would rather die than allow me to sell myself to the highest bidder, even if it would solve all our problems.

He places his hand on top of mine and rubs it gently. "I didn't know you dated someone like that. When was it? In college? Why didn't you tell me? We had a pact when you were a teenager that you would always let me meet any guy you dated, and until now, I thought you upheld that."

"I did keep our agreement, Dad," I try my best to assure him. "I just... I didn't introduce him to you back then because there was no point. I knew it wasn't going to last. It never does when a mentally ill person is part of the equation."

At my words, my father looks even more alarmed. "He is mentally ill?"

Sighing, I shake my head. "No, Dad, he's not mentally ill. I am… for falling in with his crazy schemes. He's just… rich. So rich he can buy and sell anyone."

"Well, he can buy and sell the whole world, but not you. Over my dead body." Once again, he rises to his feet. "Let's go," he says. "We'll fight him over this. I'll contact Larry right now, and we'll get to work on how we can void this entire deal. I'm… I'm ashamed of myself, but there is no way I stand to lose more than him. Just imagine what it would do to his reputation if the world finds out he is spending his time in illegal gambling dens. Even if we lose everything, I don't care. I'll—"

"Dad," I catch his hand again and pull him back down to the seat. "There's no need for any of that. I told you I'll—"

"This is my problem, not yours. You're the kid here, and I'm the adult. You didn't have to—"

I completely lose my temper. "Dad!" The sudden yell shocks him into silence. I have never raised my voice at him like that before, but we're out of time, and it's not helping.

"For God's sake, just… just sit down and listen." It takes a few more seconds for the shock to clear, but he listens to me and drops down to the chair.

"Dad," I tell him. "It's not what you think. He's actually quite a good guy at heart. When we met back in school, we were really close, but he became a bit too intense, so I pushed him away."

"So what does he want now?" Dad rushes to interrupt me.

"He wants us to spend a little time together and see if things can work between us now that we are both older and wiser. This was what he proposed to me during the house viewing, but I was too shocked so I refused."

"So... in order to get you to agree to spend a little time with him he went to these lengths? Tracked you down, found his way to this illegal game, and now he's offering you everything on a platter as part of the bargain?" Dad demands incredulously.

"I did mention that he's a bit intense, didn't I?" I shrug. "It's not a bad thing, Dad. It's what has made him what he is today. He never gives up. He goes on trying until he gets what he wants."

The skepticism and disbelief in my father's eyes begin to fade as he stares at me, assessing every word, every expression. It's as if he's trying to make sense of the situation, and I can tell that he's struggling, torn between protecting me and facing the cold reality of our circumstances.

""Dad," I call softly, "did he play fair or not?" I need him to see the situation clearly, without the anger clouding his judgment.

My father sighs with resignation. "Yes."

"He really wants the house, Dad. He just went through our agency because he saw it as an avenue to connect with me as well. He'll buy the house, and in exchange—I'll spend a little time with him and see if I missed something the last time around." I grin impishly. "After all, he's very easy on the eye."

My father glares at me, his eyes darkening. He doesn't say a word, but the intensity in his gaze speaks volumes. I wonder what's going through his head because what's going through mine is the hope I can convince him quickly so he can go home and I can meet the deadline that Ivan Ivanovich has given me.

"I'm thinking," Dad says slowly, "that I don't want you

involved with someone like this. Even if it's only for a few days."

"Dad, please be realistic. As we stand here now, you don't even have a roof over your head, the agency is gone, and I'm essentially unemployed. He will return everything you've lost in the game—the agency, your house, your car, your debt... We gain everything back while he gains nothing of physical value."

"I didn't know," my dad says, his voice heavy with disbelief. "I didn't know that anybody in their right mind would let go of a hundred and twenty million dollars simply to be able to see a woman for a few days."

"Dad, let me tell you how he thinks. He once told me that at a certain level of wealth, money becomes worthless and therefore everything he acquires is basically free."

He stares at me once again, and then he sighs, a deep, weary sound that fills the room. "If you're sure about this, then fine. You do what you need to. But you need to keep me in the loop. I don't want him to take advantage of you in any way."

"Yes, Dad," I reply meekly. "I have it all under control."

As he continues to stare at me, his lips begin to tremble, and his eyes fill with tears. Instantly, I lean forward, wrapping my arms around him tightly, pulling him into a hug.

"I'm so sorry," he apologizes, his voice cracking. "I am so sorry I put you in this position, sweetheart."

I shut my eyes tightly and hold on to him. "It's not your fault, Dad," I say softly, but he cuts me off.

"Yes, it is. It's all my fault. I am so, so sorry."

"It's okay," I reply, my voice steady. "We're lucky I know him. It will all be over soon, and everything will go back to normal."

Chapter Twenty-One

IVAN

"Well?" I say into my phone, as the door to the G-Wagon is pulled open and I step out of the driver's seat.

One of my men gives me a respectful nod as he takes my place and drives the car into the garage.

"Hello, Mr. Ivanovich," Dr. Van says quietly in my ear. "The lab has just contacted me with the results of the tests and to all intents and purposes she has been given the all-clear. I will email the results to you. I've also given her a prescription for an effective contraceptive protocol that will take a few days to take effect, but in the meantime, I believe, she is already on an acceptable method of birth control."

I end the call as Boris opens the door for me. I nod in acknowledgment. Muriel is waiting as well, along with two other staff, both male. She smiles at me.

"Dinner's ready, and as you requested, they went all out, Sir."

I glance at the two other wait staff standing beside her.

"It's been an exhausting day. I want peace and quiet. After I've eaten, everyone can retire for the night."

She nods. "Very good, Sir."

I remove my jacket and she takes it from me in a smooth practiced movement and passes it to one of the men. I take my seat at the dining table and she pours wine into my glass. "You are having seafood and fish, but I believe this red Château Caronne Ste-Gemme will be the perfect accompaniment," she murmurs quietly.

I swirl the deep red liquid in the gold-rimmed glass meditatively. Already, I can smell the complex aromas. I take a sip and let the richness of the velvety smooth Boudreaux roll on my tongue while she stands back and waits. That is the beauty of Muriel, she is more talented and knowledgeable about wines, choosing and pairing them with food than some of the best master sommeliers in Europe, but she is impressively modest and understated about her rare ability.

I nod appreciatively at her selection and she allows herself a small smile of satisfaction before filling my glass one-third of the way. One of the wait staff arrives promptly and begins to serve the meal.

"For the starter, we have edible seaweed rolled with horseradish, barbecued langoustine, and golden beets," Muriel explains.

I place a forkful of langoustine into my mouth and it melts beautifully on my tongue. It is a fantastic creation and a class act in the play of delicate flavors.

"This is superb. Who made it?"

"Anton created both the starter and main course, and Juan helped with the preparations. The preserved squid plait you will be having with your main course was sourced by James and flown in this afternoon from Japan."

"My compliments to Anton and Juan," I say as I swallow.

I realize how hungry I am. The tension of the day had masked it, but it feels like my body is reclaiming what it's been denied. Next up is jowl and throat of a cod head cooked with wild garlic, chives, and fig leaf oil served on a bone skewer and sitting on a bed of smoked tomato and pumpkin puree. The plaited squid preserved in sweet vinegar lays next to it. The presentation is worthy of a Michelin star.

I cut a piece of cod and chew appreciatively on the tender meat. It is delicious. "Is the North bedroom ready?"

"Yes, it has been thoroughly cleaned, aired, and made ready for Miss Fitzpatrick."

I grunt as I cut a piece of the Japanese squid. "Did Greta bring some paperwork today?"

"She brought a sealed A4 envelope. I put it on your desk."

"Did she bring clothes for my guest?"

"I believe she brought clothes, shoes, bags, and accessories. She also requested champagne and strawberries to be sent up to the North room later tonight."

"Good," I reply, the image of the woman who will arrive in a few minutes filling my mind. Instantly, I feel an acute anticipation building inside me.

"Would you like me to prepare anything specific for Miss Fitzpatrick to eat?" Muriel asks.

I lean back. "Probably not, but you can serve her breakfast in the morning."

"Certainly, Sir," she responds, as she refills my glass.

I press a button on my phone. "Is she on her way?" I ask in Russian.

"Yes, Mr. Ivanovich."

"What happened after I left?"

"She went back to her apartment and stayed there until the limo arrived to pick her up. There was another woman there who came out with her."

I know exactly who that was—her friend, Leila. I push my plate away. "How long before she gets here?"

"At this time of the night, I would say less than fifteen minutes."

I end the connection and feel a strange nervousness building inside me, a rush of excitement I don't often experience.

"Shall I serve the dessert now, Sir?" Muriel asks.

"I'm sure it's delicious, but I'm not in the mood for anything sweet tonight." Tonight's dessert will be Leda's hate and fury for the swan.

I sip my wine slowly while I contemplate what to do with her on her first night here. All kinds of wild and sensuous images slither into my mind, but suddenly it becomes as clear as crystal what I must do. I must not approach her at all tonight. It will serve as an unspoken torment, making her wait and speculate on my intentions. The anticipation will work in my favor. The end result will be a more explosive climax... for both of us.

I'd been thinking of waiting to receive her since we still had some details to discuss, but I decide that taking a shower, washing off all the grime and stress from the day, is a much more appealing option.

Nodding to myself, I rise to my feet and turn to Muriel. "My guest will be arriving in a few minutes. Please serve the sealed envelope that Greta brought together with the champagne and strawberries."

"Yes, Sir," she responds immediately, and I make my way up the stairs.

Chapter Twenty-Two

LARA

When I awakened that morning, I would have thought it insane of anyone who told me that before the day was out, I'd be prodded, poked, and tested for STDs to determine my 'suitability' to be a billionaire's toy for a month. But as I get closer to the billionaire's lair I recall everything the doctor said and did and feel like I'm the one who should be checked into a mental asylum.

I can't help wondering over and over again—why me?

I'm sure he could get any woman in the world, so why get an unwilling one? Okay, not unwilling, but as far as he is concerned, one who gives the impression of being unwilling. With a sigh, I turn to look out the window as I'm driven through Manhattan.

I don't even know where the driver is taking me, but I didn't expect anything else from a man who thinks because he has lots of money, he can control women. At this thought, my heart plunges. The ugly truth is I am now one of those women he can control. I feel a strange sense of disassociation fill me.

This is not my life.

This can't be my life.

I'm Lara Fitzpatrick. A little nobody estate agent trying to make my way in the big bad city. I'm not a billionaire plaything material. I'm not sexually adventurous and if I'm honest not even particularly sexual. One of my exes accused me of being a frigid prude. I don't think I'm that of course, nevertheless...

My phone rings, startling me. I pray it's not my dad as I pull it out of my purse. Despite my attempts to dissuade him from calling me every ten minutes over the past hour to check if I'm okay, he's refused to back down. I know he's hurting, so I've tried to be patient, but right now my head is too messed up to deal with his guilt and remorse.

Fortunately, it's Leila. She's more or less up to date with what's happening, other than the fresh trauma I've just endured at the doctor's office. Glancing at the driver who is purposely keeping his gaze glued on the road ahead, I put my phone to my ear.

"So you're actually doing it?" she squeals.

Shutting my eyes, I let out a long sigh. "Yeah. I guess I am."

"I'm sorry," she says softly. "You know I would gladly do it for you if I could."

"Yeah, I know. Hopefully, there's some clause in there that'll let me escape sooner," I mutter.

"Send it to me so David can look it over," she suggests.

"Can't do that," I shake my head. "I've signed an NDA. The only person I can reveal anything to would be if I hired a lawyer to represent me."

"Wow! Talk about fast. So, how was the doctor's office? You're already on birth control, right?"

"I'm supposed to be," I say, turning to stare out of the window.

"What do you mean by that?"

"I was just taking it as a habit, not as a precaution. I haven't dated anyone in two years, as you know."

"I know, but I thought you were—"

"You thought I was what?" I interrupt.

"I thought maybe once in a while when the cravings got too much during the lonely nights you'd go out and indulge in some anonymous encounters, you know?"

My voice is dry. "The only cravings I get at night are for warm waffles with rum and raisin ice cream, chopped hazelnuts, and sliced bananas, drowning in salted caramel sauce."

She laughs. "Anyway, what did the doctor say?"

"I'm in the all-clear category, but I could've told her that. It's hard to be riddled with STDs when you don't have sex.

"Do you think he's going to try to have sex with you tonight?" she whispers urgently.

"That must be the plan since he insisted I come to his house tonight rather than tomorrow like any normal person would."

"You know, at first, I didn't see the problem with this scenario. I even thought it was exciting, but now that I know just how desperate he is for you, I'm getting a little scared. The only good news is he is a public figure so he's likely not an axe murderer. But," she pauses dramatically, "get ready to collect as much evidence as you can. Everything that might protect you in the future—recordings, photos, anything."

I listen to her words of warning, but no fear creeps in. I feel it in every cell in my body that he will not hurt me. I perfectly understand what he is feeling. I feel the same thing for him. I'm furious with the way he has manipulated me, but

I want him. God, how I want him. No man has ever made me feel this way before.

"Look. I should go. Speak to you in the morning, okay?"

"Please be careful, babes," she says.

"I will," I say and put my phone away.

I know this area. We're going to the southern end of Central Park in Manhattan and heading towards Billionaire's Row. I can list off the top of my head almost every listing available here, but given how small our agency is, I've never had the chance to be involved with such a property.

We stop in front of 220 Central Park South. A man steps forward smartly and opens the car door for me. I step out and look up at the tall skyscraper. So this is where he lives. For a quick second, I feel excited to be here, curious to see what it looks like inside.

"Miss Fitzpatrick," the man says formally. "Let me help you with your bags."

"No thank you. I can manage," I say stiffly.

"Very well. Please follow me."

We go through the plush foyer and ride the elevator in silence. He opens a pair of wooden double doors and I step into Ivan Ivanovich's lair. I drop my rucksack on the floor and look around me in awe. Wow! What a magnificent space, with tall ceilings, glass walls, and a grand curving black marble staircase that leads up to more floors. But mostly my eyes are drawn to the many softly-lit beautiful paintings hanging on the walls. I don't know what I expected, but it was not this worship of beauty and impeccable cleanliness. The entire space is spotless. Not so much as a smudge or speck of dust anywhere, and every hard surface gleams and shines with polish.

A woman dressed in black approaches us. Her eyes are pale, watchful and naturally wary, but I detect kindness in them too. I know immediately that this is the woman responsible for the immaculate state of the apartment. She nods at the man next to me. "Thank you and goodnight, Steven." The man leaves and she turns to me.

"Good evening, Miss Fitzpatrick. I am Muriel Levine, Mr. Ivanovich's housekeeper. Welcome. I hope you have a wonderful stay with us."

"Thank you."

"Would you like something to drink or eat?"

My stomach growls loudly and I realize that I've been cooking and baking for hours but I haven't had any food since lunch. I don't think I can hold any food down though. I'm too nervous and stressed out.

"I'm fine, thank you," I say politely.

"Everything's ready for you. If you'll come with me, Miss. Fitzpatrick, I'll show you to your room," she says and begins to walk towards the stunning staircase. I pick up my rucksack and follow her up to the second floor.

"If you encounter any problems please let me know immediately," she says as she shows me into a cream and white bedroom with touches of soft blue. I glance around at the luxurious decor. There is a white four-poster bed with silk curtains. It all looks so luxurious that I'm momentarily speechless. On the bed is a dark red nightie, and on the table by the lounge area is a white box with a red bow, a bucket of champagne with two tall flutes, a bowl of strawberries, and what looks like my contract in an envelope.

"If you have no other requests I'll wish you a good night, Miss Fitzpatrick," she says. "Please ring that bell if you need anything at all."

"Um, are there any hidden cameras in this room?" I blurt out.

The involuntary widening of her eyes tells me I need have no such fears.

"Not to my knowledge," she says slowly, but now there is speculation in her eyes as she reassesses my status. I have shown myself to be no ordinary guest.

As soon as she exits, I rush towards the envelope, but my hand hesitates as I reach out, knowing what it contains and not wanting to face it just yet, but I know I can't just skim through it. I have to read every word carefully because sooner or later, I will have to sign this thing. I have to make sure there are no hidden traps, no loopholes that he could exploit to weasel out of his end of the bargain. I need to be sure I'm not making a mistake. Despite the strong desire in me to pretend it doesn't exist, I take a deep breath, grasp the thick expensive paper and break the logo embossed bronze-colored wax as I tear it open.

As expected, it is my contract, and it's all laid out in excruciating detail, every clause, stipulation and rule is meant to ensure that I am perfectly obedient, always on my best behavior, with no room for rebellion. It's all one-sided, all for his benefit—my behavior, my schedule, even my wardrobe, all meant to align with his expectations and whims. It's so controlling, so suffocating that I can't quite believe I've let myself into this situation.

My eyes skim over the legal jargon, the strict terms that bind me, and I feel my chest tightening with every sentence I read. The reality of what I'm agreeing to settles in more heavily with each word, and it's suffocatingly clear. He's buying a service. Nothing more. Why did he have to make it so starkly evident that it would be transaction sex?

I remind myself that this is the only way to fix the mess my father is in and focus on the words swimming in front of me. I need to read through every line and every word. I need to understand exactly what I'm signing up for.

Slowly, I begin to comb through the contract, taking it in word by word. Each section feels like a tightening knot in my stomach—stipulations about when and where I must be available, the expectations of how I should behave, the way I must look and present myself, even the things I am allowed to do in his presence. It's all there, mapped out as if my life is now a schedule he gets to dictate.

Still holding the contract in my hand, I head towards the walk-in closet. It's bigger than my bedroom, and although it isn't completely filled, it's been stocked with every piece of clothing I could possibly need for my month's stay. Dresses, shoes, bags, accessories, even glamorous lingerie —all in my correct sizes.

I notice another door. I push it open and it leads into the most breathtaking bathroom I've ever been in. The space is massive, with premium rose marble floors and gold fixtures that gleam under the soft lighting. It's almost overwhelming in its luxury, and for a moment, I'm lost in the beauty of it all. A marble alcove is lined with pristine white towels, and the scent of fresh flowers fills the air, mingling with the faint aroma of the soaps and oils carefully arranged on the counter.

In the middle of the room, perfectly positioned to overlook a window with a gorgeous view of the city's night sky, is a bathtub. It's enormous, the kind of tub you could sink into and lose yourself in for hours. I can already imagine how warm and soothing the water would feel against my skin, washing away the day's stress and the feeling of being soiled. For a brief second, I forget everything else as I picture myself sinking into that bath, letting it swallow me whole.

The thought is tempting.

Without thinking further, I turn on the faucet, choosing a

mix of the fragrant oils and bubble baths available. The scent of lavender fills the air, and I feel my shoulders start to relax just a little. I select some of the luxurious bath salts and sprinkle them into the water too, watching as they dissolve and release their calming aroma. The steam rises, and I close my eyes, letting it envelop me, imagining that it's taking away all the tension building up inside me.

I undress and step into the tub. The water is perfect—warm enough to make my skin tingle but not too hot. Lovely. I feel as if I am bathing in the sky. I sink into the water, feeling it rise around me, and then I let my head rest against the edge. The world outside feels far away, and I almost let myself pretend that this is a beautiful dream. Everything is fine. There is a gorgeous prince waiting for me somewhere in this apartment.

But reality comes crashing back when I look down at the papers on the floor.

I lay my head back and close my eyes, the water continuing to warm me, until eventually, the bath begins to feel less like a comfort and more like a trap—a reminder of the luxury that's being used to bind me, the softness disguising the control. The scent of the expensive bath salts hangs in the warm air, but instead of relaxing me, I feel a new tension growing in my chest.

My heart feels heavy as I lean back and let the water wash over my shoulders. I close my eyes and for a moment, I let myself drift, imagining another scenario. I was on a fairytale date with Ivan Ivanovich. He really cared about me. I was his girlfriend!

I shake my head at my open stupidity. He is a billionaire. Billionaires don't choose struggling estate agents to be their girlfriends. I open my eyes and stare at the ceiling. It's ornate, with a chandelier hanging directly above me—something you'd expect to see in a palace, not a bathroom in the middle of New York. Everything around me is so extravagant, so immaculate, and yet all I can think about is how much I wish I could disappear into this bath and never come out.

But I know I have to face this.

I rise slowly from the tub, water dripping from my skin, and wrap the towel on the footstool around myself. It's soft, cloud-soft, and I clutch it tightly as I walk back into the bedroom. I pull at the red ribbons of the gift box and open the lid. Inside is a blood-red silk nightie. It is beautiful, but I glare at it, knowing exactly what it symbolizes. It's another part of the game—a tool to make me feel small, controlled, like a doll he can dress up however he pleases.

I toss the nightie on the bed. No matter how much I want to tear it up, throw it in his face, and walk out the door, I don't have that option. Not if I want to save my father. Not if I want to save the agency.

This is my life now, at least for the next one month.

Chapter Twenty-Three

IVAN

It had not even crossed my mind that I'd not be able to stay away from her for the night. I never expected the wild restlessness that would consume me the way a fire consumes a dry field.

Burning, burning...

The throbbing knowledge that she is just across the corridor, waiting, all paid for, completely subject to my beck and call... and yet here I am forcing myself for no good reason to ignore the call. I pour myself a glass of strong whiskey, down it, and lay on my back, staring up at the ceiling. I can't remember the last time I felt this wound up. As far back as I can remember I have had whoever I want. The fairer have always fallen easily into my lap because of my great privilege, first as my important father's son and then as a result of my own success.

But tonight, I find myself desperately wanting a woman who actually detests me.

For two hours I endure the torment, but the frustration in

my body refuses to settle no matter how hard I try to push her out of my mind. Fuck her. I wrap my hand around my hardness and pump. It's almost painful. Pathetic, really, but still, it is what it is. I try to picture a woman, any other woman, but her image looking up at me from her awkward position on the ground from that morning refuses to budge from my mind. The more I remember that moment, the sweeter it feels. The friction becomes a good heat and a damn great release. It has me gripping the sheets, caught up in my own need. I tell myself it was not that good, that it's all in my head. It's not her, it's just the idea of a hunt.

And it is a hunt.

"Fuck," I curse softly, with an odd mix of satisfaction and frustration. I get up, heading to the bathroom to clean myself off. I pull on a pair of silk pajama bottoms and return to my room. Standing there, I stare at the bed. Sleep seems hours away. I need a distraction, something to occupy my mind. I think about going into my study and putting on some trades but realize that in my preoccupied state, I'll probably just end up losing money.

Maybe a swim will help.

I grab the envelope I left on the table, head downstairs and dive cleanly into the pool. It's well past midnight now, and it's actually my favorite time of night. The air is cool, and the water is a welcome relief. I swim twenty laps, feeling the tension in my muscles slowly start to dissipate. Climbing out, I wrap a towel around myself and head towards the lounge chairs where the soft glow of the lamp casts a warm, calming light.

I settle into a chair, the night air cool against my skin as I flip through the document to make sure my instructions were followed perfectly. I imagine her reading them, her expression when she sees the terms. Maybe she's furious. Maybe it makes her want to rip the contract into a thousand pieces. I smile at the thought. I want her agitated, unsettled. I want her angry and fierce, unable to hold back. She's so controlled on the outside, but I know an intense fire burns inside her.

I sit in silence, imagining the next month. The images are both tantalizing and immensely satisfying. Her defiance and the way she refuses to submit, is almost wonderful, a challenge I haven't felt in years.

Suddenly, I sense the creeping sensation of being watched. Slowly, I lift my head, staring into the dim distance where her shadow falls on the tiles.

"Are you going to keep watching me, or are you going to come over and say hello?" I ask, my voice carrying across the stillness.

She hesitates, then begins to move towards me. She walks slowly, and as she approaches, the details of her figure become clearer. She's wearing a long red nightdress with a lace-trimmed slit running up her thigh. The way it clings to her curves makes it impossible not to notice her erect nipples pressing at the silky material.

Almost involuntarily I respond, hardening as I take in the sight. I instructed Greta to keep her wardrobe sexy, and this outfit, I have to admit, is perfect.

"I saw the contract you left on the desk for me," she says softly.

The fragrance from her skin drifts towards me. The air leaves my lungs, but I force myself to stay composed, to act as though I'm unfazed and uninterested. I take a moment to stare at her, noting how her hair is piled up on the top of her head in a messy bun, with a few escaped tendrils framing her face. She looks both elegant and dishevelled, a combination that makes my heart beat faster.

"Have you read it?" I ask, my voice neutral. "There should

be a pen somewhere in the room, so you can sign it and hand it over to Muriel."

"Right," she says, frowning slightly, "but there are some things about it that I want to discuss with you."

I can feel the tension building, knowing full well that another argument is coming. I reach for my own copy of the contract and meet her gaze.

"What is it?" I ask.

She doesn't hesitate. "The part about removing any accidental pregnancies."

I frown, my expression hardening with surprise. "You have a problem with that?"

"Yes," she replies with a disdainful expression in her eyes. "Trust me, I have no interest in bearing any child of yours, but I don't know how I will feel about aborting a child of mine no matter the circumstances surrounding its conception—even if it is as unfortunate as the current situation."

I say nothing.

"So, I suggest we ensure it's prevented altogether," she continues in a rush. "I'm already on birth control, and am perfectly happy to go with the one the doctor suggests, but I want to use condoms as well. An extra barrier of protection for both of us."

"No," I reply flatly.

"What?" She looks shocked as if she can't believe what she's hearing.

"No," I repeat.

She glares at me, and I hold her gaze until she shifts her attention back to the contract. I can see that inside, she's close to bursting with anger. It's such a sight to behold that I can barely contain my excitement.

"In that case, I refuse to sign the contract," she says, straightening her back. "I'd like to be taken back home."

I stare at her for a moment, then rise to my feet. Before I can even take a step, however, she turns and begins to walk away. In a few long strides, I catch up to her and seize her arm.

"If you don't let go of me right now, I am going to sue you for everything you're worth," she warns harshly, not turning around to face me.

I close my eyes, breathing in her scent. It sends me insane. God, I want to bury my face in her hair and taste the sweet curve of her neck.

"Let me go," she repeats, her voice trembling. There is fear in her voice.

It is like a bucket of cold water thrown over my overheated body. I release her immediately.

Instead of running away, she turns around to face me. "I won't change my mind," she insists firmly, her eyes glittering with resolve. "And if you still say no, I'll leave right now. Let's see how much you can squeeze out of my father and me. I think you'll find us poorer than we look."

The silence between us is heavy, stretching out for several moments.

"Okay," I agree. "I won't force you to abort any child you conceive."

"I'll need it in writing," she responds. "The contract needs to be adjusted."

"The updated one will be sent to you tomorrow morning."

"Okay," she says and starts to turn away, but I catch her hand and pull her back.

"Not until tomorrow," she mumbles, but I don't hear her. Instead, I draw her closer and sliding my hand around her waist, I swoop down on her trembling mouth.

Chapter Twenty-Four

LARA

I know I should step back, and say NO clearly; it's what I should do until I have my amendment in black and white. But there's something about his barely checked power in the large hand on the small of my back that overwhelms me and bends me to his will. And there's also the undeniable fact that the man's nearly naked.

I couldn't believe it when I first walked in and saw him wearing nothing but a towel, the fabric barely clinging to his hips. All the glory of his beautifully sculpted, gorgeously tight muscles on display. I knew I'd been deceiving myself all night. I'm undeniably attracted to him, and that's the real reason I even considered this arrangement in the first place. If he had not been so attractive to me this would never have been an option. He's stunning, confident, and exudes power, and it drives me wild.

He is my dream man!

And now it is clear to both of us that I have totally and absolutely surrendered to his will. He is kissing me with an intensity that leaves me breathless. My captured lips tingle and throb. Even in my wildest dreams I never imagined anyone could kiss like this—so deeply, so desperately, and yet with a perfect balance of roughness and tenderness. He's both delicate and demanding, teasing and relentless, and he's doing things to me I've never experienced before.

I lose all sense of control. My arms instinctively circle his shoulders, pulling him even closer. It is unbelievable how much I want him, and how much I want to just surrender to this feeling.

"No, no," I whisper, as my hand brushes against his bare skin. I realize he's completely naked. At some point, the towel must have slipped off, and now my hands are tracing the hard lines of his body and creeping towards his maleness. He's rock hard, and my breath catches. I look up and meet his eyes. In this light, they seem almost black with heat and desire. Never has a man looked at me like this. As if he will die if he cannot have me. It is shocking.

I cannot look away from the naked need. For what seems like an eternity we stare at each other, almost in disbelief at the intensity of our craving. The desire is such that I actually feel a wave of dizziness engulf me and make me sway.

He catches me by my forearms. "What's the matter?"

"It's nothing. I just...I feel a bit dizzy," I stammer.

He scoops me up into his strong arms and holds me against his hard body. "When was the last time you ate?"

"Breakfast," I reply, quite happy to pretend that the almost-fainted episode was caused by a hunger for food and not him. "You might as well put me down. The dizzy spell is gone now and I feel fine."

He puts me down. "I'll ring Muriel and get her to rustle something up for you."

I swallow and step away from him. His nearness is so

distracting I can barely think straight. "No, please don't disturb her. She asked me if I wanted something to eat and I said no. She's probably asleep now. There are strawberries in my room. I'll eat them."

He turns away from me and casually walks towards his towel. Good God, I can't get enough of his naked butt. When he turns around to face me, I try my hardest to keep my eyes on his face and not on his very enticing lower half.

"Fine," he says, his tone crisp. "I'll whip something up for you."

"You? You can cook?" I ask, quite shocked.

"I'll make you my famous spaghetti *aglio e olio*," he says with a boyish grin.

The grin makes him look like a different man. One I would love to get to know. "A Russian specializing in an Italian dish?"

"I once had an Italian friend who shared his secret recipe."

"You mean, a girlfriend?" I feel like kicking myself as soon as the words are out. I sound almost jealous.

He looks at me speculatively. "No, a male friend. He died in a car crash in Monaco."

"I'm sorry," I mumble lamely. I'm such an idiot.

He nods. "Think you can walk on your own?"

"Yes."

He ties the towel back around his hips and walks ahead of me. I can't help but stare at the smooth muscles rippling on his back. It's infuriating how much that one strip of cloth can hide. I think I actually loathe it. It covers everything I want to watch.

We enter a sparklingly spotless white kitchen and I see him head straight to the refrigerator and open it. After my last *faux pas*, I decide to keep my mouth firmly shut and just enjoy the cookery show.

Chapter Twenty-Five

IVAN

I pull open the refrigerator, one I've never seen the inside of since I bought this place, and realize I haven't cooked in years. Shaking my head, I skim over the neatly arranged containers of food. I don't even know where anything is. Pasta will probably be in the pantry. Garlic is probably in one of the lower drawers. Parsley. Where would I find that?

I turn around and call her over. She comes over to join me. We are both quite the picture, I imagine—her in that sinful red outfit and me in my towel. Right on the edge, yet both of us keep to ourselves.

She lifts her gaze to look at me, there is a teasing quality to her face. "You don't know where anything is, do you?"

"Nope."

"I'm kinda still into peanut butter and jelly sandwiches."

"Right. There should be a jar somewhere in the pantry."

"Sure," she repeats, walking over to retrieve it.

My eyes devour her as she walks away. When she reaches

the door of the pantry she turns to look at me. I don't speak, but she instinctively understands exactly what I'm saying. There's no mistaking what I want.

Slowly, deliberately, her eyes move down to my naked torso. Seconds pass, but her gaze continues to linger. That's invitation number one. Then I see the outline of her nipples pressing against the silky fabric of her gown like two little unsatisfied stones. And that there, that's invitation number two.

Fuck it. I don't hold back anymore.

In an instant, she is in my arms again, but this time there's no resistance. She melts like butter against my body.

My craving hands glide down her curves, hating the thin barrier of fabric between us. I cup her ass, feeling the firm swell of it under my palms. My entire body burns with anticipation and desire, a raw need that feels impossible to contain. My towel comes loose and pools at my feet. I let her feel exactly how much I want her, how hard she makes me.

I reach between her thighs and through her soaking wet panties, find the throbbing heat of her. My fingers press against it. She gasps into my mouth and jerks back at my touch, her breath quickening, her mouth open, as if in shock. Clearly, she's startled by the way her body responds to me. Shaking her head in disbelief, she takes a few steps away. She is trying to put distance between us, but it's futile. The pull is undeniable. Even she knows that now.

I watch her retreat until her back hits the counter, trapping her, then I make my slow measured approach. Sliding my hand around her neck, I pull her in for another kiss and consume the soft, peachy sweetness of her lips. My tongue slips into her mouth, exploring and tasting the desire building between us. Kissing her makes me feel like I'm losing myself, almost unraveling. Layer by layer. Like a fucking onion.

I can't get enough of her, and it seems neither can she. I feel her arms circle my torso, her hands sliding across my bare skin like an electric charge. The sensation is intoxicating, and as her hand moves lower, I feel her brush against my cock, making me shudder with pleasure.

My body is telling me to take her hard and fast, but something about this moment forbids me to do that. It's a crazy notion for me, but this is... too special. I don't want to rush it. The plan is to let this beautiful tension keep on building and savor every second of it. Letting the strange and wonderful magic of her unfold naturally, taking each moment as it comes.

I cup her ass, pull her flush against me, and grind into her until I hear the moan that she has been desperately trying to hide, escape out of her mouth. It is a sound of pure need and it shoots through me, igniting a fire I can barely control.

Fuck control!

Like a wild animal, I rip her delicate nightie down the middle. Underneath, she is naked but for a tiny scrap of lace. Her body is smooth and creamy. Like a porcelain statue, or a lost goddess. She is every bit as beautiful as I imagined. I want to taste her everywhere until she is a shivering, begging mess in my hands. I look directly into her eyes. I want her to see that I know exactly what she's fighting.

I feel the smoothness of her skin as my hand slides up her inner thigh and I find her slick sex again. My fingers trace her soft folds through the drenched lace.

Her eyes widen.

Slowly, I rub the bud of her clit through the fabric. It's impressively swollen... undeniably aching, begging for attention. I tease it, circling and pressing, feeling her body jump and twitch beneath my touch. Her breath comes out in ragged gasps, and when I find just the right spot her eyes flutter downwards, and she lets out a moan so long and sweet that it makes my head spin.

I continue to stroke her, my fingers working her in slow, rhythmic motions, building her up until her entire body shudders violently.

"Oh God!" The words spill from her lips as she collapses against me while her hands grip my shoulders, and frantically pull me closer.

I kiss her deeply, and she responds in kind. She needs this as badly as I do. Her body presses against mine with a hunger as rabid as my own. As our tongues clash, I know that if I keep going, I'll have her coming here and now, pinned against the kitchen counter.

And I plan to.

I want to make her lose every ounce of control she has. I keep my eyes on her face, watching every expression, every bite of her lip, every flutter of her lashes. I want to see her break apart, to witness her surrender as she comes undone.

She shudders and bucks against me, her nails digging into my shoulders as I inch my fingers underneath the fabric of her panties and tug it. It's so flimsy it tears and falls away. Finally, I get to her bare pussy. She arches into me as moans fall from her mouth. Her sex is hot and wet as my fingers slide inside her.

"Don't stop," she whispers, her voice breaking.

"I'm not stopping, not even if you beg for it," I growl.

Chapter Twenty-Six

LARA

I feel my juices trickle down my thighs.

Without warning, and as if I weigh nothing, he hoists me in the air and sits me on the cold marble top. Catching hold of my thighs, he spreads me until my legs are parted into a Y and my naked pussy is open and exposed. My clit is pulsating for his touch. I'm so ready, so aroused that I'm shaking. He stands back and stares hungrily at my dripping sex. He reaches out and touches my clit and I almost swoon from the wave of pleasure that passes over me.

"Raise your legs higher and wider," he commands. "Arch your back. Show me your pussy and your ass. Show me you want this."

I obey, God help me.

"Nice, Very nice," he says and smiles with satisfaction.

I'm aware of the filthy picture I present, but I want his cock inside me so badly that I don't care. He cups my sex and I'm stunned by how violently my body responds. I should be ashamed of myself, but not one ounce of shame courses through my electrified veins. This feeling is too good, way too good. The way he touches me, the perfect balance of roughness and tenderness has me melting against him. I need more. I need him to push me further.

I grind against his hand, each movement sending electric shivers down my spine. My clit throbs painfully, swollen and desperate for more. I turn to face him, my body betraying every ounce of shame I feel.

Every time my eyes flutter open, I catch him staring at me, his gaze hungry, predatory, triumphant. I know he's won, I've surrendered, but the pleasure is so consuming that I can't bring myself to care.

"Fuck," he growls, the impatience and frustration thick in his voice.

His hands are on my breasts, squeezing them possessively. I've always known they were full, that they drew attention I didn't want, but no one has ever grabbed them like this, making me feel like he does. There is a domineering roughness about his touch that makes me ache.

He kisses me again, and it's deep, dirty, his tongue thrusting in and out of my mouth as if he is tongue fucking me. My hand reaches down between us and wraps around his length. He's hot, hard, and thick, and the moment my fingers close around him, I feel the pulse of his arousal under my palm. It makes me shudder. As he strokes me, one finger slipping inside, I squeeze him, pumping slowly, savoring the way his cock twitches in my grip. With my eyes closed, I feel every inch of him, the heat and thickness that makes my breath catch in my throat.

I look down. He's so fucking big and hard, veins straining against the silky skin, and all I want is to taste his flushed, swollen head, to pull him into my mouth and suck until he's the one losing control. I want to make him come apart in my hands and feel him shiver and break the way he does to me.

His breath is hot against my face, as he drops lower, his mouth trailing kisses down my stomach. Two of his fingers push inside me, filling me completely. It feels like an examination, like he's exploring every inch of me, learning what makes me shiver, what makes me moan.

He's between my legs in an instant, his mouth hot and wet as his tongue licks up the length of my sex.

"Oh!" A moan is torn from my lips, my head falling back as he devours me. His tongue works my clit, flicking and sucking. His mouth is relentless, driving me to the edge, pulling every ounce of pleasure from me until I'm writhing, clawing at the counter.

I hold his head, my fingers tangled in his hair, trying to push him away, but he's not stopping. His grip tightens on my hips, pinning me in place as he fucks me with his tongue, pushing deeper, exploring every part of me. He ravishes me like a man possessed.

"Ivan," I cry out helplessly, my body arching as I feel the pleasure build, coiling tight in my core.

His tongue drags against my clit, and the pressure is unbearable. I'm so close, and I know I won't be able to hold on. My hands grip the counter, my legs shaking as he sucks harder, his mouth relentless.

Chapter Twenty-Seven

IVAN

When she comes, shuddering, crying out so loud it echoes off the kitchen walls, I feel such a thrill I'm ready to come myself.

I straighten, my gaze locked on her as she lays sprawled across the counter. Her eyes are glazed, lost in the aftermath of her release, her chest is heaving, and between her spread thighs, her pussy is red, swollen and glistening. By God, she is beautiful.

"Wow!" she mumbles, her voice raw and breathy.

Completely drained of strength, she offers no resistance when I gather her limp body into my arms. In fact, she clings to me, her arms wrapping around my neck like a little monkey. With her body boneless, and her head resting on my shoulder, I carry her to the long sofa. I sit on the sofa with her on my lap.

"The doctor confirmed I'm STD-free, but I don't have any confirmation that you're the same," she says quietly.

"I'm afraid you'll just have to take my word for it."

"Isn't that unfair?" she says.

"Life's not fair."

I feel the shiver that runs through her. She stares at me, her eyes enormous, and then she reaches between us, lifting herself slightly as she positions me at her entrance. I'm ready to burst with anticipation, my cock jerks violently as I prepare to slide into her heat. But she teases only me by rubbing the head of my cock against her wet folds. She drags it across her entrance, coating me in her slickness. The sensation is so damn intense, it's sweet torture.

"You're killing me," I groan.

She smirks. "That's one humungous cock you're trying to get inside me, Mister. I'm just making sure you don't tear me in half."

Finally, she lowers herself, and I feel the tight grip of her walls as I slide into her.

"Oh my God," she gasps.

I lock eyes with her, watching as she slowly takes me in, inch by inch, her expression shifting from pleasure, to surprise, and back to pleasure. It's exquisite, and soon enough, I'm buried deep inside her. I don't move, giving her time to adjust to my size, and she leans her head back, a soft moan escaping her lips as she impales herself completely on my cock. Her skin glows in the low light. My cock throbs painfully, but I could stay connected to her like this forever.

I lean forward, pressing my forehead against hers. Her scent hits me—sweet and warm, like fruit and pastries. It's not like the usual expensive perfumes I've encountered, and the realness of it hardens me even more inside her.

Her nipples are hard, a perfect pink that I can't resist. Cupping one, I lean in and take the peak into my mouth, sucking greedily. She tastes as sweet as she smells. She moans, her body arching, and I take my time, lavishing attention on each breast, feeling her writhe against me.

I lean back slightly, giving her room to set her feet on either side of me as she begins to ride me. Her hands grip my shoulders, her hair spilling over her cheeks as she moves. I watch, entranced. She's beautiful—her flushed skin, her parted lips. Everything about her is intoxicating. Then she takes control and fucks me, breast bouncing beautifully, slow at first, and then faster and faster.

Grabbing her waist, I thrust hard into her.

"Fuck," she cries, riding me even harder, and it's my turn to surrender completely.

She's blowing my mind. Gripping her tighter I pump into her. I feel it all—every shiver, every clench of her walls around me. I fuck her mercilessly. I need to show her what it means to belong to me. Her body is mine. She is mine.

She climaxes explosively.

Now that she's had her fun...

With our bodies still joined I rise to my feet and head over to the island. I feel her spent naked body trembling against mine. The counter's height is perfect for what I want to do. I feel the thrill building inside me.

As I bend her body over the island she shivers at the coldness of marble. She's so much wetter than before. Exactly how I want her. I lower myself between her legs. With my hands gripping her thighs I spread her dripping pussy open.

As my lips connect with her swollen, heated sex, she cries out again, her head tilting back.

"Not yet. Please, I'm too sensitive," she begs.

My tongue slides over her wet folds, exploring her, and her body arches right off the counter.

"Ivan, please," she pleads.

But I don't stop. I go deeper, my tongue pushing inside her, tasting every part of her as I hold her in place.

I suck her until I know she's close.

"I'm going to come," she cries out, her voice desperate and raw.

I feel her body quivering and hear the ragged breaths she takes as she tries to hold back. Her juices pour into my mouth and run down my chin. I lap it all up. She tastes so sweet I'm getting addicted to her flavor.

I laugh, feeling the thrill of power coursing through me as I plunge into her sweet pussy. She screams with shock of the brutal entry. And then her hands come around the back of her and pull me deeper into her. We become one body and it's like nothing I've ever felt before.

"Give it everything you've got," she says.

Grabbing her by the waist, I drive into her like a wild animal. Her defenseless body jerks. The sight of my cock buried inside her naked pale body while she writhes helplessly on my kitchen counter is indescribable. I've got her. I own her now. I can do whatever I want with her. She is my possession. For the next month, my cock is going to be inside every orifice. Day and night. I'm gonna fuck her. There will be no respite.

Her moans grow louder as I ram into her. Pleasure coils tightly within me until it feels like I'm ready to explode.

Suddenly she gasps, her body tightening around me as she's pulled over the edge. Her cries fill the room, and the sound of it—her pure, raw pleasure—sends me spiraling. I'm no longer in control, and as her orgasm hits, I let my climax hit.

Everything else fades away as I lose myself completely.

In the distance, I hear her gasps, her cries, the weight of her body against mine. When it's all over I pull out and look down. The sight of my seed leaking from her swollen pussy makes me smile. She is embarrassed and tries to straighten, but I push her back down. I get on my knees and lick her from clit to asshole.

I help her up and her knees are so weak she has to lean against the counter. I look at her flushed face. She looks exhausted.

"You licked me after sex. No man has done that."

I slide an arm around her knees and hoist her into my arms.

"What are you doing?" she whispers.

"Taking you to bed. It's been a long day for you, Little Miss Muffet."

"Are you the spider?" she asks and yawns.

"What do you think?"

"I think yes," she says sleepily.

"Then that is what I am."

"You know Miss Muffet ran away from the spider, don't you?"

"Yes, I know."

She stares into my eyes as I carry her up the stairs. By the time we reach the bedroom, she looks half-asleep. I lay her down on the bed and pull the duvet over her. She curls like a cat on her side. I watch her for a moment, feeling a strange sense of satisfaction.

I don't get attached easily, and I don't take an interest in people. But I'm breaking all the rules for her. There is a frown on my face, as I switch off the lamp by her bed and exit the room.

Chapter Twenty-Eight

LARA

I feel sticky and I reek of dirty sex.

I want to get up and clean myself, but I find myself unable to move. I lie on the bed as if paralyzed. All I can do is stare up at the ceiling and loathe myself for how weak I feel.

I realize my month here is going to be far more complicated than I imagined it would be.

I've had sex before, many times, well enough to know that there's nothing too special about it. When it happens, he comes, sometimes I get to come as well, then it's lights out. But it is clear to me now that I've been living quite pathetically, missing out on something this amazing.

Rather than counting down the days towards my freedom from him, I will likely be begging him to keep me around longer. Turning onto my side, I force myself to close my eyes and stop reliving the last hour of my life.

My dreams are haunted. In it my mother is still alive and we are all having dinner in a dark candle lit cave. Ivan comes to serve us food and my father stabs him with a fork. I scream and wake up with a start.

Rubbing my eyes, I look around the room, which is now brightly lit by sunlight filtering in through the window. Again, the impression of extreme cleanliness fills me. Everything looks brand new with not a mark or stain anywhere.

I head toward the bathroom. It's time for that much-needed shower. The rain shower is pure heaven and afterwards, I slide into the fluffy white bathrobe. As I head towards the walk-in wardrobe my phone starts ringing. It must be my dad going out of his mind with worry.

I run to my bag to retrieve my phone and, of course, it's Dad.

"Lara?" he calls and his voice sounds panicked. "You're not at work. Where are you? Tell me where you are. Tell me where you are. Do I need to call the police? What—"

"Dad," I try to interrupt, but he keeps going, his voice completely broken, and I'm sure his heart is too.

"Dad!" I call out again, louder and sterner this time. I realize that I actually sound angry. I've never, in all my years of being his daughter, raised my voice at him, so he immediately goes silent.

"Dad, I... I'm fine. I was just... I was tired. I went to bed late and woke up late. I'll come in to work a bit later."

He immediately starts apologizing. "Oh! I'm sorry. I'm incredibly sorry," he says, his voice filled with guilt. "I just couldn't reach you, and I couldn't sleep, and last night just seemed—"

"I know," I say, nodding even though he can't see me. "I know. It doesn't seem real, does it?"

"No, it doesn't," he replies, his voice heavy with worry.

"Dad." I soften my tone as I move toward the seat overlooking the city. The view is quite literally breathtaking. Far below people are hurrying somewhere. Always hurrying. Trying to squeeze out a buck from a merciless machine. Only yesterday I was one of them. From up here they look like ants. Tiny and helpless.

"Lara?" my dad calls once again, pulling me back to my senses.

"I'm here, Dad, I just got distracted."

"Where are you?" he asks. "I need you to tell me where you are because I want to come and get you. I don't want you to do this for me. I'd rather rot in hell than allow him to lay a finger on you. I'll never forgive myself if you're subjected to this. I'd rather die."

"You're not coming to get me, Dad!" I cry.

"Well, in that case, come to the office right now, or I'm going to call the police, give them his name, and have him arrested. Do you understand me? I'm not joking, not for even a single second."

"Dad!"

"That's final," he says.

Panic sets in because he's about to hang up, and knowing him, he won't respond again until the ten minutes are up.

"Dad—"

"No, I don't want to hear it," he interrupts again. And when I really want to say what's in my heart, I have no choice but to yell.

"I want to be here," I shout.

It feels like I've dropped a bomb. Neither of us can believe I just said that. I certainly can't believe it, and I can't ignore how I feel about it either.

"What... what did you say?" my dad asks, and I'm certain now that he's trying to make me repeat those dreadful words. I refuse.

"Just..." I sigh. "Dad, I know you feel bad, and I know you

want to fix this, even if it kills you, but I'm telling you I'd rather it not. I'm not doing anything that will harm me. I told you that... I told you that I know him. We're close. This is strange, and he's being aggressive about it, but it's more of a friendly spat than anything else. It'll be resolved, and if he's really willing to spend this much to help us get through our problems, then I don't understand why you want to stand in the way and create an unnecessary fight."

He listens to me for a long while but doesn't say a word, and with every minute that passes, my worry deepens. "Dad," I call out again, trying to fill the silence.

"I know, based on my actions, you're convinced that I'm a complete idiot, but I'm not. And I wasn't born yesterday. No one spends that kind of money on anything unless what they're receiving in return is a pound of flesh."

I pause, swallowing hard at how accurate his words are, but of course, he absolutely does not need to know that.

"What he's receiving is the house he'll get from the deal," I tell him, trying to sound convincing. "He's just doing us a small favor by patronizing our agency instead of going to a much bigger one, and it's because he knows me. He's just making a fuss now at the beginning because I was rude to him, and that has everything to do with our past and nothing to do with you. So, could you please just stay out of it and back off? I have it all under control, and when it goes beyond my control, of course, I'll call you for help. Who else would I go to?"

He is silent again for a long while, the pause dragging on until I can feel the tension building in my chest.

"I would believe this if I didn't know who you are," he finally responds. "But I do know who you are, and I'm very aware of the lengths you will go to, to ensure that I am not hurt, and this is why I fucking cannot sleep. You know, sometimes I wish that—"

"Wish what?" I ask, my brows furrow. But he doesn't respond.

"Nothing," he says, and I shut my eyes again, frustration mounting.

"Dad—" I try again, but he ignores me.

"I'm going to fight this. This nightmare has to end. He can take everything from me, including the business, but he cannot take you."

"Dad!"

But he has already cut the connection.

Disturbed and angry, I head back to the bathroom. As I set the phone down on the vanity to brush my teeth, another call comes in.

My heart lurches as I imagine it's my father calling again to carry on his tirade, but it's Leila, and to my surprise, I'm reluctant to speak to her as well, so I just stand there frozen and let my phone ring until it disconnects. With a sigh, I pick up my toothbrush, but Leila being Leila, doesn't relent and my phone goes again. She's not going to stop until I answer. I answer the video call.

Her face is full of concern and worry.

"You okay?" she asks.

"I'm fine," I say as I start brushing my teeth aggressively.

"Are you sure," she asks.

"I'm fine," I reply after spitting into the sink. "I'm fine; everything's okay. It's just my dad spiraling."

"Want me to go check on him?"

"Yes," I reply, and she nods. "Alright, I'll drop by a little later."

"Thank you," I say, giving her a weak smile.

"How... how are you holding up? Remember, we prepared

for this. Don't hesitate to let me know the moment you want to leave, and I won't let you down. I'll go to the police if I have to. You'll be fine."

"I'm fine," I say and continue brushing my teeth. I don't know if I can endure the shame of not following my own plan from the previous night.

"That's a gorgeous bathrobe," she says conversationally. "It looks like it costs a fortune."

"It probably does," I mutter.

"You're extremely cranky."

"I'm sorry," I apologize. "I hate it when Dad and I argue. I just—"

"I think we need to get you out of there," she says, her tone turning serious. "Was it... did he try to touch you last night? Was it that bad? Because if it was that bad, you can't do this. You can't endure this. Nothing in this world is worth the psychological damage it will cause you."

"It wasn't bad," I say quickly.

"Oh," she says, fighting to control her smile.

"It's not funny," I say, and she lets out a laugh that echoes across the room.

"Actually, it is," she manages to say.

I turn away from the sink and start walking back to the bedroom.

"Wow!" she gasps.

"What?" I ask.

"Just taking in the space you're in. I'm not even going to ask for another close-up, but just for the record, it's breathtaking. Take some pictures for me, please, so I can use it for inspiration for my own bathroom and bedroom."

"As if we could ever afford marble bathrooms," I scoff.

"Oh, come on, Lara, just try to make the best of this situation. Just treat it like a one-night stand of sorts."

"Well, it's lasting more than one night, isn't it?" I retort. "How is this supposed to be temporary when—"

I stop myself.

"When what?" she prompts curiously.

"When I couldn't say no," I confess. "I wanted him, Leila... with all my heart."

"Listen to me, Lara. If you want him then, hell girl, enjoy the month. Do everything you want with him, and when it's over you'll have had something that 99.99% of women could never even dream of having. Trust me, we only regret experiences we don't take, not those we do."

I listen to her words silently.

"You know I'm right... don't you?" she asks.

I give her a slow nod. Again, I don't know if her words are entirely accurate, but they feel good. They are the only thing that's made me feel remotely okay this morning, so I accept and embrace them.

"Okay," I say, my voice softening. "Okay."

"So, you can stop feeling so bad and just let go. Enjoy yourself."

"Yeah," I reply.

Chapter Twenty-Nine

IVAN

It turns out it's extremely hard to sleep when you have a raging hard-on that won't go away because you can't stop thinking about a woman. Which is crazy because the sky is literally falling on top of me. The fires cannot be put out and they are spreading so fast that soon they will burn to ashes everything I worked so hard and so long for, but all I can fixate on is how good it felt to be deep inside her.

I have an important breakfast meeting at the Four Seasons that I'm already running late for, but what I'm itching to do is turn back and go fuck her. I'm fucking obsessed with the smell and feel of her and it's driving me absolutely insane.

My phone starts vibrating. Likely a reminder of more fires I won't be able to put out today. With a sigh, I pull my phone out of my jacket pocket, but it is Lara. Instantly, my cock gets hard and my body throbs for her. I want her so badly I can barely contain myself. Out of frustration, I grab my rock-hard cock through my pants and squeeze, seeking some relief.

"Hello," she says with annoying nonchalance.

Irritated, I resort to sounding as gruff as I possibly can. "What is it?" I bark.

I can picture her reaction. Her brows scrunching up, her lips drawing into a stern line. She looks fierce when she gets like that, but that only makes her even more sexy and fuckable. A ridiculous phenomenon that has no logical explanation.

"I'm calling to ask about the contract," she says stiffly.

"What about it?"

"You said the new one would be revised this morning..."

"My secretary will be over with it later this morning. Anything else?" I ask, my words clipped and sharp, sending the clear message that I am irritated by her call, which isn't the case at all. I'm irritated by how unaffected she is.

"There will be no further—" she clears her throat, and I can hear the discomfort. "There will be no further... interactions between us until it's been issued."

I can't hold back my mocking laughter. If we were having this conversation face to face, I'd take her right there without the contract, just to prove how susceptible she is to me. It would completely humiliate her and make her even fiercer.

"Isn't it a bit late to be making such a stipulation?"

The line goes dead on me. I stare at the phone in disbelief. She hung up. I don't like it one bit, but I guess I can't really complain since I was taunting her.

I place a call to Greta. "Are you in the office yet?"

She responds in her usual perky manner. "Good morning, Sir. I got in about half an hour ago."

"I'm sending an amendment to Lara's contract. Once you've updated it please send a copy to the house for her to sign it."

"Got it," she replies crisply.

"This is an urgent matter, so it should be resolved before I return from the Four Seasons."

"Of course."

I end the call and just send off the email with the amendment to her when I see I have another call. My mother.

"Mama," I greet.

"I've sent multiple messages. Why haven't you responded?"

"I've been busy." She can't really complain further or contest this.

"The committee never received your RSVP. You are coming to the gala tomorrow night, aren't you?"

I frown. It's in my calendar, but I was hoping to avoid it.

"Ivan, are you listening?" my mother demands crossly. "I need a response."

"I told you I'd try my best."

"Ivan, you promised," she complains. "I really want to see you. A lot of people want to see you. You're never at these events."

"For good reasons, Mother. Anyway, I only promised I'd be at your birthday getaway in France this weekend, not the gala."

"No, you also agreed to the gala as well," she lies blatantly.

I sigh deeply. "Can't I just write a check?"

"No, I don't want your money. I want your presence. The whole family will be there."

"Even my father?" I murmur.

"Not him," she says with cold fury. "He's probably at some sunspot with his latest slut." She takes a deep breath. "I actually just called to confirm your attendance, not to go back and forth about the guest list. Please don't disappoint me this time."

Without giving me a chance to respond, she ends the call.

I put my phone back into my pocket and stare reflectively

out of the window. There is so much bitterness in my family. We can't even be in the same room anymore.

I lean back and think about my next meeting. Yeah, it's important, but I can already guess with 90% certainty what James and Steven are going to say, and it can wait until tomorrow, Wednesday, or Friday, or even next week.

I know it's an absolutely terrible idea, but I cannot help myself. I rap on the partition glass and meet the chauffeur's eyes through the rearview mirror, his expression expectant, waiting for my next instruction.

Chapter Thirty

LARA

Uggh... that man needs a punch to his smug face. Why does he have to be so damn hateful?

I don't know what I thought, but after what happened last night, I certainly did not expect him to be so cold and impatient, as if he couldn't wait to get rid of me. As if I was an irritating nuisance interrupting his busy day. He makes me feel so stupid and foolish, even when I'm discussing serious matters. We have a crazy arrangement between us so obviously I'm going to want to make sure I'm not signing anything that would cause me regrets for the rest of my life. Throwing the phone onto the bed, I take a deep breath and let go of my annoyance.

Main thing is, I made my stance clear.

Let him get on with running his great empire, I need food. I'm starving. I think back to the meal we were planning in the kitchen before we both lost our heads. I go over to the strawberries and bite into one of them. I can honestly say, I have never had a sweeter, juicier fruit in my life.

I move over to the window. Marveling at the amazing skyline and the city spread out under me, I eat a couple more, then take a shower. Under the heated cascade, it's hard not to think of his touch on my body. After the way he spoke to me, it seems like I must have dreamed it. But in this enclosed space, with my eyes closed, I can still feel his hands on every inch of me so intensely that it becomes nearly impossible to breathe.

He was exactly as rough as I wanted him to be, and then he was soft and sensual when it mattered. It felt like he understood and knew my body better than any man I've ever been with, hell, better than even I do. At one point during my climax the sensations that gripped me were so intense and overpowering I thought I was dying. I might even have blacked out for a bit. That has never happened to me before. Ever.

And yet, we haven't even had a proper conversation. Other than mutually wanting to tear each other apart we don't even have anything in common. And yet here I am wanting his body inside me. Shaking my head at the almost surreal situation I find myself in, I step out of the shower. This constant emotional rollercoaster is driving me crazy, but at this point, I'm more than willing to blame my weakness and frustration on hunger, so I focus entirely on getting on with the day.

On the vanity, there's an assortment of expensive-looking lotions and creams gathered neatly on the spotless glass surface. I pick up a jar of moisturizer, unscrew the lid and bring it to my nose. It even smells costly. As I lather the sumptuous cream onto my skin, I have to admit, I'm really surprised by the detail and care put into my stay here. Obviously, he's not the one who personally picked any of these out, so I wonder who did. Was it Muriel?

Heading into the closet to find something to wear, I have to decide that it's absolutely not her because the style of the clothes doesn't match what a woman of her age would care for. I wouldn't call them slutty, because they are clearly exclusive, beautiful and opulent, but they're all deliberately sexy. Clothes designed to turn a man on. But as I move through the rails I have to admit there are also a multitude of formal and perfectly decent options available. I suppose I should thank whoever had gone shopping for me because never in a million years would I have been able to afford such luxurious and costly outfits.

I choose a black camisole and a classy pair of cream linen trousers. Both are comfortable and when I pair them with a striped pale green linen dress shirt, I feel quite happy with the result.

Grabbing my phone, I head out of the room and make my way down the stairs. In the bright light of day, I can admire the magnificent apartment even more. The sunlight filters through the ceiling-to-floor windows, bringing the place to life like magic.

I also have more time to study the paintings. His collection is exquisite. Each piece is special. From what I can see he is not into modern art. It seems to be mostly impressionist. I almost get carried away inspecting the pieces and trying to identify them. I'm pretty sure the combined value of them could easily buy the house itself.

The air smells like cherries and something else—something warm and inviting. I can't stop taking deep breaths, savoring the scent for no reason other than that it feels so refreshing. It's easy to forget that I'm right in the middle of busy New York. This place feels like an escape, a still sanctuary far removed from the city.

As I finally reach the bottom of the stairs, I notice a few maids in uniform cleaning places and items that are already clean. They smile at me politely and nod obsequiously, but don't utter a word. Not even when I wish them a good morning.

Eventually, I arrive at the kitchen, and everything from the previous night flashes back to me. The wild moments, the slow ones, the ones so sweet I can almost still hear my moans and cries in my own ears.

I'm forced to pause as a particular memory of grinding against him, feeling every ridge of his rock-hard cock, comes rushing back. My entire core tightens. I try to catch my breath as Muriel walks in, carrying a covered dish that looks like a casserole. All I can do is stare at her, unable to meet her eyes, given the filthy images flooding my mind. I'm not even sure I'll be able to face Ivan himself when he returns.

"Good morning, Miss Fitzpatrick," she greets with a warm smile. "Did you sleep well?"

"Good morning. Yes, thank you," I reply awkwardly.

She nods. "Good. Where would you like to have breakfast? In the sunroom or in the formal dining room?"

"Uh... Sunroom sounds good."

She nods again. "I thought you might. I didn't know what you usually have, so I took the liberty of setting up the buffet table. If you'd like to follow me..."

"Okay, thanks," I reply, giving her a wide smile. Breakfast is usually a couple of slices of buttered toast or cereal for me, but I follow her willingly as I am ravenous and also very curious as to what kind of food rich people eat.

I gasp as I take in the spread. It looks like one of those heaped tables you see on cruise liners. Every single thing looks delicious. As I walk along the long table, some items are familiar. Finger sandwiches and sliced meats, but others are more exotic. There are the pastries with fruit oozing out of them, itty bitty cupcakes, sausages, bacon, caviar, little eggs, a tureen of porridge, chocolate with churros, congee, a selection of dim sum, and at the end of the table a huge tray of fruit that look so perfect they could be straight out of one of the paintings I've just been admiring. My eyes are caught by a bunch of dark purple elongated fruit.

"Are those grapes?" I ask, pointing at them.

She nods. "Yes, they are organic moondrop grapes. Sometimes called witches' fingers. They were flown in from Spain yesterday."

I instantly reach out to pluck one, hesitating briefly as I wonder if it's rude, but she nods encouragingly.

"It's okay. Please, feel free," she invites kindly.

She watches me as I bite into the fruit.

"Mmmm. Freaking good."

She smiles. "Help yourself to coffee, tea, or orange juice. If you want anything different please ring."

"No, this is more than fine, Muriel." Impulsively, I reach out and lightly touch her arm. "It all looks amazing—thank you so much."

There's a glint of surprise in her eyes as she straightens her spine. Her voice is formal. "Well, then. I'll leave you to enjoy your breakfast in peace."

"Thank you for everything," I say again.

She nods and retreats quietly and I contemplate the array of options laid out before me. With no audience to witness my gluttony, I pick up a plate and begin piling on a little of everything. The fragrant smells coming from the plate make my mouth water and, even though there is no more space on my plate, I heap on top the heirloom tomatoes stuffed with truffle-infused cheese.

Relishing my solitude in the stunning high-ceilinged room I then sit and eat like a Queen. Once my plate is polished clean I lean back and find myself unable to tear my eyes away from a curved staircase. From where I am sitting, I can see lush plants, leafy palms that should be growing in a tropical environment. There must be a conservatory up there.

I take the stairs up and come to a space on the roof of the entire building: a room made entirely of glass. The floors are made of weathered yellow flagstones and there are charming rugs with intricate patterns on it. An antique chandelier hangs from the arched roof and there is a wrought iron table, a gorgeous curved cream sofa and chairs next to a pond, where red and yellow koi swim serenely. The air is filled with the sound of running water from a little stone fountain.

Sunlight filters in through the leaves, making the space look like a magical forest.

Over my years as an estate agent, I always notice these architectural features that make a space special. This apartment feels like an absolute treasure. I have never seen anything like this in my life. I find myself falling in love with the secret forest despite myself because my preference is the shabby chic, but this is beyond beautiful. Its beauty feels timeless and unique.

I can't help but wonder who maintains this garden. It feels too personal to be contracted out to a gardening company.

Pulling out my phone from my pocket, I'm about to send some messages to the office when I hear Muriel's voice calling. Feeling almost guilty to be up here, I quickly go down the stairs.

There is a classically beautiful blonde in a fitting black suit standing next to her. Something about her... Instantly, my guard goes up.

"That will be all, thank you, Muriel," she says coldly, and Muriel walks away, her face expressionless.

"Miss Fitzpatrick," the woman says, her gaze locking onto mine with a hint of disdain. "Mr. Ivanovich sent me. I've brought your amended contract." I notice she has a foreign accent and that she doesn't give me her name. I refuse to play her game. Whoever she is, I genuinely don't care. I say nothing.

"Are you his secretary or something?" I ask rudely, mirroring her condescending tone.

Her eyebrows shoot up and I can see the fury in her icy blue eyes. "I'm his PA."

"I see. You can leave the contract on the table. I'll go through it when I'm ready."

Her frown deepens, and it hits me. She's the one who purchased all the clothes in my closet. It makes sense; the style matches her own—forced to be proper but undeniably sultry.

"Please sit down," she says coldly. "There are things I need to explain to you. It's important. Mr. Ivanovich expects certain things."

Lifting my chin, I walk towards one of the chairs at the table and sit down. She follows suit.

"Mr. Ivanovich has a packed week ahead, and you'll need to accompany him to many of his events," she begins immediately, her tone all business, as she pushes an envelope towards me. "I've already filled your closet with everything you'll need. I tried my best to gauge your size, but if there's anything that doesn't fit or needs taking in, I'll give the seamstress's contact information to Muriel, and you can arrange it yourself. Please ensure that you're presentable at all times. Mr. Ivanovich has a very respectful image to uphold, and it mustn't be tarnished for any reason."

Her words are sharp, almost demeaning, almost proprietorial, as if Ivan belongs to her, but I cock my head and raise an eyebrow. I want to say something sharp in return, but I restrain myself. After all, my fight isn't with her—it's with no one, really. The deal I've entered into is my choice, and I've decided that it's worth what I'm being offered in exchange. So why should I feel ashamed of that? Especially after the way Ivan had nearly rendered me incapable of walking last night.

"Don't worry," I tell her, my tone quiet but pointed. "I wouldn't dream of it. It's such a short period of time, and he's paying an obscene amount for it, so why would I cause any trouble? I'm making more money in a month than most women ever will in a lifetime, and all I have to do is fuck the most fuckable man I've ever met in my life."

The color drains from her face, and I take a moment to relish it. I don't give her a chance to respond before I turn my attention to the contract that I pull out of the envelope. Calmly, I start reading the contract, cross-checking that no major changes have been made to the version I originally read.

"I need to get back to work," she says abruptly. "Some of us have real jobs to attend to. If everything is in order, just sign here."

I glare at her and I'm about to tell her to fuck off when she jumps to her feet, startling me in the process. It takes a moment for me to realize why she's reacted so suddenly.

"Mr. Ivanovich," she says. Her voice has lost all its disdain. She sounds positively flustered.

My heart jumps into my throat, and I nearly rise as well, but as usual with him, my legs freeze. My entire body turns heavy, as though the weight of his presence alone is pinning me to my chair. It's an unbelievable feeling, like the air itself is thickening around me, and when I finally manage to turn my head, I take in the sight of him. He is not wearing a jacket. His tailored pants are cut perfectly to his physique and his soft blue-striped shirt makes him look impossibly refined. The way his sleeves are rolled up despite his polished look is so disarming that I find myself grasping for control over my body, particularly my breathing.

It's easy to understand why I've been so captivated. He's

everything. Intensely powerful and magnetic. I stop judging myself for my reaction and realize that he is worth it. He's worth every bit of this overwhelming attraction, every moment of self-hate.

I turn my face away, trying desperately to ignore him. After all, I'm not required to acknowledge him like his secretary does—I don't work for him.

"Oh, you're here?" his PA exclaims, clearly thrown off by his unexpected arrival. "You have a meeting in Manhattan."

"Something urgent came up so I called and canceled," he replies with a careless shrug. The sound of his voice is so rich, so deep, that my entire being seems to vibrate in response.

"You cancelled it yourself—" she repeats, confusion evident in her voice.

"Yes, I knew you were busy with the contract. You can reschedule the meeting for next week," he says calmly.

She frowns. "Something urgent came up? What's more urgent than the meeting you had?" she presses in an amazed, almost disbelieving voice.

"Something of a personal nature." His words send a wave of satisfaction through me, though I try to suppress the smile creeping onto my lips. I can feel his gaze on me, even though he's addressing her.

Her reaction is telling—her posture stiffens, and I can tell that my earlier suspicion about her feelings toward him was correct. She clearly desires him, and now she's faced with the reality that his attention has been captured by someone she considers a two-bit slut.

I meet his eyes again and it's like the world stops spinning. Everything and everybody just falls away. There is only him and me. His gaze is intense, unwavering, and I feel it on me like a physical touch. I want to hold his gaze, to show that I'm not intimidated by the sheer intensity of the emotions swirling inside me, but after a few moments, it becomes too much. I break eye contact, looking away quickly as though I've been burned. How does this man have such a strange ability to make me feel completely out of control? Almost as if my body reacts without my permission.

Suddenly desperate to do something with my hands, I grab my cup of green tea, though it must be cold by now, only to realize it's empty. Needing to escape I stand.

"I'll be in the conservatory if you need me," I mutter and almost run up the winding stairs.

Chapter Thirty-One

IVAN

I've done something I've never done—breaking my work ethic for the most frivolous reason. Even Greta, who is usually composed, looks visibly shocked because she knows there is no emergency.

"Are you done here?" I ask.

She recovers quickly, like the professional she is, but boy is she's flustered—more flustered than I've ever seen her.

"I, uh... I was waiting for her to sign the contract."

"I'm here now. I'll get it signed."

"Okay, I'll head back to the office then," she says stiffly and starts walking towards the door.

I pick up the contract from the table, grab a bottle of water from the serving tray, and head out to the conservatory to join Lara.

I find her sitting on the edge of one of the chairs. She looks nervous and edgy. An image flashes into my mind of bending her over the table and fucking her until I get every ounce of frustration out of my system. I sit across from her and place the contract on the table between us.

"Greta says you haven't signed."

"Greta," she repeats, nodding. "That's her name, huh? She didn't bother introducing herself."

"She's busy."

A flash of irritation comes into her eyes and her voice is sarcastic. "Of course, she is. Everyone is. Which makes me wonder why you came back. Why did you come back, Ivan?"

"To fuck you, of course."

Her eyes widen in shock. "What?"

I stand, growing impatient. "Sign the papers, Lara. I have to get back to work in thirty minutes."

She frowns, then snatches the document up and stands. As she reads through it she paces around the room. I relax and take in Muriel's extraordinary garden. It's been so meticulously maintained and is now bursting with so many plants, flowers, and fruit. I have never been in here ever since I bought the apartment, and now, for the first time, I realize the effort she has put into this space. It's transformed from a glass room with an indoor garden into an enchanted mini forest. And now the forest has a delectable sprite walking through it.

"I have one more stipulation," she says.

I don't stand because if I do, she'll see how hard I am. The only thing I can think about is the feel of her skin under my hand as I grab her hips and fuck her senseless. My desire for her feels almost crazed, maybe even unnaturally possessive. Yet she's taking her time as always, torturing me. I curse under my breath.

"I... I hesitated to bring this up because I imagine it carries some negative connotations, but that's not the case. I just really need the extra clause to protect myself."

"And what is it?" I ask quietly, not turning around.

"Um... I need it explicitly stated that I'm allowed to leave before the thirty days if you lose interest."

I frown. "Haven't we already discussed this? Isn't this one of the first things I mentioned? You're free to leave as soon as I lose interest. Why would I want it any other way?"

She stares at me, and then something clicks in my head and I realize what she is up to. I smile nastily. "Were you perhaps planning on finding a way to make me lose interest so you can leave earlier?"

She shifts uncomfortably, confirming my suspicion. I truly can't believe her audacity, but at the same time, I'm not surprised.

"I just... I just want all the terms to be clear so there's no misunderstanding whatsoever."

"You can leave today if you want to," I say.

Her head snaps up. "What?"

"I'm not one to hold a woman against her will. Sure, I was more than a little insistent on having this arrangement, but I was convinced it was fair. But after last night, I think the time and energy I've spent has been well worth it and I'd like to continue fucking you, but if you'd rather not be touched by me anymore, then go ahead and leave."

She looks at me, and I can see the surprise in her eyes. I feel annoyed because I've canceled a meeting for this. I feel dumb and out of control and can hardly believe I have reduced to behaving like a fool for a bit of pussy. I realize it's the effect she has on me, and I really don't like it at all. Shaking my head, I turn around and head for the exit. Before I can cross the threshold, she stops me.

"Wait."

I don't stop or turn around. She's wasting my time,

playing games. She affects me like nothing else, and now my challenge is to find a way to get rid of this worrying lack of self-control so I can focus on the rest of my day and be as effective as possible.

I hear her footsteps behind me, hurrying to catch up. Just as my hand touches the old-fashioned metal handle, hers lands on mine, stopping me. I look down into her beautiful eyes swimming with a mixture of uncertainty and, God help me, desire, and my heart starts racing again. Fuck, I hate her. Just as much as I fucking... want her.

"Don't you want me to sign the contract?" she gasps.

"Sign it or don't sign it. I don't care. I've already told you this. What more do you need from me? I've already gotten what I wanted from you," I say with deliberate cruelty.

"Well, I haven't," she says.

"Don't worry," I say, my tone cold. "I'm not going to renege on our agreement or your financial compensation just because you want to leave as quickly as possible. I am a man of my word, and I will keep it, even if you decide not to honor yours. And don't think you've outsmarted me. My purpose for getting on in life is to have control and power. If I want something, I get it, even if it's just once."

"Oh, shut up for God's sake," she suddenly says.

I freeze. No one has ever spoken to me like that. "Excuse me?"

"You said you came to fuck me, but you're just whining about something I didn't even say."

"What the fuck do you want, Lara?" I growl.

She lets out an exasperated sigh. "You're doing it again. Talking instead of fucking me."

I let out a laugh of disbelief. This woman! First, she pushes me away and now she pulls me back into her web. But it is galling to think how much I want to be back in her dangerous web. For a few seconds, I stare at her. The moment feels like it is frozen in time. The sound of water fills the air. Right behind her head is a hanging orchid plant in full bloom. It is as if the plant had lived all its life to fill its purpose for this instant to adorn her face. I want so much to walk out of here. To end it all. Right now. She has too much power over me. She is no good for me. She is nothing but trouble. Any fool can see that. And then... a voice stronger than all the other objections flying into my head. It says: She belongs here. Without her, this conservatory would be barren. Everything is barren without her.

I turn away from her. I cannot let her see my face, my thoughts. I walk back towards the sofa. I stare down at it as I control my breathing. This is a transaction. An arrangement. She gives me sex and I pay her for it. Nothing more. I sit on the sofa, lean back comfortably, and look at her coldly.

"You want to fuck. Show me how much you want to. Let's see if I still enjoy your company."

She starts moving towards me slowly, a look of complete disbelief etched into her features. "You want me to prove myself to you?"

"Exactly. Show me you're worth all this money I'm paying out."

Her eyes widen. "You're joking."

"I was never more serious in my life. You can't be the only one reaping all the benefits. Why don't you put yourself to work and try to convince me that you're worth the headache you come with?"

She reaches me and I feel a small flare of satisfaction. Her eyes are guarded, but I can see that she is visibly startled and understands now she holds no power over me. Slowly, her gaze begins to travel down my body, lingering on my hard cock.

I spread my legs even wider, giving her a full view.

"Say something," she urges in a small whisper.

But I shake my head slowly. I hold all the power in this relationship and it's about time she realizes it.

Chapter Thirty-Two

LARA

Okay, I'm a lifelong feminist. I started at six years old when I boxed Jason Appleby in the ear when he told me girls can't be astronauts, so the man sitting in front of me should be enemy number one, but to my horror, he's not. I'm not the least bit turned off by his declaration that he's bought me at all. In fact, his caveman attitude and the thought of being his sex toy tempts me and fills me with a strange and crazy excitement.

It feels more like a challenge. He wants me to give him his money's worth. Sure. I'll show him how hot and heavy I can get. This is the most illicit relationship of my life, so why not? Why the hell not?

"All right. Let's go to bed then," I say and begin walking towards the entrance, but there is no movement behind me. He isn't following me. When I turn back, even the mocking smile has vanished from his face. He is dead serious about doing it here. I literally have to give him his money's worth.

"I'm a real estate agent, not a hooker," I tell him.

His response comes as quickly and brutally as a slap. "And I'm a businessman, not a bank. But you've managed to make me one to fit your needs, so I suggest you adjust to mine now or call it quits."

I look at the contract and shake my head. "I can just leave," I say. "You said it yourself—you're not holding me hostage here. Doing that would be kidnapping."

He crosses his arms, his face smug. "Go ahead. I'm not stopping you."

Smug bastard. I know he's pushing me, daring me. I glance back at the door. "Muriel might come in at any moment," I say, searching for an excuse.

"I don't hire stupid people," he replies callously.

That's that excuse gone. I bite my bottom lip. My heart races as I'm still torn between the instinct to retreat and the inexplicable pull of his magnetic eyes. His gaze is fixed on mine, unwavering and full of that same intensity that always makes me feel exposed like he can see right through me. Every breath feels heavy, every second longer than the last as the air between us grows thick with tension. He's watching, waiting for my next move.

I walk towards him, all the while holding his gaze. Lowering myself to my knees, I place my hands on his thighs. His eyebrows raise slightly as I silently begin to unbuckle his belt.

My hands tremble slightly, and to hide this, I try to move faster. I have my hand on his zipper, ready to pull it down. I glance up at his face then. His face is deliberately expressionless, and I cannot tell what he is thinking.

I realize I want to surprise him.

For once, I want to see him not be in complete control of everything—of his emotions, of his mood, of his desire. I want to see him under my control, even if it's just for a moment.

The zipper comes down easily, revealing dark briefs and the hard bulge beneath them. I pause, feeling the tension between us.

"Can you help?" I ask, my voice low.

It takes him a moment to react, his eyes narrowing as he studies me. "Intimidated?"

"A bit," I confess. "We are strangers, after all."

He holds my gaze for a moment before reaching into his briefs and pulling his cock out. "We're strangers?" he repeats, his voice low. "We're not strangers after last night. I know what you taste like—every aspect of you. Your skin, your tongue, your pussy."

I cannot stop the hot heat rushing up my neck and into my cheeks. Trying to hide it I bend my head and my attention is immediately caught by his cock. I knew it was huge; after all, I felt every bit of it the previous night. But seeing it now, in broad daylight, is an entirely different experience.

He is massive, with a lush pink head and thick veins snaking around the shaft. He's so hard it looks almost painful, and it makes me realize just how much he wants me, just how intense his desire is for me. I've never had such a big dick in my mouth before and I don't know if he is going to fit inside my mouth.

"Are you going to get to work, or was all this a waste like my entire morning has been?"

Smug asshole! I'm tempted deeply to get up and kick him, but as I look down once again at the gorgeous cock and the need to take him is greater than the need to kick him. I want to taste him so bad I can't think straight. My mouth waters as I think about what I'm about to do.

My lips hover inches from him. I can feel the heat of his skin. His cock, still hard but pulsing with a vulnerability I've never seen from him before, catches my gaze.

With my hand resting on his thigh I brace myself and his body tenses. From the corner of my eyes, I catch the way his jaw clenches as I wrap my fingers around the hard shaft. He's solid and thick, and I can feel every throb in those greenish veins against my palm. The anticipation is building inside me as I lean closer, letting my breath brush against him.

I start slow, my lips barely touching the head of his cock.

His breath hitches. Just for a second, but I know I've already got him. His I'm the big I am, macho talk was just that. Talk. He will be jelly in my hands. A thrill runs through me, a sense of power that I haven't felt in a long time. I stretch my lips, taking him in, feeling the velvet heat glide across my tongue. His taste, salty and musky, floods my senses, and I close my eyes as I sink further down, letting him fill my mouth.

He groans a deep, guttural sound that reverberates through my body. His hand slides into my hair, not pulling, just resting on my scalp as if to ground himself.

"That's it," he mutters, his voice rough.

I can't tell if he's praising or commanding me. The tension in his body is palpable, and it's intoxicating to know that I'm the one making him feel this way. I swirl my tongue, slow at first, testing his reaction, and when he moans again, low and deep, I feel a surge of satisfaction.

I pull back, letting my tongue trace the ridge of his head, savoring every moment. His fingers tighten in my hair, and I glance up to meet his eyes, finding them dark with hunger. I pause, my lips still touching him, and his gaze locks with mine. That look makes my stomach flip.

"You're good at this," he says, his voice barely a whisper. "I hate to think why that is."

I smile inwardly and let my hand stroke him slowly, teasingly as I take him deeper, my mouth hot and wet around him. His head falls back, and he lets out a long groan.

I quicken my pace, hollowing my cheeks as I move up and down, feeling him slide between my lips. His body is taut with tension, and I know he's holding back, trying not to let go too soon. I take him further and further into my throat. He swears under his breath, and I feel victorious, like I've got him exactly where I want him.

But there's something else there too—something softer. I slow down, savoring the feeling of him in my mouth and his fingers relax slightly in my hair. I let my eyes drift closed as my tongue swirls like a snake around him.

I pull back just enough to breathe and find him staring at me, his gaze awed. His thumb strokes my cheek, and for a moment, it feels tender, almost affectionate.

"You're a walking disaster when it comes to selling a house, but that's one hell of a blowjob technique you've got going there," he says, his voice low and ragged.

I don't answer. Instead, I slide back down on his cock, while pressing my tongue flat against him and moving a much faster rhythm. I can feel him getting close to going over the edge, simply by the way his grip in my hair tightens and his hips start to move. He's fucking my mouth.

Instantly, I go faster, my hand moving in time with my mouth, and he lets out a sound that's half a growl, half a plea. I can feel him throbbing, so close.

"Don't stop," he mutters, his voice rough and needy.

I increase my speed until he's there, his body going rigid, his breath catching in his throat. I feel the pulse of him against my tongue, the way he grips my hair like it's the only thing keeping him anchored. He calls my name, his voice breaking.

I swallow, taking his cream, feeling the heat of him slide down my throat.

When it's over, I pull back slowly, my lips lingering on his skin. Like a cat I lick his shaft with small delicate licks. All the while we just stare at each other, breathing heavily, the air between us electric and charged with something I can't quite name.

"Not bad for a stranger, huh?" I tease, but my voice is hoarse and unsteady.

"Yeah," he says, but his voice is oddly different and there is a strange look in his eyes. "Not bad at all."

It would have been a great end to my performance if I could have stood up and walked out of there with my head held high, and I would have loved to be able to do that, but when I stand my knees feel week. I collapse on the sofa next to him.

I don't know what just happened between us, but giving him that blowjob affected me in a way I did not expect. It makes me want him even more. I loved doing it more than I ever did sucking another man, and I am now convinced I'm in a lot of trouble.

I stare at him speechlessly. "I should go," I whisper, and start to stand, but he grabs my hand and pulls me back down. I don't fight back.

His eyes are half-lidded and mysterious. It leaves me feeling off balance like I'm teetering on the edge of something I can't quite name. The sunlight filters through the leaves, illuminating the planes of his face, casting shadows that make him look even more dangerous and... alluring.

"You're not done," he says, and there's a promise in his voice, something raw and deep that makes my body respond immediately. A shiver runs down my spine, and I can feel the heat gathering between my thighs, my skin tingling with anticipation. I know what he means, and the thought sends a rush of adrenaline through me.

Of course, I'm not done.

My panties are soaking wet and my clit feels so swollen and hot. I want his mouth on me again... and again. My eyes meet his, and I'm sure he can see it—how badly I want him, how much I need this. "I... uh..." My voice falters, and I hate how vulnerable I sound. His fingers curl into the waistband of my trousers. Before I can react, he tugs them down, the fabric sliding down my skin and pooling at my feet. He kicks them away and catches me and pulls me onto his lap.

When I am astride him, he draws my feet up to either side of his thighs, then slowly lowers my body backwards until my head is resting on the cold stones between his feet. I can smell the polish from his shoes. He seizes my knees firmly and slides me further along on the stones, then when I am in the position he desires, he parts my knees wide open. I have never been in this position before. A spray of tiny cream flowers dip from the canopy of green overhead and I watch it in a haze of anticipation and excitement.

He drops his head forward and eats at me through the lace. I grip his knees and gasp with the shock of sensations that course through me. Licking, sucking and even biting. Then he tears the lace with his teeth and eats hungrily. Far more ravenously than he did last night. As if he is starving. Like a wild animal. A wolf no less. Making slurping, growling noises as he feasts voraciously on me.

The heat from his mouth feels like fire, and I can't stop the way my hips instinctively roll against his feral mouth, searching for more of that delicious friction. His hands are everywhere—gripping my hips, running down my sides.

The sensations are almost too much. His tongue works against me with a skill that makes me cry out, the sound loud and uninhibited. No more thoughts of Muriel. In fact, every coherent thought has slipped away as I grind mindlessly against his mouth. I start to see the sunlight filtering in through the leaves as shining spots of light, like twinkling stars, the spray of little flowers seems to glow, and I know I'm losing myself. There is no going back.

He pulls away, his lips glistening, and hoists me up into a sitting position on his lap. What? I almost start begging him to finish the job. My body aches with need.

"Take me inside you," he commands in a voice that sends shivers through me.

With my hands on his shoulders, I lift myself, align my hips, and impale myself on his erect cock. I cry out at the jolt of sensual pleasure as he stretches me to the full. I take him in, inch by delicious inch. When I think I can't take anymore, he grips my hips possessively and pushes me down so his cock thrusts deeper and deeper into me. His eyes lock onto mine with a look full of pure lust. When I'm finally fully seated, he allows a pause, the perfect moment suspended in a shared breath as if the entire universe has stopped just for us.

His hands slide up my body.

I can feel the warmth of his touch through the thin fabric. It's almost reverent the way he looks at me like he's savoring every second, every inch of my skin that he's about to uncover. His eyes lock onto mine, and the intensity in them sends a shiver down my spine, making me ache for more.

Slowly, he tugs the straps of my camisole down, letting the fabric slide over my shoulders. His fingers graze my skin, leaving a trail of heat that has me trembling, my breath catching in my throat. When the camisole slips down further, exposing my breasts, his pupils grow and his gaze becomes dark and heavy with desire. It feels like he's memorizing every detail, every curve.

He leans in, his mouth finding my skin and presses soft kisses along the line of my collarbone, and then lower, until his lips brush over my hard nipples. The sensation is electric, and I gasp, my fingers tightening in his hair as he circles my nipple with his tongue, teasing and tasting. It's a slow, torturous rhythm, one that makes my body arch toward him, silently begging for more.

His hand moves up to cup my other breast, his thumb brushing over the sensitive peak, and the combination of his mouth and hand is almost too much. He sucks gently, then harder, his tongue flicking in a way that sends sparks of pleasure shooting through me. My head falls back, and I let out a high-pitched call, unable to hold back the sounds of my own need.

His hands roam over my body, sliding down my sides, his fingers tracing the curve of my waist, before they move back up to my breasts, squeezing and caressing. The warmth of his touch, the way his hands feel against my bare skin, is indescribably sweet. He's taking his time, savoring every inch of me, and it makes me feel more desired than I've ever been before.

His mouth moves from one breast to the other, sucking and teasing, and I can feel the heat pooling between my thighs, my body responding to every touch, every kiss. His hands hold me steady as I tremble beneath his touch. I arch into him, my fingers curling around the back of his neck, pulling him closer, wanting to feel every bit of him against me. This is heaven.

When he finally pulls back, his breath warm against my skin, I'm left feeling raw and hungry for more. His eyes meet mine, and there's a possessiveness in his gaze that makes my heart beat like a trapped bird. It's like he's telling me without words that he's not done, that there's so much more he wants to explore, to feel, and I find myself aching to give him everything.

"Ride me," he groans, his voice husky and strained, and I know he's just as lost in this as I am. I start bouncing on his hard cock. It's fast, frantic—each movement bringing me closer to the edge. I can feel every inch of him inside me, hitting all the right spots. I cling to him, my fingers digging into his shoulders as I throw my head back, lost in the feeling.

His hands move to my ass, squeezing and guiding me as I ride him harder. His mouth finds my breast, and the sensation of his lips, his tongue swirling over my skin, is enough to start the first waves. I'm losing myself, the pleasure building higher and higher until it's almost unbearable. I can't think; I can only feel—the heat of his body, the way he fills me so perfectly, the wet slapping sound of our bodies coming together.

"Faster," he urges, and I obey, my movements becoming more frantic, more desperate as I chase the release that's so close I can taste it. His touch becomes rough and fierce, but so, so good, and when he thrusts up hard, I come undone. My body shudders and breaks into millions of pieces as my cries echo through the conservatory.

Those cries... they are his name!

The explosive climax goes on and on and it is like nothing I've ever experienced. And I know then that he has ruined me for all other men.

He follows right after, his grip tightening as he spills inside me, his head falling back against the chair, a deep, guttural groan ripping out of him. I feel the heat of him filling me, and the sensation only prolongs my pleasure, drawing out every last bit of my climax until I'm shaking, my body spent.

For a long while, neither of us move. We're both breathing heavily, our bodies still tangled together, the aftershocks leaving me feeling raw and exposed. I can't look into his eyes. I collapse against him, resting my head on his shoulder as I catch my breath. His arms wrap around me, holding me close, and for a moment, it's not just about the sex—it's something deeper, something that scares me as much as it thrills me.

We stay like that, our bodies pressed together. Neither of us speaks. We would only spoil it with our snipping and bickering. I can feel the warmth of his skin against mine, the way his fingers trace patterns on my back. I close my eyes and pretend we are not what we are. We are real lovers. For once, I don't want to think about what comes next.

I just want to savor this perfectly beautiful thing that happened in a magical forest in the middle of New York City.

Chapter Thirty-Three

IVAN

Heading back to the office after the time I spent with Lara at my home feels strange. Something happened in that conservatory. Every step I take is heavy as if I left a part of myself behind with her. I can't stop thinking about her—no matter how hard I try.

It's distracting, maddening even.

The way she looked at me, the way she trembled, her lips on my skin. She lingers in my mind, refusing to go, like a shadow that follows no matter where I turn. I've had much more experienced partners but none of them managed to get under my skin like she has. She's there, embedded in my thoughts, and I find myself unable to focus on anything else.

When I finally reach my office, I sit behind my desk, staring blankly at the paperwork piled in front of me. I should be diving into the day's agenda. The New York Stock Exchange opened hours ago and I have a couple of risky open trades that I should monitor, but all I can think about is her.

I keep replaying everything in my head, trying to make

sense of my obsession with her. They circle in my mind like a whirlwind. Round and round. It doesn't make sense. This won't do. This is meant to be a purely sexual escapade. I try to force myself to focus, but all I see is her pale body stretched out on the stone floor, her pussy open like the most beautiful pink flower imaginable. My cock starts to stir.

I'm lost in those thoughts when there's a knock on my door.

Greta strides into my office, her sharp heels echoing off the hardwood floor. The sight of her cold beauty snaps me back to reality, away from thoughts of Lara's vulnerable innocence. Greta is professional as always, holding her folder to her chest. Her expression is neutral, carefully composed. There's no hint of what she thinks about the way I have bought and paid for Lara—just business.

Her voice is crisp and professional as she walks over to my desk. She flips open the folder. "I've made the necessary adjustments following your changes this morning."

I lean back in my chair, nodding, trying to appear like I'm paying full attention, but she looks alien to me. Everything feels wrong. In my head Lara's gorgeous eyes are looking up at me from the stone floor.

I'm fucking hooked. It's an addiction I never saw coming. I thought I was buying her! Ha, ha, what a joke. The joke's on me.

"Your breakfast meeting at the Four Seasons has been rescheduled to Le Bernardin's drinks bar," she continues, her tone detached, almost clinical. "The appointment is confirmed for 7:30 p.m."

Le Bernardin. It's a perfect place for closing deals with its quiet elegance and impeccable service.

"Good," I reply. Even my voice sounds different. I tap my

fingers on the desk. "Make a reservation for two at the restaurant afterwards."

Her pen pauses over her notepad, and I can sense her curiosity. "For another business matter, Sir?"

"No, not business."

She tries to hide it, but there's a flicker of something. Displeasure, maybe. She doesn't like Lara. Greta is superefficient, capable, and loyal, but she can't understand why I'm behaving this way with Lara. Why I am willing to pay so much just for a woman? She's probably already decided Lara is temporary, just another woman passing through. She doesn't know what's really going on in my head, she doesn't know about the way Lara lingers even when she's not around.

"Understood," she says. "I'll make sure to get the best table for Miss Fitzpatrick and you."

She's holding back, I can tell. There's an edge to her tone, as if she disapproves but knows better than to say anything. Her job is to manage my life and keep it running smoothly, not to interfere in it in any way.

"Is there anything else, Greta?"

She flips with unnecessary violence to another page in her folder. "Your mother called regarding the charity gala tomorrow evening. She wanted confirmation that you will be attending. What shall I tell her?"

I think of that carefully staged social nightmare, of all the eyes and conversations I'll have to navigate. It's always a carefully staged dance.

"Yeah, tell her I'll be there."

"Do you need me to arrange anything for the occasion?"

"Arrange for Steven to chauffeur me."

"Of course," Greta replies, jotting it down. Her professionalism is impeccable, but I can feel the undercurrent. She's watching closely for any changes, for decisions that deviate from my usual routine.

"And about the trip this weekend," she continues, "your mother's birthday in France. Shall I finalize the travel arrangements?"

"There might be an issue. The DA's office is still poking around. I need to make sure they won't interfere with my plans."

She gives me a quick nod. "I'll keep the flight details flexible until you confirm."

"By the way, there will be two of us on the trip."

I see the slight lift of her eyebrow. This time the disapproval is more obvious. She doesn't think it is proper for me to take Lara to my mother's birthday, but her voice is carefully neutral. "Right."

"That's it. Will you get the DA on the phone for me?"

She nods, turns smartly, and leaves with her back ramrod straight. Strange. She is bristling with suppressed jealousy. As if... Is she in love with me? I dismiss the thought immediately. Of course not. I've known her too long. There would have been signs. I lean back in my chair with a sigh. It's infuriating the way DA is circling, looking for a way to pin something on me. They never have anything solid, but they keep pushing, hoping I've slipped up somewhere.

My phone bleeps and I pick it up. "David Madley on the line," Greta says and clicks off.

I keep my voice friendly, casual. "David, good to speak with you. I wanted to check on the status of the investigation. I have a trip planned, and I want to make sure there are no restrictions."

His voice is smooth, too smooth. "As of now, there's nothing stopping you. If anything comes up, you'll be the first to know."

I grip the phone tighter. It's all politics and leverage with him. A game that people with limited amounts of power play.

"Good to hear."

He laughs, and it grates on my nerves. "No problem, but be careful. Anything can come up, anytime."

He has nothing and he knows it, but it's always the same: veiled, unspoken allegations and threats while he tries his damnedest to find something, anything that he can use against me.

I end the call in a sour mood. I know they're waiting for me to make a mistake. I'll try to move money from one jurisdiction to another or something else equally desperate. But I won't. I've played by the rules. Done nothing illegal.

My record and conscience are clear.

Chapter Thirty-Four

LARA

I lie on the bed staring at the ceiling. In shock.

I can still feel the imprint of his touch. I don't understand what's going on. We've only had sex twice and he's already managed to get under my skin. Far, far more than I'd like to admit. It's starting to feel like… God no!

I'm not falling in love with him. No way.

I don't even want to be thinking about such a thing. That way lies madness.

I get up, feeling restless, and pace the room. Maybe I should go to the office. But I can't face Dad, his guilt or misplaced anger. But I have to do something or I swear, I will go crazy. I feel like calling him. I feel like hearing his voice, but I know better to call him at work. I can still remember how cold and horrible he was the last time I called him.

But now that I have thought of calling him, I'm itching to pick up the phone and speak to him. I come to an abrupt halt and shut my eyes again. I am just being pathetic and clingy. No man wants a desperate woman. And yet I find myself walking towards my phone, my hand hovers over it. *Don't do it, Lara.* But I pick it up and flick it open. My index finger hovers over his number. *Don't do it, Lara. You'll regret it.*

"Damn you, Ivan," I mutter.

I bite my lip and just as I'm about to press the button, there's a knock on the door. The breath I was holding comes out in a rush. Saved by the bell, it seems.

I open the door and find Muriel standing outside with a tray in her hand. "I thought you might want some scones hot from the oven and Chef's raspberry jam," she says, smiling warmly. "You barely touched breakfast earlier."

Barely touched breakfast. I ate enough to feed two horses, but her kindness touches me. "Oh... thank you, but you shouldn't have gone to all this trouble."

She steps inside and sets the tray down on the coffee table. "It's no trouble. I know how overwhelming it can be when you're in a new place." The fragrance of the freshly baked scones fills the room and the comforting scent is just what I need.

I nod, eternally grateful for the distraction. "You're very thoughtful. Thank you. Are you responsible for the fairytale garden on the roof?"

Muriel lights up as if the garden itself fills her with life. "I am. It's one of my passions. I grew up in a squalid council estate in England, but I've always loved gardening so when Mr. Ivanovich has been generous enough to give me complete freedom with it, I went for it."

I arch a brow, genuinely intrigued. "So you're from England."

"Yes."

"Have you known Ivan for a long time?"

Her gaze softens, as if the memories themselves are as fragrant as the flowers she grows so beautifully. "Oh, yes. I've been with Mr. Ivanovich for eleven years now. He had just left Russia and was setting up his base in London. I was supposed to be based in his London apartment, but after a while he began to take me everywhere he went."

"I see," I say softly. "So he's a good employer?"

"He is family. I'd trust him with my life," she says simply.

"Oh!" I exclaim.

Ivan Ivanovich's housekeeper regards him as family and trusts him with her life. Wow. I'm quiet, trying to reconcile this side of him with the man I've encountered. It feels like peeking behind a curtain, seeing a glimpse of a person I never expected. I thought he was just another powerful man who coasted through life, buying his way through everything. There's more to him than I thought.

A small pang of envy flows into my body. She's known him for so long, and she seems to have this unspoken bond with him. It's effortless and pure, untainted by sex and wanting and resentment. It is something I'll never have with him.

"I've always wanted a garden," I say, more to change the subject than anything else. "But I'm afraid plants don't like me too much. I tend to kill even the supposedly hardy houseplants I put on the windowsill."

Muriel's eyes brighten. "Well, you're welcome to learn while you're here. It's late summer. I'll be happy to teach you everything I know."

I feel a buzz of excitement at the prospect "I'd love that. Can we... sorry if I'm being too forward, but can we start today? Like now..."

She grins and it lights up her whole face. "Of course. But after the scones."

"Deal."

She waits while I cut a scone in half, butter it, spread a

generous amout of clotted cream and jam on it, then eat it in three mouthfuls. It's delicious. Then I grab my phone off the bedside table and follow her out of the room, feeling a sudden lightness, like I'm breaking free from the weight that's been sitting on my chest.

We walk down the grand staircase in silence, the soft patter of our steps echoing in the quiet hallways. The afternoon light filters through the windows, casting warm shadows as we head toward the conservatory, the tension I've been carrying since Ivan left eases off.

As soon as we enter the conservatory it's like walking into another world again. This time, I notice the vines that have been skillfully trained to drape the walls. Sunlight pours through the glass ceiling, bathing the sofa where Ivan took me in a golden glow. I turn my head away quickly.

Muriel leads me deeper in. The conservatory is bigger than I first thought. Her steps are quick and confident like she knows every corner, every leaf. The garden stretches out beyond the forest-like plants, and I'm surrounded by a patchwork of flowers and herbs—small clusters of marigolds, basil, rosemary, and rows of tomatoes. I take a deep breath, inhaling the mix of fresh earth, and blooming flowers.

"When I first got my hands on this place," Muriel says, her voice soft, "it was just sad, you know? They discarded all the gorgeous miniature trees and lovely greenery they had used for the showing and only left behind a few house plants that had seen better days. I had to start from scratch."

She points at the marigolds, their fiery orange petals almost glowing. "These are my summer fighters. Late bloomers, and they just fill up the space with this burst of color. It makes everything feel alive, even when other flowers are fading."

Her hands sweep toward the wooden box full of lavender.

"Lavender's my favorite. There are no bees so I pollinate them all myself with a brush. I love their calming scents so much that I use the flowers to make little sachets for the pillows. Keeps things smelling fresh."

I nod. "Aha! That's what I was smelling last night."

She smiles. "Yes."

"You've planned this place like a story," I say, noticing how everything seems to flow.

There's a twinkle in her eye. "That's exactly it. It's not just a garden; it's an ecosystem. The basil grows well next to the tomatoes, and the rosemary keeps the pests away. Everything works together, and in return, it all thrives."

I feel myself relax as we move through rows of flowers—dahlias, climbing roses, and these bright purple flowers. Each patch feels like it has its own personality, its own mood, and I'm getting lost in her stories about them. It's not just flowers and plants to her; it's her whole world.

I touch a velvety leaf, it's like satin under my fingers. "It shows. You've put your heart into this, haven't you?"

She laughs, a warm sound that feels as comfortable as the garden itself. "I have. It's my passion, you know? It's my little haven. A sanctuary—somewhere you can step into and the plants will heal you."

I realize I'm not thinking about Ivan or the tension that's been brewing since I met him. For the first time, it's quiet inside my head. This isn't anything like the chaos of the city or my small apartment with its half-dead cactus on the windowsill. This is something else entirely.

"Honestly, it does feel like a sanctuary," I admit, a little surprised at myself for saying it out loud.

Muriel smiles, and I sense her pride and love for the truly marvelous space she's created. "It's my joy. So if you really want to learn and there's plenty we can cover while you're here if you're happy to get your hands dirty."

I find myself smiling back, a real smile. "I'd love that. This is more than I ever thought I'd get to learn."

As we wrap up the tour, my phone buzzes in my pocket, pulling me. I take it out, and my heart does a little jump when I recognize the number that flashes across the screen. It's Ivan's coldly beautiful PA.

"Miss Fitzpatrick," she begins, her voice as sharp as nails. "You're having dinner at Le Bernardin tonight. The chauffeur will pick you up at seven sharp. Don't keep him waiting and make sure you dress appropriately."

My temper is immediately aroused. Where does she get off talking to me in that bossy tone, and making out as if I don't know how to dress appropriately for dinner at a good restaurant? But I don't betray my resentment. I keep my voice cool. "Dinner with Ivan?"

"Yes," she confirms, her tone irritated. "He has a prior meeting so you will be joining him after. Please be punctual. Mr. Ivanovich hates to be kept waiting Oh, and I'll call you tomorrow to discuss arrangements for the Gala."

I'm almost amused by how annoyed she is with me. "Sure, whatever," I say nonchalantly, knowing that my casual attitude is guaranteed to piss her off even more.

As I expected, the call briskly comes to an end and I stand there holding my phone, my nerves all a flutter. Dinner with Ivan. Like a date. Well, well. I slide my phone back into my pocket, trying to keep the fluttering in my chest at bay. Dinner is hours away, but knowing it's going to happen makes me feel restless.

Muriel notices the look on my face. "Everything alright?"

"Yes, everything is just fine," I say, a big, happy smile on my face.

"Good."

Later on, as I return to my room, I can't help but feel the thrill growing inside me. It's ridiculous—just dinner, nothing more. I look at the time and realize I have only a couple of hours to get ready and I feel a sense of urgency. What should I wear? And why do I care so much? In order to keep myself in check, I go to my room and deliberately scroll through my Instagram to look for garden ideas so I can resist the urge to run to the closet and browse through the available options.

Chapter Thirty-Five

IVAN

"As I was saying, the new site near Chicago would significantly cut down transportation costs for the Midwest distribution," Levi says, his black eyes watching and shrewd over his glass of whiskey.

My eyes slide towards the window. "Sounds promising. I'll get one of my guys to look over the legal side of things."

The view outside shows the steady movement of traffic, yellow cabs weaving in and out, and the warm glow of streetlights bouncing off the passing cars. The restaurant, positioned right in the heart of Manhattan, has a perfect view of the city streets. It is the kind of place where deals get closed and fortunes are made, but right now, all I'm interested in is the black sedan I've been waiting to see pull up.

I catch the glint of its sleek exterior, and my attention sharpens. The doorman steps forward as she emerges from the back seat. She's wearing jeans and a tucked-in black t-shirt, paired with heels—casual but effortlessly striking. Her hair is loose and flowing as she steps onto the sidewalk. I thought she'd dress up. It's dinner at a top-tier place, not some corner café. Greta should've told her that.

I force myself to turn back to the clients. "Let's wrap this up for today. I'll have my team review it by next week and get back to you then."

Both men in front of me nod, pleased with the outcome of our meeting, but my mind is already elsewhere. As soon as they leave, I call Greta.

"Greta, didn't you tell Lara where we were having dinner?" I ask, keeping my voice calm.

"Of course, I did. I also told her to be punctual. Is she not there yet."

"It's all good. She's here now," I say and hang up.

She's defying me, and it's obvious. I look across the room and catch sight of her approaching the hostess. Even so, I can't deny it—she still looks breathtaking. The jeans hug her in all the right places, and the casual look somehow makes her stand out even more. But I wanted her in something different tonight, something that I had paid for. I wanted to see her skin exposed, her cleavage enticing me throughout dinner. Something that I could simply pull up and eat her out in the back of the car on the way home

However, once again, she has robbed me of this fantasy. I wonder what to do about this. Maybe I should punish her. The thought of punishing her excites me. I think of putting her on my knees and smacking her bottom until it is red…

I wave to the waiter. "Bring her over to the table."

As she approaches, I watch her every move. There's a confidence in her stride, a spark in her eyes—a defiance that sets my nerves on edge. When she meets my gaze, I feel it: a challenge, an unspoken dare. And it's not just defiance; there's something else there, too, something I can't quite name, and it gnaws at me.

"You look...different from what I expected."

She lifts an eyebrow, her expression almost daring me to continue. "What did you expect?"

I don't mince my words. "A dress? Some effort?"

"Well, I didn't feel like playing dress-up," she says, her tone casual.

"Making an effort for dinner is playing dress-up?"

She looks up at me. "Yes, it feels that way. I should be able to wear what I want."

I lean back, trying to keep my cool, but the irritation rises. "I'm paying you to look the part. Very heftily, I might add. And yet you can't dress up for dinner."

Her eyes flash, and I know I've struck a nerve. She sits down, her movements deliberate, controlled.

The tension between us builds, a palpable thing. She's upset. No, more than upset. She's wounded. It's in the way she looks past me, like she's shutting me out. And that stings, more than I care to admit. I want to take my cruel words back, to say something kind that will undo the hurt in her eyes, but I can't. Years of living walled up in my own world makes me turn away and signal the waiter over.

"Drinks list for the lady, please."

The waiter hands it to her and she takes it and smiles her thanks to him, but her fingers hesitate on the pages. She's not even really looking. "

"I have no idea what to choose," she says finally, her voice flat. "Everything looks expensive, and I usually just drink the cheap stuff."

"Choose anything you want," I say, but I am shocked. Shocked by how affected I am that I have hurt her.

She pushes the menu back across the table. "Whatever you recommend."

The waiter stands by, waiting.

I skim the list, but the names blur together. She's nothing like what I thought she was going to be like. She is not following directions; she's making a point. I shouldn't let her get to me, but she does. "Just bring us a bottle of Château Margaux."

She pretends to flip through the food menu, but it's obvious she's not reading a single word. She's closing herself off, like she's building a wall between us. I pick up my own menu, pretending not to care either that our first dinner together is already ruined. I know it's my fault. I started it, but fuck her. I've paid a fortune to have her company.

"What's the special tonight?" I ask when the waiter returns.

He starts listing the options off in a ridiculous French accent—every dish is made to sound impressive and extravagant so that it all sounds like it's straight out of a Michelin kitchen.

"The grilled summer peaches with Serrano ham to start and the Black label fillet steak to follow," I decide, shutting the menu. "For both of us."

She looks up, and there's fury in her eyes. "I wasn't ready to order."

I clench my jaw.

She holds the menu out to the waiter. "Fine. I'll have the same."

It feels like every choice we're making tonight is a battle, and I don't even know why. Every time I think we're getting somewhere, she finds a way to pull back, and it drives me insane.

The waiter leaves, and the silence between us feels heavy, like a weight pressing down on my chest. I hold her gaze, searching for something, anything that might break through.

"Why is it that every time I think we're making progress, you do this?" I ask, my tone rougher than I intend.

Her eyes don't waver. "Maybe because your version of progress is just you getting what you want."

The words hang between us, and I feel the sting of them, like a slap I didn't see coming. I want to argue, to push back, but I learned a long time ago. Only the truth hurts. I've always been in control—of everything. But she's turning the tables on me. I don't know if I want to fight her or pull her close, but it's now obvious that every time she challenges me like this, it makes me want her even more. The silence stretches, thick and charged.

For the first time in my life, I feel like I'm losing control, and it terrifies me.

Chapter Thirty-Six

LARA

I sit across from him, feeling a mix of hurt and defiance. I thought I looked fine—good, even. It's not that I didn't want to wear a dress, but the way Greta instructed me to dress appropriately irritated me. So, I chose this—jeans, a tucked-in black T-shirt and heels. I even tried a halter neck top before I left, but I didn't want to look like I was trying too hard to be sexy. Now, he's sitting there, looking all annoyed, as if what I'm wearing is a personal insult.

And then he ordered for me, which is a big no-no for me. It actually made me want to get up and leave. But the truth is, I'm hungry and I was planning on the steak anyway as I'd never had black Argentinian label steak before. Plus, the way that French waiter described the grilled peaches sounds too good to pass up.

I tell myself it's not all bad, seeing him irritated like this. About time he realizes he can't control everything about me. Also, he's starting to grow on me unexpectedly and unnaturally fast, and it's good to remind myself we are totally and absolutely incompatible outside the sack. We are almost like two different species. We can come together to mate, but that's it. After that, we must go back to being strangers.

We settle into a tense silence that neither of us wants to break. When the food arrives, I pick up my fork and concentrate on my peaches. A fine choice as it happens. I try to ignore how easy it is for him to behave as if I'm not even there. He doesn't make any effort to fill the silence, and I'm tempted to just let it ride. I see the papers stacked neatly on the table, and I realize he's been working. I miss working. I miss feeling useful, like I have a purpose. It reminds me of what I wanted to ask earlier.

"I've been thinking," I start.

He glances up at me, his eyes expectant.

"Would it be possible for me to work while I'm under contract? I mean, go back to my job during the day while you're at work."

At first, he doesn't respond, just keeps chewing as he stares at me, as if he's deciding on an answer. "I would have been friendly enough to consider it," he says eventually, voice cool. "But the simple fact is I'm paying you to be idle while I'm away and busy while I'm around."

I roll my eyes, but I can't hide my disappointment. "I found a book in the library about poisons," I say, trying to sound casual. "I could start learning how to make them."

He stops mid-chew, raising an eyebrow. "I don't have a library."

I give him a look. "You don't say."

He bursts out laughing. A deep laugh that's so surprising and so contagious an unintended laugh slips out of me too. Instantly, I lower my head to hide it, feeling a flicker of warmth in my chest.

He leans back. "What the hell is wrong with you?"

"Why do we have to argue over a dress?" I mutter, feeling defensive. "I'll dress up tomorrow. That's an actual event."

He studies me for a moment before nodding slowly. "Okay, I'll look forward to it."

I raise an eyebrow. "Why does it even matter? You've seen me naked already. It's not like a dress is going to change anything."

"What kind of guys have you been dating?"

"We're not dating?" I remind tartly.

"No?"

My heart skips several beats. I hate how he does that. How he can turn everything around with just one look, one word. I focus on my plate, trying to ignore the warmth spreading through me. I decide to change the subject, to steer us back to something safe.

"In case you're worried, I won't actually make poisons, but please don't order for me again."

He takes a sip of his wine. "I never order for my date, but something about you brings out the worst in me."

"Is that you saying sorry?"

"Yeah, that's me saying sorry."

"Okay. I'm sorry too that I pressed all your buttons and made you go haywire."

He smiles.

"By the way, I spent some time with Muriel in the conservatory today. She agreed to teach me to garden. Maybe gardening will keep me busy."

He stares at me curiously. "You liked her."

"Yes, very much."

He nods and smiles. "I hope you're not planning to steal her away from me."

"I got the impression I couldn't even if I wanted to. She's totally devoted to you."

He looks surprised. "Good. I hope she never leaves me. I've had her as my housekeeper ever since I left Russia."

I want to ask more about his life in Russia, about his family, but I hesitate. I shouldn't want to know more about him. It's not part of the deal. Instead, I let my eyes drift over him. He is wearing a brilliantly white shirt, a blue tie and a navy suit jacket. In this light, he looks good enough to eat. God, I hate how sexy he looks. I hate how, once again, I'm feeling the magnetic pull of him.

Black label steak arrives. It is the best steak I've ever eaten.

"Good choice," I say.

We lapse into silence and I wonder what he's thinking, but again, I resist the urge to ask personal questions. It's safer to stick to neutral topics.

"So, what's the gala about tomorrow?" I ask instead.

He wipes the corner of his mouth and sets down his fork. "It's for my mother's charity event—it's an annual gala that brings together some of the most influential figures in the community. They focus on supporting cultural preservation and women's initiatives. It helps build connections and raises significant funds for various charity organizations back in Russia."

I nod. "I take it you're not one for parties?"

He leans back in his chair, tilting his head as if considering my question. "What makes you say that?"

"Just a feeling. You seem like the type who'd rather be behind the scenes, pulling the strings and letting the puppets take all the glory."

He raises an eyebrow, a hint of amusement flashing in his eyes. "You think you've got me figured out, huh?"

I shrug, leaning forward slightly. "I don't know... do I?"

He leans in, his expression softening. "Sometimes, you

have to show up. Not because you want to. You go because your mother expects it."

I laugh. A bit of skepticism creeps into my voice. "And maybe it's just a game, showing off to people who know how powerful you are."

His eyes flicker and I get the feeling he is disappointed in me. "Sometimes, playing the game is the only way to win."

I sense that I have lost him. I had him and I lost him. Maybe he really is going just because his mother expects his presence, but I can't stop myself from poking the bear. "Winning is everything to you, isn't it?"

"Isn't it for everyone?" he counters. "We all want to feel like we've accomplished something, that we're moving forward. What about you? Why do you make your videos? You want to accomplish something with them, don't you?"

I feel a slight prick of annoyance, but I meet his gaze. "Well, one of them got you to notice me, didn't it?"

A smile tugs at the corner of his mouth. "You certainly accomplished that."

For some reason, his words don't feel as satisfying as they should. There's a hollow note to them, like he's pointing out something I didn't want to admit. I look down at my glass, feeling a twinge of uncertainty. My videos never sold any houses, all it brought was a man who wanted to buy me for sex.

He must notice my unhappy expression because he brings his glass to his lips, taking a slow sip before tilting his head. "Let me guess, now you hate me."

I shrug, feeling a mix of exasperation and amusement. "You know exactly how to get under my skin."

"Part of my charm," he says, his eyes twinkling.

"Charm, huh?" I challenge, crossing my arms. "More like a talent for infuriating people."

He lifts his glass. "I could say the same about you."

I raise an eyebrow, intrigued. "Oh really? How exactly am I doing that?"

He pauses for a moment as if considering his next words. "Maybe you're making me lose my sanity."

The way he says it, quiet, almost vulnerable, makes my heart skip. "Well, maybe we're even then."

Chapter Thirty-Seven

IVAN

I want to fuck her. Right now. "Ready to leave?"

She blinks, surprised. She thought we'd stay longer and talk a bit more. "Okay, sure."

I call my chauffeur and pay the bill quickly. We step outside together, our bodies not touching. The night air hits me, cool and sharp, but it does nothing to douse the heat inside. She stands there, illuminated by the glow of the city lights, and for a second, everything else fades. She's gorgeous—the way her hair catches the light, the translucence of her eyes.

My driver pulls up and gets out, opening the door for her, and she slides in, casting a look over her shoulder at me.

As the door closes and the driver settles in up front, I can feel her presence. Smell her skin… her shampoo… her pussy. The city moves around us, the hum of traffic and distant horns, but it's like everything outside the car is just a blur.

My eyes flick to her hands resting on her lap, her fingers tapping lightly like she's nervous. The temptation gnaws at me —if only she'd worn a dress.

She shifts beside me, and our eyes meet. There's a look there—curiosity, maybe even a challenge. It's like she knows she's driving me crazy.

I lean in, just a little, my voice low. "You know, you're making this really hard."

Her lips twitch like she's holding back a smile. "Am I?" she says, her tone playful, but there's something else there, something that makes my pulse quicken.

I glance up at the driver, feeling the heat rise in my chest. The tension is building, and I can't ignore it. I'm tired of pretending I can wait.

"You have no idea," I mutter, shifting closer until our knees touch. My hand inches toward hers. She doesn't pull away.

Instead, she looks at me, her eyes wide and questioning.

I lean in, the scent of her filling my senses. "I don't know how much longer I can hold back," I whisper, feeling the thrill of the moment, the urgency, the need to forget everything else and just take her.

She glances at the driver, then back at me, and there's a flicker of hesitation. "Here?" she asks, her voice barely audible.

"Why not?" I reply, and the thrill spikes. We both know it's risky, that the driver is right there, but it's exactly that—the closeness, the fact that we're supposed to hold back—that makes me want to break all the rules.

I slide my hand up her thigh, feeling her muscles tense, the hesitation in the way she leans back against the seat. Her eyes flicker to the front where the driver sits, and I can see the conflict there, the reluctance.

"We're not alone," she whispers, her voice tight. "The driver—he'll know. This isn't private."

I lean in close, my lips brushing her ear. "It's called privacy glass. He won't see or hear anything." I press a button and the partition goes up. "There. It's just us now," I murmur, my fingers tracing up her inner thigh. "No one else."

She bites her lip, eyes searching mine. "This still feels..." Her voice trails off, and I can tell she's wavering, the battle between her desire and her reservations playing out in her head.

"Trust me," I say, and kiss her, slow and deep, coaxing her into the moment. Her hands grip my shoulders, and I feel her start to respond, her mouth opening and her body melting into mine as she finally lets go.

The heat between us ignites, and I pull her fully onto my lap, feeling her settle against me. She hesitates for no more than a heartbeat, then her hands reach for my shirt, her fingers tugging, desperate.

"Ivan..." she whispers, and I can feel the urgency in her voice too. It's enough to drive me over the edge.

I grab her T-shirt, yanking it off her shoulders. It lands on the seat beside us.

I pause for a moment to take in the sight of her. I squeeze her breasts gently, feeling the weight of them.. Under her lacy bra, her nipples harden, and I circle my thumbs around them, watching her eyes flutter shut as a shiver runs through her. She's so responsive, so open, and it drives me wild. It's as if every touch, every movement, brings her closer to me, and I can't help but want more.

I lean down, kissing the swell of her breast, my lips grazing her skin as I trail kisses, savoring the way she trembles beneath me. I take my time, dragging it out, wanting to memorize every reaction, every soft sound that escapes her lips. I pull her bra cup down and suck a nipple into my mouth, feeling it tighten against my tongue. She gasps, her back arching, pressing herself closer.

My hands roam her body, gripping her waist, pulling her

in. I can feel the urgency in the way she moves. Her hips shift against me. I pull back slightly and my eyes lock on hers. There's something intense there, something that matches the fire burning in me.

She whispers my name again, and I feel her hands slide down to my shirt, tugging it up. Her touch is eager, it makes my pulse quicken. I watch her as she pulls my shirt tails out. She grinds against me, her jeans tight and rough against the fabric of my pants. I can barely hold back. My fingers trail up her back, and I reach for the clasp of her bra, undoing it. It snaps away, and I watch, mesmerized, as she pulls it off, tossing it aside.

She's bare now, her chest rising and falling with her quickened breaths, and I run my hands over her breasts again, feeling the softness, the way they fit perfectly in my hands. Her nipples pebble under my thumbs, and I take one into my mouth, sucking slowly, feeling her hands clutch at my shoulders. She moans, the sound vibrating through me, and I can't get enough.

I trail my kisses lower, down her belly, and she shivers as her hands slide into my hair.

"You make me lose my mind," she breathes huskily.

I lift my gaze to hers, feeling the truth in her words. It's the same for me—I'm lost in her. Nothing else matters.

She moves against me, and I guide her, lifting her just enough so I can reach between us, unzipping her jeans. I slide them down her hips, feeling the way she shifts to help me, her breath catching as the cool air hits her bare skin. I run my hand up her thigh, savoring the feel of her, every curve, every shiver.

"Tell me you want this," I whisper, my voice low, needing to hear it, needing her to say it.

"I want it," she says. There was no hesitation.

So we fuck. We fuck like animals. So hard, the car vibrates as it snakes through the city.

Chapter Thirty-Eight

LARA

The sun is high in the sky and the air is exceptionally warm but not oppressive in the conservatory. Muriel teaches me a surprising method of growing apples and oranges. Remove the two ends of the fruit, and rub garlic on the exposed part. Cut one-quarter of a medium-sized tomato into a little plastic cup, fill it with water, and stand the fruit on top of the water. And voila it's done. She says I can expect roots on my plants in seven to ten days.

Muriel moves away to speak to one of the maids, and I stand back and look at my row of potted plants with satisfaction. I have potted an orange, an apple, a bougainvillea cutting, and a green chili pepper.

The scent of earth and flowers fills my senses as I set about sticking the labels on the pots. I'm glad for the shade from the wide-brimmed hat and the long sleeves of the gardener's attire Muriel insisted I wear. I know it's to prevent sunburn, but today it feels more like armor, a way to hide. I need to hide because every time I think back to last night, my body tingles and my mind races.

I pat the soil, feeling the coolness beneath my fingertips. Then I gently water my plants. This is exactly what I need—something to keep me busy and distract me from the memory of Ivan's hands on me and the velvety sound of his voice in the dark.

Muriel is not back and I gaze curiously at an exotic plant with big fleshy leaves, normally only found in South American jungles. Muriel says it only flowers once a year and only at night. By day the flower has faded. She says she has seen the flower before and it is worth staying up for.

My thoughts wander. Flashes of last night play in my mind. I can't forget the way he looked at me as if I was the object of his entire attention. One of the maids comes into the conservatory with a tray of freshly squeezed pineapple juice and a tall glass filled with ice cubes. When I thank her, she nods with her eyes cast down and leaves quickly.

It's hard to ignore the feeling that the staff are gossiping about me. Not that I can blame them. I certainly would if I were them. My presence here must be very odd. How many of them know or have heard about what happened in the car last night? A part of me is mortified, but the other part... well, it doesn't give a damn. Let them think or say what they want. They don't know what it's like to feel the irresistible and seductive pull of Ivan Ivanovich.

After last night, Ivan and I parted without a word. I think both of us are in a bit of shock and need space to process whatever this is between us. It's clear that we hate each other's guts and yet we can keep our hands off each other.

I couldn't sleep for ages, my mind replaying how complete and absolute my surrender was. He could have done anything he wanted with me and I wouldn't have objected. When I finally drifted off, it was a restless, disturbed sleep. I dreamed I was getting married and my mother and I were going shopping for bridal dresses. She looked like she did in her thirties and my dad was there too. It was a good, happy dream. When I woke up this morning, tangled in the silky sheets, I found myself staring at the empty space beside me and feeling strangely alone.

But once I was dressed and making my way through the house, I realized Ivan was still around. He was clearly on his way out but had stopped to talk to one of his staff. I stopped dead in my tracks. For a few moments, our eyes met in the mirror. My breath caught, and I felt a rush of emotions—desire, confusion, and something powerful left over from last night. I almost turned around and fled back to my room, needing to escape before he saw how much that single glance affected me. But he turned away and headed out of the door.

This is why I'm hiding out here in the garden today, just in case he comes back early to prepare for the gala or something. I hear quick footsteps on the stone floor and my heart lurches into my throat. When I swing my head around, I see Greta striding toward me, her face pinched and annoyed, her heels clicking sharply. She's a stark contrast to the garden's tranquility, her presence breaking the quiet peace. I don't even have the energy to be snappy with her.

"Miss Fitzpatrick, I've been calling you for hours. What on earth are you doing?" she snaps, her voice slicing through the calm.

I wipe my hands on my jeans, feeling a twist of anxiety in my chest. I switched my phone off because I didn't want to speak to my father just yet. Not today. Tomorrow I will face his recriminations and guilt. "I'm just here gardening. What's wrong?"

"What's wrong?" she repeats, practically waving her phone

in my face like a weapon. "The gala is tonight at seven. It's already three o'clock! You need to get ready. There's an entire bunch of professionals waiting for you. Hair, makeup, nails—all of it at your suite at the St. Regis."

I stare at her in shock. The St. Regis is one of the most luxurious hotels in Manhattan. There's a mixture of emotions swirling inside me. He got her to arrange all of this for me? I stop with the dreamy train of my thoughts and tell myself it's just for show. All part and parcel of the image he needs me to project, but I can stop my heart from soaring a little. It feels... different. It feels as if he cares.

I push down the strange fluttery feeling in my chest. "Okay."

Greta nods curtly. "Good. Now, let's go. We're already behind schedule."

I follow her, leaving the tranquil peace behind, and we head to the waiting car. I lean back against the plush seat and watch the city rush past the windows. The ride is quiet, the tension between Greta and me unspoken, but thick and impenetrable. She's glued to her phone, typing furiously. I stare out at the city, feeling like I'm on the edge of something I can't quite name.

Walking into the St. Regis is like stepping into another world. The lobby is a masterpiece of sumptuous elegance. The floors gleam under crystal chandeliers and the staff move around with practiced efficiency. Everything about it feels glamorous and luxurious, removed from anything I'm used to.

My mind drifts back to the innocent, uncomplicated life I was living in my tiny box-like apartment just days earlier. My walls are a discolored beige so no matter how much sunlight streams in through the windows the place looks dull, but my rental agreement doesn't allow me to make changes. The corridor has a worn-out carpet and air almost smells of old coffee and stale smoking. Everything about that life was about small spaces and tight budgets repeating day after day.

But now here I am... in the middle of Manhattan, about to mingle with some of the city's elite. It feels surreal, like I'm caught in a current I can't escape, and I'm not sure if I want to resist or just let it take me wherever it's going.

Greta leads me up to the floor where the spa is located, and soon enough, I'm wrapped in the warmth of luxury. The staff greet me with practiced smiles, guiding me through each treatment as if I'm royalty. As they work, their hands knead into my muscles, releasing the tension knot by knot. The scent of eucalyptus, rose, and musk fills the air, and it's impossible not to feel the heaviness slip away. After a short while, I let myself sink into it—the clean sheets beneath me, the warmth of the oils soothing my skin. It's like floating, my body surrendering to pure indulgence and comfort. Even though a small voice whispers that I don't belong here, I push it aside. Sorry, but today I do.

When I feel almost too boneless to walk, I'm taken to the suite Ivan reserved. It's breathtaking—high ceilings, tall windows that overlook the city skyline. The deep red dress I chose waits for me on a hanger. Also waiting are the hair and make-up professionals. They set to work immediately.

Two hours later I stand in front of the mirror in my suite and stare at the stranger reflected back. The transformation is unbelievable. My hair is styled into a soft, romantic chignon, with delicate curls left loose to frame my face, making me look softer, almost ethereal. It is a style that feels both timeless and elegant, the kind you'd see in fashion magazines but never imagine having yourself.

The make-up artist has swept a rose-tinted blush over my cheeks, giving them a natural, flushed look, and lined my eyes with a smoky shadow. It makes my eyes seem twice as large and smolder mysteriously. And deep berry lipstick. I've never really used such bold colors. I never thought I could carry it off. But apparently, I can. I look sophisticated and classically regal; the likes of Carolyn Bessette-Kennedy.

I almost reach out to touch the glass, just to make sure that's really me. This isn't just about looking beautiful; it's about becoming someone else entirely—someone who belongs in this world, if only for tonight.

My hand flutters towards my stomach. I feel excitement and nerves, but also dread. I had fought this, and now it terrifies me to think that I might never want to leave, that, at the end of the day, I'll find that he was right all along.

I do want this. But more than this I want Ivan.

I run my hands down the smooth fabric of my dress, adjusting it, feeling the soft rustle of the material as it hugs my curves.

There's a knock on the door and my heart leaps. For a moment, I hesitate, then, my feet in their new gold shoes run towards the door. My hand hovers over the handle. I know who it is. I take a deep breath, steadying myself before opening the door.

Ivan stands there, and the sight of him steals my breath away. He's in a tuxedo, perfectly tailored, the crisp lines emphasizing his broad shoulders. He looks every bit the part—powerful, controlled, but there's something in his eyes when they meet mine. It's like a spark, an intensity.

For God knows how long we just stand there, our eyes eating the other up, the air between us charged. I feel the heat in his gaze and it makes my skin flush.

"You look..." he starts, and for once, he seems to search for the right words. "Stunning."

"Thank you, but you don't look too bad yourself," I manage to say, my voice no more than a whisper.

To my surprise, he flushes. Amazing. My simple compliment embarrasses him. There's so much I want to ask, so much I want to say, but the words catch in my throat.

He steps closer, his hand reaching up to brush a stray strand of hair behind my ear. The touch is gentle, almost hesitant, and it sends a jolt through me. "Are you ready?"

I nod, even though everything inside me feels like it's spinning. "I think so."

Chapter Thirty-Nine

IVAN

I walk into the hall with her on my arm and every set of eyes in the room seems to turn our way. I can't blame them. She looks... breathtaking. She actually rendered me speechless when she first opened the door.

I must admit I was concerned when Greta told me Lara spent the whole day working in the garden—out in the sun, of all places. Considering how she dressed for dinner last night I pictured her arriving with flushed cheeks, exhausted, or maybe even disheveled. But instead, here she is, her skin glowing with health, her cheeks sun-kissed and radiant.

She's dangerous for me.

I realize that now, more than ever. She is like a secret I'm desperate to keep. The kind you never share with anybody. Not because you're ashamed, but because you are afraid they will try and take it away from you. I'm aware that everyone is watching and speculating. I don't want her here—at least, not here in front of all these people. I want her back in my bed, away from this crowd of piranhas. They'll cheerfully consume you down to your skeleton if you let them.

As we move through the room, various people approach. High-profile executives, highly placed government officials and celebrities. An internal bunch of globetrotters, but they all have one thing in common: they want something from me. Each one comes forth with charm and smiles, but every one of them is curious about Lara.

"Mr. Ivanovich, so glad to see you. And this is...?" One of them asks, raising an eyebrow, the implication hanging between us.

"This is Lara," I say simply, ignoring the unspoken question in their gaze.

The awkward silence that follows is delicious, watching them expect something more—a title, an explanation—but I give none. Lara stays silent, her arm looped through mine, meeting their curious gazes with a polite smile.

After a few strained pleasantries, they get the message and drift off.

Then the icing on the cake, my mother floats over, her stern and regal demeanor demanding attention as always. Her eyes land on Lara immediately, but she doesn't acknowledge her.

"Ivan, darling," she says, her voice a smooth purr. "Have I missed anything?"

I can already see the flicker of irritation in her eyes as she finally turns her gaze to Lara, assessing her for the first time.

"And whose daughter is this charming creature? I don't believe I've seen her before," she says disapprovingly.

Before I can respond, Lara laughs, the sound light. You'd think she's been dealing with Russian snobs all her life. "You're right, you've never met my parents or seen me before," she says with a smirk, causing my mother's eyes to widen in surprise. "I'm his new girlfriend for the month. Actually, more like a lover... maybe an escort even?"

I feel a burst of amusement and glance at Lara, my lips curling into a fond smile. She's good at this, better than I expected.

The shock on my mother's face is priceless. For a second, she is too outraged to react. Then, her back stiffens and she turns to glare at me. "Did you bring a whore to my Gala?" she asks in a fierce whisper.

"Relax, Mother. Lara has a strange sense of humor. She's an estate agent."

"Sorry about that," Lara says, her voice sounding not the least bit sorry. "I'm an estate agent. I help people find their dream homes."

My mother's eyebrows lift in subtle judgment. I'm not sure she's convinced yet that Lara is an estate agent. "And how did the two of you meet?"

"He found me on social media," she says in a bright happy voice. "Decided he had to have me."

It's hard to tell if my mother believes us. Her eyes dart between us, searching for some kind of confirmation that this is not some kind of joke we are playing on her, but neither Lara nor I offer her that satisfaction.

Clearly annoyed, my mother purses her lips. "For the love of God, at least mingle," she mutters to me, before turning on her heel and walking away.

Lara leans in closer to me, her breath brushing against my ear. "I think I upset her."

I chuckle softly, glancing down at her. "You think?"

I'm starting to really like this girl. I admire the ease with which she handled my mother's condescension. Here, under the golden glow of chandeliers and surrounded by people who only see the version of me I choose to show, she's the only one who feels real.

"What?" she asks, one eyebrow cocked.

"Nothing. Come on, let's find our table," I say, putting my palm possessively on the small of her back and guiding her through the soft buzz of voices talking and laughing above the muted sounds of Mussorgsky's piano's concerto.

The table is near the front of the ballroom, of course—where all eyes can find us easily. A prime spot reserved for people who matter. Like my sister, Natalia, and my half-brother, Nikolai.

My eyes lock with Natalia's first. There's no warmth in her expression, just that distant, assessing look she always wears ever since she found out that every man she meets is only after her money. She's eight years older than me, an investment banker with a razor-sharp mind, and she is also my father's favorite child. We used to be quite close—before the family divisions... before she put her inheritance first and sided with our father. That connection is a memory now, something fractured beyond repair. She glances at Lara briefly, her gaze unreadable, then she turns away, getting pulled into a conversation with someone else.

Before I can pull Lara away, Nikolai approaches us with his usual charismatic smile. I stretch my lips into a smile. I have no beef with my brother, but he is a notorious womanizer. That is almost exclusively what he does. And his greatest sense of achievement and victory comes when he can steal another man's woman. "Ivan!" he exclaims. Perhaps he is genuinely pleased to see me, I can never tell. "And this must be the infamous..."

"Lara."

"Lara," he says, looking at her almost in awe as he rolls her name on his tongue. "What a beautiful name. It's an absolute pleasure to meet you."

I nearly roll my eyes. What a smarmy bastard. I'll never understand how women can fall for such cheap tricks.

He then takes her hand and kisses it. Where does he think he is? The Tsar of Romanov's court? Idiot. But for some reason, Lara indulges him and allows him to kiss her hand. His charm, seemingly, is hard to resist. Even Lara is not immune to it. I control my rising irritation.

He gazes at her, his eyes sparkling with mischief, and lies blatantly. "I'm Ivan's older brother, Nikolai. We share the same father. I'm sure he's told you nothing about me, but I've heard *so* much about you."

"Oh, really?" Lara says, playing along with his lie.

I can't believe her. My hands clench and itch to sock his pampered, good for nothing jaw, but I'm not here to spoil my mother's pride and joy, grand gala. I let the interaction continue without stepping in.

"I hope it's all good," she says.

"All good and then some." Nikolai grins, still holding her gaze, flirting openly with her. "You've got quite the reputation."

A light chuckle escapes her lips. The sound that gets under my skin. It's not for me. "From the looks of it, nothing compared to yours," she says.

Nikolai laughs, an assessing glint in his eyes.

I know that look. An unfamiliar sensation tightens my chest. I want to protect her, to take her away from this parasite, from all these people who consider her to be beneath them. But Lara, to her credit, has handled herself well so far and doesn't want to run away, and neither does she seem intimidated.

"You've been holding out on us," Nikolai says, looking at

me with mock accusation. "Ignoring calls, pretending you're too busy. Have you finally decided to live it up a little, hmmm?" His eyes flick coquettishly again to Lara.

"You'd know all about that, wouldn't you?" I mock.

But Nikolai's skin is thicker than a crocodile.

"Oh, for sure," he agrees with an easy laugh, his eyes twinkling amiably as he returns his attention to Lara. "Well, it's good to finally meet the woman who managed to melt my brother's heart. Be good to him. He works too hard. And Ivan, don't be a stranger. We've got to catch up soon. Family reunions are not the same without you." He nods toward a table nearby, where a few familiar faces are looking our way with interest. Then he steps back, his movements as graceful as a male ballet dancer, his smile still in place. He waves, a romantic gesture. "See you both later."

Lara smiles again—this time, genuinely. It's the first smile I've seen from her tonight that isn't guarded or tinged with sarcasm. She bought his bullshit. She thinks he's one of the good guys. For a second it makes me feel like an outsider, as if I'm watching something from a distance.

The announcement for the ceremony to begin echoes through the hall, cutting off all conversation. I lead Lara to our table, but my eyes stay fixed on Nikolai as he moves to his seat. I notice with a jolt that he's on the other side of her. That, I know for sure, is not an accident. The annoying little shit asked the planners to seat him there.

I pause, weighing my options. The thought of Lara sitting next to Nikolai all night is enough to spoil my mood, so I act before anyone can question it. "Let's switch seats," I tell her.

"What? Why?" she asks, surprised.

I don't answer directly, just pull out the chair next to mine instead, gesturing for her to sit down. "I want you next to me."

Lara hesitates, and I glance over at Nikolai, who merely

shrugs at me. Lara nods and slips onto the chair. I have now ruined the male-female arrangement. Instead of me sitting next to Natalia, Lara will be. Natalia gives me a sideways glance. She doesn't like it, but I keep my attention on Lara.

Everyone at the table has witnessed what I have done and the curiosity in the air is palpable, but I don't care. Nikolai is experienced and has spent many years perfecting and turning seduction into an art. Under no circumstances will I allow Nikolai to prey on Lara.

Chapter Forty

LARA

"You know, whichever way I sat, I still would have ended up next to you," I say, glancing at Ivan. My voice is light, but the edge in it is clear. I'm not trying to make a fuss, but it wasn't exactly nice to be moved away from Nikolai in that horrible manner. Everyone was looking. He behaved as if Nikolai was poison. He's a little over-the-top, sure, but there is something about him that made me feel like I could loosen up a bit, and maybe even enjoy myself. And just as I was starting to, Ivan stepped in and stopped it. I start to wonder if he is worried Nikolai will reveal dark secrets about him or their family to me.

"Don't sulk," he says as the rest of the venue settles in for the event to begin.

"Why did you do that, anyway?" I mutter quietly.

"You wouldn't understand," he says shortly.

That really annoys me and I glare at him. "I see," I hiss. "I suppose you don't really want me sitting next to your family."

He turns to me, but I don't meet his gaze. I'm whining

like I actually care when I should have no business whatsoever in doing so.

"The one beside you is also family," he says. "That's my sister Natalia."

My heart jumps into my throat then. For a moment, I wonder if he is joking with me, but he looks deadly serious. This makes the atmosphere even more awkward. The proud woman sitting next to me looks like she has been carved from a block of ice. She is by far more intimidating than his mother. She refuses to even engage in eye contact, turning her body firmly away from me, she converses with the person on her left. I sneak another look, unable to help myself, but her indifference is complete. She is determined not to acknowledge me.

Then the lights dim and Ivan's mother takes the stage and makes her speech. I hear, but I don't listen. People clap and I follow suit. More elegantly dressed men and women make their carefully rehearsed speeches. Words flow easily about charity, legacy, and the importance of family. But I don't really keep up, my thoughts are too loud, trying to piece together the tension I feel humming between Ivan and his family.

Once, just once, Natalia meets my eye, and she shakes her head slightly, almost to herself, as if she cannot believe the trash her brother has picked up and brought to one of their family's most important events. The rest of the night passes like a dream. Odd and confused. I eat things that I don't taste properly. There is dancing, but Ivan has to make an important call so we leave.

In the car, he seems preoccupied with his own thoughts and I say nothing. I'm still lost in my thoughts. Somehow that slight head shake hurt deeply. More than if she had said something cutting. Then I could have responded. Said something cutting back. There is a bitter taste in my mouth as Ivan heads towards his study or office to make his call. He says he will join me in an hour.

Leila called me earlier so I sit on the floor of my closet and call her back surrounded by clothes I'd pulled out earlier while I was trying to decide what to wear. The mess is comforting in a way—chaos that I can control. Leila's face is on my phone screen, eyes bright and mischievous as always.

"Tell me everything," she demands.

I give her a brief rundown of the night.

"Mmmm..." she says as she munches on grapes. "Didn't you watch *Succession*. That's what all moneyed folk are like."

"That's a TV series?" I say, raising an eyebrow.

"Nope, that's based on Rupert Murdoch's relationship with his children," Leila replies, popping another grape in her mouth. "They are all cold as ice. It's a power thing. They act like they're better than everyone else, but they are all psychopaths. Come on, look at the Davos lot. They screech at us to buy reusable groceries bags, and use less of everything to save the environment while they fly in 3000 hookers to entertain them. There's probably a few murders and deaths in the Ivanovich family."

I sit up straighter. This is a severe shock to me. "What? Now you're just making up stuff."

Leila smirks, clearly enjoying my shock. "Just think. This guy's family was closely connected, if not directly related to the Romanov's dynasty. You know, Rasputin and shit. There must have been murders. Bound to have been. I'd bet next month's wages on it."

Just as I'm about to respond, the door to my room swings open, and Ivan steps in. My heart nearly leaps out of my chest.

"I knocked," he says, his eyes scanning the mess of clothes and the phone in my hand.

I quickly hang up on Leila and pull out my AirPods, trying to regain composure. "Sorry, didn't hear you."

His expression is unreadable, but there's something in his eyes that makes me uneasy. "We're going to France this weekend," he says offhandedly, like it's no big deal.

I blink. "Okay... Wait, We're going to Europe?"

"Yeah. My family has a vineyard in the countryside. It's my mother's birthday. She's having a small party," he explains, but there's something off in his voice. He seems preoccupied, distracted even.

Before I can say anything more, he turns and walks out of the room, leaving me sitting there on the floor, surrounded by my clothes and confusion. Well! We're not going to have sex tonight? France? A family vineyard? His mother's birthday? I call Leila back, and she is so excited at the update that she nearly screams my ear off.

"France? A Vineyard? Oh my God, let's get started on your outfits. Pull everything out."

It's the last thing I want to do, but her excitement is contagious. Plus, she's extremely good at fashion and it will save me the trouble of having to put outfits together, so I concede and let her make the choices.

Chapter Forty-One

IVAN

The hum of the jet's engines is muted, but the frantic chaos in my London office on the other end of the phone is deafening.

"How the hell did they get a warrant that quickly?" I snap.

My lawyer mutters some legal jargon about national security. Ah, the go-to of all tyrants around the world. Two little words and you can do anything you want. Raid an innocent man's office, drop a bomb from the sky on a wedding celebration. Anything.

"This... this is a fucking joke. What are they taking?" I bite out, my voice tight with fury.

"Looks like everything. Files, papers, hard drives, the works. Anything they think will help make their case."

Outside the windows, fluffy clouds envelop us. In my ear I can hear my team thousands of miles away arguing with the authorities, my lawyer trying to hold his ground, but it's clear —the situation is slipping out of control. They have the legal right. There is nothing my lawyer or my staff can do.

They are going on a tip from an anonymous source. There is no sense to the raid except pure spite and jealousy. I'm a billionaire so I must be corrupt. Whoever fed them this information knew exactly how to light the match and there is not a damn thing I can do about it. I'm not used to feeling so helpless and vulnerable.

I rub my temples, frustration coiling inside me like a vice. "Let them take everything they want," I growl, exhaustion creeping into my voice. "Let them take it all. We've got nothing to hide." I end the call and put the phone down on the table. My movements are slow and controlled and do not reflect the fury and frustration simmering just under the surface.

I've been so consumed by the chaos, I forgot... Lara.

I turn my head and catch her watching me, a frown on her forehead, her eyes curious. She quickly looks down at her open book and pretends she wasn't staring, but there is tension in her shoulders. She is also gripping the book too tightly.

I buzz the flight attendant and she arrives immediately. "Bring me a whiskey."

I need the burn of it, something sharp to settle me. She returns quickly with a glass generously filled with amber liquid, the scent of peat and smoke filling my nostrils as I take a sip. The warmth spreads through my chest, but that doesn't ease the gnawing sense of impending disaster inside me.

My eyes flicker toward Lara—still book in hand, still so tense the air around her crackles. I hit the do not disturb button on my console.

"Lara," I call, my voice guttural and raw with emotion.

Her head jerks up, and her eyes are enormous. And I remember again, that time I found her on the floor at my feet and I fell hard even though I didn't know it then. She's so innocent. So pure.

"Come here." It sounds like a demand, but it's a desperate need to lose myself in something beautiful. The command lingers, hanging thick in the air between us, a reminder of everything unspoken and unresolved between us.

Slowly, she sets her book aside, her fingers lingering on the cover for a moment as if considering her options, hesitating, her eyes searching mine. Then she understands the unexpressed. It's not sex I need, it's her. Only she will do. Only she can drown out the fury tearing at my guts. Only her touch, her skin, can make the prospect of losing everything acceptable.

She holds my gaze, a strange expression on her face. Is it pity? I don't think so, but even if it is, I don't care. Right now, all I want to do is lose myself in her sweet smell. Then she rises from her seat and walks toward me, her head held high, her movements graceful and sure. Every step she takes sends my pulse hammering harder.

"Take off your clothes." The words rap out like a harsh order, but underneath, I can hear the tremor, the unspoken vulnerability.

Her lips part, like she's about to say something, but she doesn't. Underneath that stubborn, fiery exterior she's kind. She can feel how on edge I am, how desperate. So she nods and reaches back, fingers trembling, and slightly pulls down the zip of her yellow dress. She slides the fabric down inch by inch, revealing her shoulders, the swell of her collarbones and then she lets it go. It glides down her curves like water until it pools silently at her feet.

Underneath she is completely nude, Not a stitch in sight.

It sends a shock wave of heat through me, and just like that the tension flies out of my system. Fuck them! They are nothing but cackling hyenas. Scavengers. Well, they can steal everything away from me today and in a few years, I'll win it all back again. Every last cent. Will she be here then, though?

There is a catastrophe happening in real-time outside this cabin, but my mind is focused only on her. Oh, Lara, Lara, Lara. Goosebumps start to appear on her skin, but she stands there, motionless, her eyes locked on mine, her chest rising and falling in a steady rhythm. Her naked body trembles in the dim light of the cabin and yet she cuts a proud figure. She is the strong one. I watch her nipples harden as my gaze rakes over her, devouring every inch of her as lust surges through me.

"It's okay, my great and beautiful swan, Leda is here," she whispers soothingly, and lowering herself on the opposite chair she opens her thighs wide to show me how slick and swollen her sex is.

My breath escapes in a hiss. Suddenly the need for her is unbearable, igniting something raw and uncontrollable inside me. My hand moves on instinct, slipping inside my pants. I grasp the aching cock and pull it out. The cool air hits my skin. I can't look away from her dripping pussy.

In turn she watches me avidly, hungrily.

Griping myself tightly, I stroke myself. A groan rumbles from deep in my chest, rough and ragged, as the pleasure starts to take over. Knowing she is watching, my thumb glides over the swollen head, smearing the bead of precum that's already formed there, slicking the motion when I pump my hand up and down.

The sound of her quickening breath fills the air, and it drives me further, my hand moving faster, tightening with each motion as the tension coils tighter inside me. I'm completely lost in the rhythm, the pressure building with every stroke, the need to release overwhelming, but I hold back just enough, knowing nothing will feel really good until I am buried inside her soft body.

"Come here," I say, but now my voice is a growl.

She gets up and her scent reaches me before her body does, sweet and intoxicating. When she comes to stand in front of me, I lean back and growl, "Ride me."

She straddles me, her thighs warm and soft as they press against mine. Her eyes flutter shut for a moment as she lowers herself with a quiet gasp onto my cock. The tight heat of her makes me groan deep in my throat. All I can feel is her—the way her body clings to mine, warm and wet, the sensation overwhelming me as she begins to move.

She surrounds me, enveloping me as she slowly lifts herself and sinks back down, setting off electric jolts of pleasure through my entire body. My hands find her hips, gripping her tight, guiding her movements, bouncing her furiously on me. Driving me deeper and deeper into her with each thrust and drowning me in the pure, visceral pleasure of being inside her.

Her hands brace against my chest, her fingers digging into my flesh as she rides me harder now, her breath coming in quick, shallow bursts. My eyes are glued to her face, the way her lips part with each soft moan, the way her brows knit together in pleasure, and the way her eyes flutter closed as she gets lost in the moment. She's as consumed as I am, and every sound she makes, every movement, pushes me closer to the edge.

I wait for her to climax. It's beautiful watching her come. I stare at her and memorize it all. Then I bury my face in the curve of her neck and while breathing in her intoxicating scent of her I ram up into her. Harder, faster, driven by nothing but the raw need to lose myself in her completely. She gasps at the brutality of my need. She jerks like a living doll on my lap.

And then, with one final, shuddering gasp, I feel myself unraveling, the pressure exploding as I lose myself in her, the world around us fading to nothing as I reach that release I've been chasing.

Here, there is nothing but Lara.

Chapter Forty-Two

LARA

The descent into France feels bizarre. I'm sore between my legs, my clit is still throbbing and swollen, and I'm still confused by what happened midair. I don't know exactly what Ivan is dealing with, but I know whatever it is is a legal problem and it's big. Big enough to make him lose his customary cool. Now, as we taxi on the private airstrip, the beauty of the French countryside sprawls before me.

A sleek black Bentley is waiting for us outside the plane. A formally uniformed, sour-faced chauffeur holds the door open for me. I murmur my thanks and slide in beside Ivan. As the door closes, I smell it. Ivan and I reek of sex. I steal a sideway glance at him, but he is almost unaware of my presence.

For the last hour, he's been busy on the phone. Even now his fingers fly across the screen of his laptop as he deals with whatever it is that has gone wrong. He hasn't said much since I climbed off him and got dressed, and I doubt he will anytime soon. This is a different part of him I am seeing. I can't help but be worried for him. We're not friends and we'll probably never see each other again after the month is out, but I don't wish him harm. Underneath, I am convinced he is a good man. I trust Muriel's judgement. I remember my mother used to say, you can tell a man's character by the way he treats waiters.

I turn my gaze toward the window instead and try to distract myself with the sights of France. The drive to the vineyard is quiet, save for the occasional muttered curse from Ivan. I try not to listen or pry, but the urge to ask him what's going on is very strong. I tell myself it is none of my business.

Instead, I focus on the scenery unfolding outside the window. The golden fields stretch for miles, rolling over gentle hills, dotted with ancient stone houses that speak of centuries of tradition. The sun is low on the horizon by the time we approach the Ivanovich's family estate, well one of them anyway.

I've never seen anything like it.

Set on higher ground the chateau looms against the late afternoon sky. It is a massive pink and white mansion surrounded by sun-warmed stone walls that glow in the low sun. Around it, are vineyards as far as the eye can see, the neat rows of grapevines lining the hills like soldiers. It's breathtakingly beautiful, but Ivan doesn't even lift his head to appreciate the beauty and privilege his family have acquired.

The car door opens, and as I step out, we're greeted by the scent of sweet grapes and earth—a heady, intoxicating mix that hangs in the air. A stiff, unsmiling man in a black suit, I presume to be the butler, waits by the tall doors. He greets us formally by name in an English accent.

"I trust you had a good flight," he says quietly to Ivan.

"Yes, thank you, Philip." Ivan turns to me. "This is Philip Barnes, my mother's butler."

"Hello," I say awkwardly. I've never been in such a situation.

He nods formally, then addresses Ivan. "Your mother has requested the west wing for you and your guest, Sir. It is nicest this time of the year."

"Very good."

He nods again. "This way, madam," Philip says, leading us inside.

The interior is nothing like the bustling, modern, glass, and chrome world we had come from. The grandeur nearly knocks the breath out of me. It feels like I've stepped back in time into a golden era where Kings and Queens surrounded by their courtiers ruled. Mesmerized by the grandeur of the place, the history, the way every gilded detail has been so lovingly shaped by master craftsmen, I look around in awe at the high ceilings, the grand staircase, the fine oil paintings that line the walls. Everything speaks of old money. Suddenly, New York feels brash and loutish.

A young woman in a black dress and a white apron appears bearing a tray with two glasses of some pinkish liquid.

"Aperitive, madam?" she asks, with a smile.

Ivan refuses, but I take one and try to appear composed even though I am anything but.

Ivan says he has to quickly do something on a high-speed computer and leaves, and Philip hands me over to another staff member, a young man, who escorts me through the chateau up to our room. He opens the door and I step in.

Behind me, I hear the man say something in French. I turn around and shrug. "No speak French."

"Ah. No speak English," he says with a grin and leaves.

I grin back then close the door and look around. Very impressive. The walls are pale blue and adorned with intricate gold trim. No built-in cupboards here. The furniture is all antique and polished to perfection, and the bed is high and full of fluffy pillows. Tall windows overlook the endless stretch of vineyards outside, and I watch as the curtains sway lazily in the gentle scented breeze coming through the open door to the balcony. I could lose myself in this life.

It's hard to believe this is my reality. Little ole me scuttling around the subways trying to sell cramped, cockroach infested-apartments as wonderful places to live. I didn't know better. But now that I do, how could I go back to that?

I put my untouched drink on the table, sit on the edge of the bed and sink into the soft luxury. Just as I begin to unpack my things, there's a knock at the door. Before I can respond, another staff member enters, carrying bags. Mine and Ivan's.

My heart skips a beat as the realization hits me. We're going to be sharing this room.

I hadn't expected this. I assumed we'd be in different rooms in his mother's place. We never even slept together in New York. Not once. There's a part of me that craves his closeness and needs the comfort of his presence, but there's another part, the rational part, that feels uneasy about it all. We're not real lovers and the closer I get to him the more painful it is going to be when it is time for me to pack my bags and go.

Quickly, I shower and change into something more casual —shorts and a loose, button-up shirt. Leila's choice.

I glance at my reflection in the mirror, nerves twisting in my stomach. The person staring back at me looks out of place here, in this world of wealth and power. The luxurious room seems to swallow me whole, reminding me of just how far I am from everything I know.

Another knock at the door pulls me from my thoughts.

"Dinner is at eight. Drinks at seven-thirty," comes the voice from the other side of the door.

Dinner with his family. It's daunting, to say the least. The mother is horrible, the sister worse, and I like the brother, but Ivan seems to hate him. I change out of the shorts into the only demure black dress I could find in my new wardrobe and pair it with dark red lipstick. I look at my reflection in the mirror and feel satisfied. Leila would approve. Taking a deep breath, I steel myself for what's to come. My phone rings and Ivan says he is stuck on the computer and will not be able to make it for drinks, but he will meet me in the dining room at eight.

I decide to skip the drinks too and sit on the balcony and watch night fall as I will probably never again be able to witness such a beautiful sight. At five minutes to eight I rise reluctantly, and taking one last look in the mirror, I leave the room.

As I walk downstairs, my heart grows heavier with the anticipation of what's waiting. The dining room is stunning, set on a wide terrace overlooking the vineyard, the soft glow of the setting sun casting everything in hues of gold and pink. The table is long, covered in fine damask linen and candles, and each place setting has a gold plate with a crest on it. It's as if every detail was carefully designed to impress.

I count fifteen people already seated, their quiet murmurs filling the space, and I feel a pang of self-consciousness as I approach. To my horror the butler announces me.

"Miss Lara Fitzpatrick," he says, his voice ringing in the still air.

His mother courteously acknowledges me, but her voice lacks warmth and like me, everyone at the table must have felt it too, because they smile and nod politely, but I feel their eyes on me, assessing, weighing. A waiter steps forward and shows me to my seat.

There's a formality to it all that makes me feel like more of an outsider than ever. Natalia, in particular, seems even colder than back at the event. This time, though, she doesn't completely ignore me as her eyes flick over me with an almost reptilian-like interest. I can't quite tell what she is thinking, but it makes me uneasy. She reminds me of a half-submerged crocodile waiting patiently in the water for its prey to arrive.

The seat next to mine remains empty. Ivan's seat.

I sit down, trying to look as if I'm not shaking like jelly with nerves inside. My mind is stuck on Ivan—the tension that's clung to him ever since we boarded the jet, the way he's been glued to his phone, and now he's disappeared, probably to handle even more troubles.

Everyone around me starts talking in different European languages or maybe even Russian. I can't tell the difference. All I know is I don't understand a word. I can't help wondering if it is deliberate.

The first course is served, and the dishes are as exquisite as the view. Foie gras with fig compote, thin slices of herb bread still warm from the oven, and a light salad with delicate dressing that smells like summer. It tastes as rich as it looks, but I can barely focus on the food. My fork moves automatically, but my mind is elsewhere—drifting between worrying about Ivan and the strangeness of being here at all.

And then Nikolai arrives.

His easy, charismatic smile is like a balm against the awkwardness. He greets me warmly, his eyes twinkling as if he's genuinely glad to see me. I can't help but feel a wave of relief wash over me. At least there's one familiar face in this sea of strangers.

"Lara!" he exclaims, taking the seat beside me with an effortless charm. "I'm so glad to see you again. How are you finding France?"

I smile at him gratefully, finally, someone I can actually talk to. "It's beautiful. Absolutely breathtaking."

He grins boyishly, leaning back in his chair. "I knew you'd appreciate it."

He introduces me to the others, his sister Natalia, and a few other relatives whose names I instantly forget. They're polite, offering smiles and nods, but they look at me with speculation and curiosity as if I was a strange creature that they cannot comprehend.

Just as Nikolai settles into the conversation, there's a voice behind us. It's cold and clipped.

"Move," Ivan demands, his expression unreadable, but his tone so harsh that everyone at the table stops their conversation and watches us.

I hate to admit it, but I feel so happy now that he's here. I try my best to hide my smile that he has returned. I like Nikolai, but without Ivan, the last place I want to be in this world is at this table.

Nikolai laughs lightly, making a joke about Ivan being possessive, but he obliges, moving to the seat on the other side of the table while the waiters quickly move his plate, glasses and cutlery for him. Ivan takes the seat next to me, his presence immediately commanding the space. I can feel the tension rolling off of him, but he doesn't say a word, just nods briefly as a server pours him a glass of wine.

The silence between us is thick, and for the first time, I wonder if I should get involved with his affairs. Something is clearly very wrong. Should I ask him what is going on? But the words don't come, I guess, because it is not part of our deal and he looks so forbidding I'm afraid he will tell me to fuck off and mind my own business.

Chapter Forty-Three

IVAN

As we continue to eat, I catch Lara sneaking glances at me. Each time her eyes flick towards mine, I can feel the weight of her concern, and it stirs something inside me, but the last thing I need is to have her worried about me. I don't want my burdens to become hers. I want her to be how I found her. Innocent, sexy, kind-hearted.

"I'm fine," I say softly, glancing at her.

Her lips part slightly as if she wants to say something, but instead, she nods, her eyes dropping to her plate. I catch a glimpse of my sister Natalia watching us from across the table, her gaze sharp as she looks between the two of us. I don't have the time or patience to figure out what her scrutiny means.

As the plates are cleared away our champagne glasses are filled and Nikolai rises, clinking his knife on his glass. He's always liked being the center of attention, and tonight is no different. His smile is full of effortless charm, the kind that he wears when he's about to take the spotlight.

"Everyone," he begins, his eyes sweeping over the family and the few close guests gathered, "it's rare that we're all together like this. So before the evening takes us away into more wine and conversation, I want to take a moment to honor someone very special."

He raises his champagne glass high. "To my stepmother, Svetlana Ivanovich, the heart of this family. Your grace, strength, and love have held us together, and tonight, we celebrate not just you, but the legacy you've built for us."

There's an undeniable warmth in his words, my mother smiles graciously and the table bursts into applause. There's a collective murmur of appreciation, heads nodding in approval as glasses are lifted and champagne is consumed. Nikolai's gaze lingers for a moment on one of our older relatives, an uncle with a notorious reputation.

"Uncle Mikhail," Nikolai says with a smirk, "let's try not to make it like last year, hmm? Leave some wine for the rest of us." His teasing tone brings out soft laughter from the family, and Mikhail, sitting at the far end of the table with his fifth or sixth glass of wine, stands unsteadily and bows playfully.

"Also... and before we go any further," Nikolai says with a mischievous gleam in his eye, his voice shifting to a lighter note, "I'd like to give a special welcome to someone new at our table tonight—Lara."

At once, all eyes shift to Lara, and there's a moment of uncomfortable silence as Nikolai, clearly relishing the moment, smiles wider. "We don't often get the chance to have new faces here, so Lara, maybe you'd like to say a few words?"

I can feel Lara stiffen beside me, and before she can respond, I raise my hand, my voice cutting through the charged atmosphere. "This is a night to celebrate my mother, not my lover, Nikolai."

The air around us changes instantly, the energy shifting with my words. Nikolai lets out a small chuckle and lowers his glass. "Of course, Ivan. I was just trying to make your guest feel welcome."

How victorious he looks now that he has got under my skin. I catch a few sidelong glances in my direction, but I don't care. I've had enough of his silly little games. A subtle but palpable shift settles over the table. The remaining toasts of tribute to my mother are polite but lack the earlier ease. The ugliness between Nikolai and me has tempered the mood. The cake is wheeled out, and we all sing for my mother, the candles are blown out and the night continues.

Afterwards, we move to the patio for the cognac and cigars for the men and cake and sweet port for the women.

The night is cooling, and the soft glow of lanterns lights the path as we walk. The vineyard itself is scenic, stretching for miles out under the moonlight, but I barely notice any of it. My mind is tangled up with what is happening back in London, with the constant calls from my lawyers, the updates that keep coming in about the properties and assets being seized. The authorities appear to be moving at lightning speed. Just an hour ago they impounded my yacht moored in the Bahamas.

I move away from the gathering, finding a quiet corner in the vineyard's lounge, away from the garrulous chatter. Pulling out my phone I dial and the call connects almost immediately.

"Ivan," my lawyer's voice is clipped, on edge, "we're doing everything we can, but it's not looking good. The French authorities have tightened their hold on the chateau, and the British are relentless with the Mayfair property. They've frozen everything under suspicion of financial misconduct."

"Are they not even going to wait and go through the mountains of evidence we've provided?" I ask in disbelief, pacing in the dim light.

There's a pause on the other end, the hesitation grinding on my already frayed nerves. "They're digging their heels in, Ivan. They've been tipped off about irregularities with Chinese steel deals, and I'm afraid the US is getting involved now too. They're looking at everything—the finances, the acquisitions, your connections to Russian interests."

My grip tightens on the phone, the mention of the steel deals only stokes my anger even more. "What irregularities?" I demand, trying to keep my voice steady. "Everything is above board and they know it. I've kept this business clean—there's nothing for them to find."

"The British authorities don't care. They are on a witch hunt. It's political. Given your background they thought you were an easy target and they've spent a lot of time and money chasing you and now they need to show results," he replies. "And now they've got the Americans sniffing around too, looking for connections to illegal Russian funds."

A curse escapes me as I pull at the collar of my shirt. There are not fucking serious. Connection? Whatever connections there are, are weak at best. I want to shout, but I realize that doesn't matter to the authorities. Perception is enough. They'll drag this out for as long as they need to, ruining everything in the process.

"How long will all this take? How long can they legally keep my assets?"

"Sorry, Ivan, but the answer is: indefinitely. Legally they're combing through the documents and there is a lot, and they are bureaucrats so they have a good excuse to drag this out for years."

"Years?" I spit the word out. "I'm not waiting years."

I hang up abruptly and have to quell the desire to smash my phone to the ground. Fuck! The chateau, the yacht, and the Mayfair flat—they're all tied up in this mess indefinitely! They're acting as though they have all the evidence needed to build their case against me, as though it's solid, and I don't understand why. Their goal is clear: to cripple me and steal what I have worked so hard to earn. I take a deep breath. They won't beat me. Hyenas cannot take down the king of the jungle. The lion, in its prime, can hold off a whole cackle.

The problem is actually not what is happening now, but what will happen once the American authorities begin to follow suit. They are much more aggressive than the Europeans. Then I will really be in deep shit. I'm not the first Russian billionaire who has been harassed like this—it's normal, but I'm the first guiltless billionaire.

When I turn back toward the others, I see Lara watching me from across the room. She's been keeping her distance, and I can't blame her. I've been distant all night. Without a word, I get up and head toward the door, walking briskly to the office where I've spent my time since I arrived. I need space. I need to think and I need to plan.

I can feel Lara trailing behind me, her figure silent but persistent. As soon as we are out of earshot of the rest of the party I turn towards her, my voice rough and strained. "Go back, Lara. I need time to think."

But she doesn't move. Her eyes, wide with concern, lock onto mine, and she steps forward instead of retreating. "What's wrong?" Her voice is soft, careful, like she's walking on fragile ground, trying to understand what's going on inside my head. "I know it's none of my business but ..."

Her expression stops my heart. I realize she is what I need.

I want to hold her close, want to tell her all my frustrations, but... I can't. I've never confided in anyone before. I always solve all my problems on my own. I am the lone lion, roaming the savannah on his own. I can't let her in. She is already too close. Anyway, it looks like soon I won't be able to afford to keep her. The thought sears me. There is nothing I cannot afford.

I take a deep breath, shaking my head. "Just go," I say, more forcefully this time, but it's more for my own sake than hers. I'm trying to push her away, trying to stop her from seeing more than what I want her to.

But she shakes her head and stands her ground. She comes closer, eyes defiant. "No, I'm not leaving until you tell me what's wrong."

I let out a heavy sigh, running a hand through my hair, the tension in my shoulders knotting tighter. Before I can say anything else, she snatches my hand and starts running towards the house. I could have tugged once, and she would have come to a sudden stop, even slammed into me, but no, I run with her. In the cool night air, we run like two lovers towards the summerhouse by the lake. Out of breath, she opens the door and pulls me in. Then she shuts the door. The soft click of the latch feels final, sealing us in together, along with everything unsaid between us. She leans against it and in the dim light from the lamp outside stares at me.

"This fuck is already paid for. Why not get your money's worth?" she says softly.

What irony. I paid for the houses, the yacht, and the cars too, but instead, I'm getting fucked by Western governments. But she is right. This fuck is paid for. I close the distance between us, my hands finding her waist and pulling her to me in one swift motion. She gasps, her body stiffening with the savagery of the movement, but she quickly melts into me. Her lips part as I swoop down on her mouth hungrily.

Her hands slide up my back as she kisses me back urgently. It's as if she's trying to pour whatever little care she may feel for me into the kiss, hoping it will reach the parts of me that are too locked away to let her in. I can feel it, but I can't acknowledge it, not now.

My hands make quick work of the long zip on the back of her dress. One tug and the silky thing falls away to the floor. Underneath she is exactly how I want her: beautifully naked. Her chest heaves as she looks at me, waiting, wanting, knowing exactly where she's headed.

There is a table pushed up against a wall and I swipe my hand over the odds and ends on it and let it all crash to the floor. She gasps, the wood creaking, as I lay her on her back on it. I part her legs roughly and my mouth is instantly on her. Her fingers tangle desperately in my hair. I eat her wet pussy until she comes, gushing her juices into my mouth, her open mouth screaming silently.

I straighten and look down at her. Pale, naked, her legs wide open on a wooden table in my mother's summerhouse. I'm losing everything but I still own her. They can take everything else away, but not her. Bending my head, I take one of her delectable pink nipples into my mouth and suck hard. The little kitten sound that escapes her lips is everything I need. It fuels the fire raging inside me, driving me faster, harder.

I work my belt and I free myself. My cock is hard and throbbing with the need for her. Her eyes flick down, taking in the sight of me, and she bites her lip, her body rising slightly, eager, ready. There's no time for teasing. No time for slow. Grabbing her ankles, I lift her hips right off the table. I position myself at her entrance, and with one ruthless thrust, I'm inside her.

Her body arches as I start to pump, hard and fast. The sound of our bodies colliding fills the room—rough, raw, animalistic. I bury myself in her, each thrust sending waves of pleasure through me, and I can feel her responding to every movement, her breath coming in quick, shallow bursts. Her nails dig into my shoulders, her grip tightening as she pulls me closer, her body meeting mine with every thrust.

"Ivan..." she breathes, her voice trembling with intensity.

I lean down, kissing her again, but this time it's different. This time, her lips are slower, deeper, pulling me in with a tenderness that doesn't match the raw intensity of what we're doing. It's as if she's trying to tell me something, trying to reach the part of me that I've been keeping locked away.

I drive into her harder, faster, my hands gripping her hips as I lose myself in the heat of her body. Her moans grow louder, her body trembling beneath mine. I push deeper, my release building, the tension coiling tighter and tighter inside me. And then, with one final, shuddering gasp, I explode deep inside her. For a brief few seconds, everything else disappears. There's only this, only her and me.

But it all comes tumbling back again. The hyenas are waiting outside the door.

As I pull away, adjusting my trousers, Lara sits up and drops her feet to the floor. I watch her bend to pick up her dress with hands that are shaking slightly. She meets my gaze and her lips stretch into a small smile, but there's something in her eyes, a sadness that wasn't there before.

She doesn't say anything as she pulls on her dress. I zip her up in silence. The room feels thick with unspoken tension, the weight of what just happened pressing down on both of us. I feel a pang of guilt and want to reach out to her, to tell her what is going on, but the words stick in my throat. Before I can find the words, my phone buzzes in my pocket. I can't ignore it.

"I have to go," I tell her.

She nods but doesn't move.

At the door, I pause for a moment, glancing back at her. "Aren't you coming?"

"No, Ivan," she says softly. "You go ahead. I'll come in a minute."

Chapter Forty-Four

LARA

I really don't know why I'm upset. What else was I expecting? That he would suddenly confide in me, spill all his problems like we're equals in this, like we share more than just passion?

The door clicks shut behind him. Once his footsteps die outside, silence fills the room. The air feels suddenly too suffocating and warm and I feel the need to escape, to breathe. My hands move towards my hair, smoothing it down, but my mind is elsewhere, stuck on the hollowness of our exchange.

Why do I feel this way? Hurt and disappointed. I wanted more than just his body, even though I should know better. After all, this is what I signed up for, right?

Shaking my head, I push those thoughts away and leave the summerhouse. I walk back to the house and see that everyone is still on the terrace. Many lamps have been lit, there is music, and from where I am it looks like everyone is having fun and enjoying themselves. Instead, I grab a glass of wine from the counter, needing something to distract me. I walk towards a waiter holding a tray of champagne flutes. It makes me long for some alcohol.

"May I have a glass?" I ask, making a drinking gesture with my hand.

"Of course," he says in English.

I walk to the edge of the terrace and hidden away from everyone by a laurel bush, sit on the stone steps to enjoy my drink. I take a sip of the bursting bubbles and gaze out into the gorgeous night sky.

"Beautiful, isn't it?" a voice asks suddenly.

Startled, I glance up and find Natalia looking down on me.

My throat tightens, and I nearly choke on my drink, but I manage to compose myself just in time. She's watching me, her eyes sharp but unreadable. I've been avoiding her penetrating gaze all evening. And now, here she is, standing over me, wanting to engage in conversation.

"I'm not trying to pry," she says, her voice smooth, detached, "but I can't help but wonder why Ivan brought you here. Are you both serious about each other?" She pauses, her eyes scanning me as if I'm something she's trying to figure out.

Her words hang in the air between us, and for a second, I don't know how to respond. I stare at her, wondering why there is no love in Ivan's family. Why does he seem so distant from the people who should be supporting him in this difficult time?

"I'm just the girl of the moment," I say, trying to sound nonchalant, though the words taste bitter in my mouth.

Natalia looks at me, her expression unreadable. She takes a sip of her wine. "He must really like you to bring you here. I've never met any of his women before, though he's had many."

I drain my glass. "I can assure you, it's not serious. We're just having fun."

Natalia watches me for a moment longer, as if she doesn't believe me, then, with a faint shrug, she turns and walks away.

I glance back at the party, taking in the scene—the magical lighting, the music, the servants bearing trays of more drinks, the carefree laughter from the elegantly dressed people. And I feel a new worry. Something is eating away at Ivan, something far bigger than he usually deals with, and none of his family know about. It saddens me because I don't know what it is. And it depresses me that I might not ever really know him.

A voice behind me interrupts my dismal thoughts, and I turn to see Nikolai approaching.

"I'm sorry for putting you on the spot earlier," he apologizes, leaning against the stone balustrade. "Ivan has a way of making everyone's intentions seem... untrustworthy."

"Don't worry about it," I dismiss. I feel a bit more at ease with Nikolai than I do with anyone else here. He's charming, yes, but there's a sincerity in him that draws me to him.

"What's going on with your family? Why is everyone so distant with each other?" I ask. The questions slipping out before I can stop them. I've been wondering all evening after seeing how detached they all seem.

Nikolai raises an eyebrow, but he doesn't seem offended by the question. Instead, he sighs and takes a sip of his wine before answering.

"Well, money does that to you," he says with a wry smile.

I blink in confusion, and he elaborates.

"The family was ripped apart when my father and Ivan got into a bitter feud. It was so bad they refused to be in the same room together. Sadly, they both made us choose sides."

"I see," I say slowly. "Did you pick a side?"

He shook his head, and I can see the pain behind his easy-going demeanor. "No, Ivan picked it for me. He cut me off so my father wouldn't hate me too."

I listen quietly, my heart aching for Ivan as he continues.

Nikolai's expression darkens. "I've been trying to get along with the family ever since, but it's pretty impossible. As for Ivan and Natalia... well, they used to be close. Very close. But when things got ugly Natalia made her choice. And she chose my father. Can't blame her, my father is a very rich man."

I take it in, feeling like I'm finally beginning to understand the fractured dynamics at play here. It's no wonder Ivan is so closed off. He's been walking this tightrope between his family and his own ambitions for years, and it's clear that no one has made it easy for him.

Nikolai nods. "That's our story. What's yours? You're not Ivan's usual type."

"What's his usual type?"

He smiles suddenly. "How do you say it in America? Bimbo?"

I smile. "Ah."

The music changes in the background into a fast tune. Nikolai grins and offers me his hand. "Care for a dance?"

I hesitate, glancing around at the guests, the family.

"Come on," he urges. "You have to dance when you are in France."

I look into his eyes and I see no malice, no ulterior motive, no sexual come-on. Nikolai is just a nice guy and he means no harm. Maybe I can help mend the rift between him and Ivan. I take his hand and let him lead me towards the merrymakers.

He is a great dancer and I find myself relaxing, even laughing a little. It's a strange contrast to everything I've been feeling, but it's a welcome distraction. As the song ends, Nikolai twirls me one last time, grinning down at me.

"See? That wasn't so bad."

But before I can reply, a cold voice interrupts us. "Mind if I cut in?"

"Papa," Nikolai exclaims in shock, and immediately steps back. I stare at Ivan's father curiously.

His tone leaves no room for refusal, and Nikolai literally scuttles away like a frightened rabbit, and I'm left staring into Ivan's mortal enemy. He looks a bit like an older version of Ivan, but his presence is commanding, almost chilling, like that of a general, and I feel a wave of nervousness wash over me as he takes my hand formally.

"It is good that my son has picked a girl that can waltz."

My eyebrows rise with surprise.

"What exactly is your relationship with my son?"

My heart pounds in my chest. Everyone keeps asking me this question. "We're... we're just having a... casual relationship," I say, but the words feel strange on my tongue. The more I say them the more I hate saying them.

He raises an eyebrow, his expression unreadable. "If it were casual, he wouldn't have brought you here."

He doesn't know about the nature of our relationship, our arrangement, and I'm not the person to enlighten him.

I clear my throat. "I'm his real estate agent," I explain lamely. "We... sort of became friends."

He nods, but I can't tell if he believes me. He lapses into silence and I can't think of a single thing to say either. When the song ends, he releases me with a curt nod.

"Goodnight, Miss Fitzpatrick." Then he's gone, almost as if he was a figment of my imagination.

Chapter Forty-Five

IVAN

To my shock, I look out of the window and see the astonishing sight of my father dancing with Lara. For one wild irrational second, I want to run to them and push his poisoned hands away, but a strange wave of emotion washes over me and I stare at them. The truth is I love my father. When I was growing up he was the person I most dearly loved and admired in the whole world. And even after we fell out and he tried to crush me and made my family choose between him and me, I still couldn't bring myself to hate him.

It is a laughable idea to even think for a moment he will try to poison Lara or ask her to choose between him and me. I watch them curiously. My father is a good dancer and he leads her well. As for Lara, she carries herself brilliantly. A warm glow fills my chest. The dance ends. My father walks away and I see her head back towards the house.

My phone rings and I take the call. It's only more bad news. It is almost certain now that the Americans will move next and it is too late to get my money out. Moving that much money around could raise a lot of red flags. I still have some in Russia. That is my only safety net for now. I call an old friend from Cambridge and ask him for a favor. He agrees readily.

"I'll get on it first thing in the morning," he promises.

"Thanks, James. I won't forget."

"No, worries. You can count on me."

"Good night."

It's late, I'm exhausted, and I have a headache as I make my way through the silent house up to the west wing. I open the door and there she is. Sitting by the lounge, her legs tucked beneath her, wearing a white silk nightdress that clings to her body in ways that send heat spiraling through me. Her eyes flick toward me as I enter, but she doesn't say anything, doesn't move.

In spite of everything that has happened, my desire for her burns brightly.

"Nikolai told me about your feud with your father and how bad he feels about not being close to you."

She really ruined my mood with those words, but my voice is pleasant. "Did he now?"

"Yes, he did. He's a nice guy, Ivan. And his family. Families should stay together," she says.

I'd come in here wanting her, missing her, thinking I'd find sanctuary in her body, and instead, I find she has taken Nikolai's word for gospel truth. After the horrendous day I've had, I lose it. I feel fury burn like fire through my body.

"Well, if he's such a nice guy, go fuck him then," I snarl.

Her face turns white as a sheet.

"What a horrible thing to say," she gasps and leaps up. Moving toward the bed with purposeful steps, she grabs the blanket at the bottom of the bed. She's going to sleep on the day bed. That... that just pisses me off.

"You're really going to ignore me?" I ask, my voice low, a dangerous edge creeping in despite myself. My frustration from the entire night, the entire day, is bleeding into this moment, and I can't stop it.

Still, no answer. She carries the blanket past me, and something snaps in me. I step forward and snatch it from her hands, my movements sharp.

"Lara," I growl, my grip tightening on the blanket.

She jerks the blanket back, fire in her eyes. "Is this the part where you get violent?" she snaps, sarcasm dripping from every word. But I hear the undercurrent of fear beneath it. She is a woman in a foreign country with a man she doesn't know much about.

I let go immediately. The anger drains from me in an instant, leaving behind something raw and aching. "I would never hurt you, Lara," I say, my voice full of remorse. "I'd rather burn myself alive than hurt you."

The words surprise even me, but they're the truth. They spill out, raw and unfiltered, and she just stares at me in shock.

"I mean it," I repeat, stepping closer, my hand reaching for her. I touch her face gently, cradling her cheek in my palm, my thumb brushing over her skin. "You're the only good thing I have right now. The only thing keeping me from losing my fucking mind."

She doesn't say anything, but her expression softens, and the tight tension between us shifts. She reaches up, her fingers resting lightly on my hand. The simple touch sends a wave of warmth through me.

"I know you're going through hell," she whispers, her voice so soft I almost don't catch it. "I wish I knew how to help you."

"You help just by being here," I murmur, my other hand coming up to cup her face, pulling her closer.

I kiss her. Slow at first, but it deepens quickly, the old passion bubbling up to the surface. I kiss her like she's my lifeline, like I need her more than air right now.

And God, I do.

I pull her into me, my arms wrapping around her waist, and her body fits perfectly against mine, like a key into a lock. The fury, the frustration, it all fades away, replaced by this need—this need to feel something real, something that isn't slipping through my fingers.

But then the headache takes over.

The throbbing becomes so hard I can't ignore it anymore. I pull back, collapsing onto the bed and rubbing my temples. I can't even think straight.

"Hey," she says, sitting beside me, silent for a moment. Then she offers me a glass of water. I down it in one go and lean back, closing my eyes. The silence stretches between us, but it's a soothing silence.

"I'm sorry I made things worse for you, Ivan," she says quietly, breaking the silence. "I feel so useless. What can I do for you?"

I reach for her hand, squeezing it gently. "You're not useless, Lara. You're helping more than you know."

She looks at me, her eyes filled with uncertainty, and I realize that for the first time in a long time, I want to tell someone everything. I need to tell someone everything.

So I do.

I tell her about the growing list of governments breathing down my neck, believing my wealth is tied to the Russian government. I tell her about the sanctions, about the lies someone's feeding the authorities, about my connections to Russian money. I tell her about the yacht, the chateau, the properties in London and Paris, the Coutts bank account—all unfairly impounded. And I tell her how everything is falling apart faster than I can fix it.

And she listens. Really listens.

She doesn't interrupt, doesn't push me to explain more than I want to. She lets me fall apart without judgment. She just listens, her eyes filling with compassion and becoming kinder with every word I say. The more silent she is, staring intently into my eyes, the faster the words roll off my tongue. I have never in my life spoken to anyone this way. Maybe it's just because I want to tell someone, anyone. Maybe I can speak this freely because I know she will be gone from my life in a month. Or maybe it's because I can no longer deny how I feel about her and I want to show her the real me, come what may.

"I wish I could do something," she whispers almost to herself when I'm finished. "I want to help. I know I can."

Her words linger in the air, hanging between us.

The exhaustion of the day pulls at my limbs, but something else—a raw, unspoken need—keeps me tethered to this moment. The vulnerability in her voice and the quiet confession of helplessness cuts deeper than I expect. I can see it in her eyes. She really wants to help me and that soothes me more than she will ever know.

I reach for her, pulling her closer, needing her warmth against me. I cup her face in my hands, the softness of her skin grounding me, calming the chaos inside me.

"Lara," I whisper, my voice hoarse, "you've already done enough. Just being here… that's everything."

Her lips part as if to protest, but I stop her with a kiss, soft and slow, pouring every ounce of gratitude, every unspoken word of thanks, into it.

"Just lie next to me. I'll face tomorrow when I wake up."

Her arm curls around me. "Okay, my great, big white swan. Let's sleep now. Together."

A few minutes pass, and the drowsiness creeps in, thick and heavy. My eyelids grow heavier, the quiet peace of the moment sinking into me. With her pressed against me, I feel the pull of sleep stronger than ever before.

I didn't expect this—I never thought I could fall asleep so easily with her in my arms. The world outside the room fades away, and all that remains is us.

Just Leda and me.

Chapter Forty-Six

LARA

On our flight back to New York, I call my dad and he assures me all is well. He is going to his addictions group therapy, and the office is ticking along nicely. I end the call with him to take Leila's call.

"What's going on with you?" she demands.

I stare at her familiar face on the phone screen. It should calm me, but it only amplifies the mess in my head. I don't know what I feel... numb? No, that's not right. I'm overwhelmed. Completely. Everything is swirling together—the past few days in Ivan's world are like trying to hold water in my hands, and I don't know how to explain it.

Leila's voice is louder this time, sharper. "Lara, did you hear me? What's going on? Are you all right?"

I snap out of my daze. "Yeah, sorry. I'm fine." It's an obvious lie, and we both know it. The last two days feel like a whirlwind that I still can't quite wrap my head around.

Leila tilts her head, raising an eyebrow in that unique way she does when she knows something's up. "Don't give me that horseshit. What's going on? You're acting all... I don't know. Different. Weird. Please tell me you're not falling for him."

Falling for him. That's very much already baked into the cake. My mind pulls me back to earlier this morning. To Ivan. The memory floats in, vivid and intimate.

It was one of those perfect mornings where everything felt easy. Ivan and I had stayed in bed longer than usual, the early sunlight filtering through the windows, casting a golden glow over us. He'd pulled me close, his arms wrapped securely around me, the weight of the world temporarily forgotten. His skin was warm against mine, his breath steady as he mumbled something in Russian I didn't quite catch, but I didn't need to understand. The softness in his tone said enough.

Then he started sharing bits of stories I'd never heard, and I found myself lost in the way he spoke, his words unguarded, his laughter warm. And then he picked up the book I'd been reading. "Romance, huh?"

I nodded. "Yeah, I can't get enough."

"Is the hero Russian?" he teased.

I smiled secretively. "Of course."

"Is he tragic and brooding?"

I nudged his arm. "No, I have that in real life."

His eyes had flicked to mine, playful but with an edge of something deeper. "Maybe. But I'm working on my happy ending."

We both laughed, but beneath the surface, I felt something shift. It was subtle but undeniable—this pull between us, a connection I couldn't ignore. And then he kissed me. Not the passionate, hungry kisses from before, but something softer, almost... careful.

"Hey, what is that around your neck!" Leila calls, her voice pulling me from my thoughts.

Leila's eyes are wide with curiosity "Oh my God, is that a gift?" she squeals.

I touch the little ruby pendant lightly, feeling its warm weight against my skin. "Yeah," I admit, my voice quieter, almost shy. "He gave it to me this morning."

Leila's mouth drops open in awe. "Lara, it's so pretty! Oh my God. You are falling for him."

I hesitate for a moment, but I decide to just tell her. "it's not what you think. There's a story behind it."

"Well, come on. Out with it?"

"It's not an ordinary pendant. It has a tracker inside. He said he'd be able to find me if there was ever any trouble."

Leila's eyebrows shoot up, her excitement replaced by a hint of skepticism. "Wait, what? Isn't that... a little... um... creepy? I mean, he's tracking your movements now?"

I try to laugh it off, it sounds forced even to me. "Yeah, normally I would agree with you, but some stuff is going down right now with him and he doesn't really trust anyone here in Paris."

"What stuff?" she asks skeptically.

"I don't know. Heavy stuff with the governments. I can't really talk about it."

"What the fuck!" she screams.

"Don't get your panties in a twist. It's cool. He just wants to make sure I'm safe. New York is not all that safe nowadays, you know. There are kidnappers everywhere," I add airily.

"Have you gone totally mad?"

"Look, it's just a precaution, okay. Drop it for now, Leila. I'll explain everything fully when we get back, okay?"

Leila takes a deep calming breath, but there's still a hint of unease in her eyes. "Well, I get that a man can be worried about his girl, but still... a tracker?"

I nod slowly, the weight of the pendant suddenly feeling

heavier against my chest. "I know it sounds crazy," I admit, "but with everything that's been going on, it oddly makes sense."

There's silence on the line, and I can see Leila trying to process everything, just like I've been trying to. Her skepticism fades into something warmer, a protective sort of worry. "Fine, I'll leave it until you get back. Just be careful, okay? I don't want you to get hurt."

"I will," I promise, but the words feel thin, insubstantial.

"Are you in love with him, Lara?" she asks outright.

"I don't know. Maybe," I admit honestly. "He confides in me. It's... hard not to feel something when someone lets you in like that."

Leila leans closer to the screen, her expression shifting to concern. "Girl, look out," she warns, her tone serious but playful. "This is the man who made you sign a contract."

"I know."

"I guess I'm just letting it play out. He's different than I thought. It's not just... It's more than that."

Leila sighs, leaning back. "Just be careful, Lara. Guys like him..."

"I know," I whisper, more to myself this time. I feel like someone who's crossed a line she can't come back from.

I end the call, and slipping my phone into my pocket I go and splash cold water on my face. It's supposed to help, but it doesn't. Nothing really does. The book I've been holding onto for hours? I haven't even read a single sentence, not really.

I step out of the bathroom and return to my seat, and it hits me like a wave. The lights are dimmed down low, but the air is thick with tension. Ivan's face is tight, frustration written in every hard line of his jaw as he speaks rapidly into his phone in Russian.

I'm careful not to disturb his conversation, but it's hard

not to stare. He looks... worn down. His posture rigid, his hand gripping a half-empty glass of whiskey. Whatever's happening on the other end of that phone, it's bad. I can feel it.

I sit quietly, refilling my glass of wine, watching him from the corner of my eye. He doesn't notice me. He's too wrapped up in whatever storm is brewing around him. And as much as I want to reach out, to ask him what's going on, I know better. I'm just here, on the edge of it, watching him fight battles I don't understand.

The rest of the flight passes in a blur. Eventually, the phone calls stop, and Ivan slumps in his seat. His exhaustion is palpable in the tense set of his shoulders, and the way his fingers tap restlessly against the armrest.

Then, before I know it, we've landed back in New York.

Chapter Forty-Seven

LARA

The next few days merge together in a haze of routine and uncertainty.

Ivan is always busy, constantly on the phone, lost in meetings, his attention divided between the chaos unfolding around his businesses and trying to find solutions. Yet, somehow, every evening, no matter how late, he makes it home for dinner. We don't plan it, but it's become our unspoken ritual. Muriel sets up the table as we are having a formal dinner, with gorgeous flower arrangements, candles, good chinaware, and antique linen. We sit across from each other, often in silence, but as the meal progresses, I see the weight of the day slowly melt away from his face.

He's different now. Tired in ways I hadn't seen before. He wears his strength like an armor, refusing to let it crack, but I can feel the strain beneath the surface. The lines on his face have deepened. His smiles, when they come, are fleeting. Even so, he reaches for me. Every night, he slides into bed, pulling me close, like I'm his last tether to something real, something grounding.

We fall into each other then. There's heat, always, but it's laced with something softer, something unspoken. In those moments, I feel like we're drifting into our own world, separate from the chaos outside. I've started to count the days with dread. I would have laughed if someone had told me I wouldn't be celebrating, but dreading the day my contract ends.

When he falls asleep, his body is warm and heavy against mine. I listen to his breath, steady and deep, and then at some ungodly hour he wakes up. A phone call, the London stock exchange is opening, or a Zoom call from Shanghai. There's always something. I start to appreciate how hard Ivan works. That he earned the right to be proud of his success. His money is not inherited. Nikolai is fun and charming and he dances very well, but he lives an idle life of luxury on his father's dime.

During the day, while he's out, I lose myself in Muriel's garden. It becomes my sanctuary—my escape. Both my apple and orange have started to root and bear shoots. It's the most beautiful thing to see. The feel of the earth between my fingers, the scent of the flowers blooming under the sun, it's grounding. I spend hours there, letting the simple act of tending to the plants bring me a sense of calm. I hope I can infuse the same calm when Ivan comes home.

Sometimes, I wonder if he's thinking about me while he's out, dealing with whatever new attack has come up against him. He never expected or planned for any of this to come down on him. At first, I felt somewhat bitter and robbed that it all kicked off during our time together, but now I'm glad. If I was not here he would have to go through this ordeal alone and I would never wish that on anyone let alone him.

Then one night he left the bed at two in the morning. I get

up a few minutes later and follow him to his office. I find him sitting in front of six computer screens.

"Whatcha doing?" I ask from the door.

"Taking some scalps to pay the bills," he says.

My eyes widen. "What?"

He leans back against his black leather chair. "Scalping is slang for when a trader goes into the marketplace, takes a trade and is out quickly, before the trade can turn against him."

"I thought you couldn't trade anymore. Your accounts at the exchanges were frozen."

"An old friend from Cambridge set up an account in his name for me. I use a VPN to hide my location and I only scalp because I have studied Robert's trading record and I adhere strictly to his risk appetite and loss rate. So no placing big trades that could raise red flags. The last thing I want to do is to get him in trouble."

"Can I see what you're doing?"

He smiles. "Sure. Come in and sit on my lap."

I go and sit on his lap and watch quietly while he works.

"This is the Bitcoin chart. A very volatile asset. Fantastic for scalping," he explains.

There are numbers blinking everywhere and his fingers move at lightning speed chasing a pulsating dot on a one-second screen. "Wow, how can you know the exact movement when it is about to change direction?"

"The market is like a woman," he says. "To persuade her to dance with you have to learn how she moves and move with her. Then she will embrace you and give you riches you never dreamed of."

I turn to look at him in the blue light from the screen. "You're special, you know. Really special."

He smiles. "So are you."

"No, I really mean that. I'm just an ordinary person.

You're not. You're truly exceptional. I never said that to you before and no matter what happens always remember, you're extraordinary."

"That's it for tonight," he says, clicking the red sell button on his screen and lifting me into his arms. "Now it's time for you to see just how extraordinary you are."

* * *

Then one night, everything shifts.

He doesn't come home for dinner. I eat alone and go to bed, certain he will return soon, but I fall asleep alone and wake up, groggy and disoriented, reaching out for him instinctively. But the bed beside me is cold and empty. My heart stumbles in my chest as I sit up, glancing at the clock. It's well past midnight. Where is he?

Panic prickles at the edges of my mind, but I push it down, forcing myself to stay calm. I get out of bed and wrap my robe around me as I walk toward the window. There is a full moon in the sky and the city is alive and buzzing with bright lights.

Where could he be?

The anxiety bubbling in my chest tightens, and I need to move, to do something, anything, to clear my head. I need something to calm me down. Perhaps a swim in the pool. I get into my bikini and leave my room. I decide to go through the kitchen but stop in my tracks when I see Muriel sitting at the island. She is pouring tea from a blue and white flowery porcelain teapot into a cup with a matching pattern. She's not usually up this late, and the sight of her in the kitchen feels oddly out of place.

"You're up late," I say, my voice gentle, not prying but curious.

"Yes. I couldn't sleep. I thought a cup of chamomile tea would do the trick."

I shift from one foot to another. "Ivan isn't back. You wouldn't by any chance know where he is, would you?"

Muriel sets her cup down. "No, I was worried when he didn't come back for dinner too."

I pause, surprised. It's not like Muriel to talk about Ivan like this. She's always professional, and I never expected her to express concern for his whereabouts.

"You were worried?" I ask, unsure of how else to respond.

Muriel's mouth quirks downwards. "We all are, Lara, I've worked for him for years, and I've never seen him like this. But I'm glad you're here, especially now."

Her words take a moment to sink in. I'd never thought about how Ivan's staff might feel about what's going on.

"Who's 'we all'?" I ask, the curiosity pushing me to dig a little deeper.

"The staff," she says with a small shrug. "Everyone who works for him. It's not just that we've seen the news, but we all talk. We all care about him and we can all see he's under pressure."

There's a pause as I let her words settle in. I hadn't considered that Ivan's staff might actually be concerned, that they'd notice when things were not right.

"We've been talking about how we can help. If it comes to it, we're willing to pitch in however we can financially."

I blink with shock. "Financially?" It feels strange to even suggest that they would want to support him like that. Most people will have no idea of how they can be of use like how I was, or make vague offers to help, but financially? To offer your own hard-earned money... that's real commitment.

"You are surprised because you don't know our history with him. He's helped us all over the years. Some of the staff have even talked about remortgaging their homes if necessary. He helped them buy those homes in the first place. It's not just about loyalty—it's about giving back to someone who's always been there when we needed him."

I lean against the counter as her words settle in. "I didn't know any of that," I admit quietly. "Ivan never talks about helping people. It's almost like he's kept this part of himself hidden from me."

Muriel smiles softly. "Ivan isn't one to boast. He does things quietly, and most of the time, people don't even realize it. We are spread about in all his properties. His chefs, his chauffeurs, his gardeners, his butler in England, his staff in Russia—there are so many of us that he's been so generous with over the years. Do you know he bought me a cottage with a garden? It's meant to be a place for me to retire when I'm too old to work. It's in Devon by the sea. Well, I don't need it. Let him have it. He can sell it or mortgage it or whatever. Living here with all my bills paid for, I have saved quite a bit. Let him have that too. He's not alone in this."

My eyes widen with shock and I stare at her, feeling something shift inside me. I've always seen Ivan as closed-off, someone who keeps people at a distance, but this... this changes everything. The way his staff think about him, their willingness to help—it's not something you earn with money or power. It's something deeper, something real.

"Have you told him this?" I ask softly, wondering if Ivan even realizes how much his people care about him.

"No, not yet," Muriel says, her eyes full of the wisdom she has gained over decades. "He's a proud man with a deep well of resources and talents, and I'll only step forward if and when I see that those petty men have abused their office and might to unfairly crush him. Only when I see that it is absolutely necessary."

I don't know what to say. I feel like I'm learning a whole new side of Ivan and Muriel. And it makes me feel closer to both of them in a way that I can't quite explain.

I smile at Muriel, feeling a strange sense of comfort. "He is lucky to have you," I say quietly.

"And he's lucky to have you. He needs someone like you right now." She picks up her cup and saucer and stands. "Well then, I'm off to bed. Goodnight, Miss Fitzpatrick."

"Lara. Call me Lara."

She shakes her head. "No. It wouldn't be proper. I come from a long line of servants. My grandmother served as a charwoman in Winston Churchill's home. I am what I am. I don't need to pretend to be something I'm not. I'm proud to be here serving Mr. Ivanovich and you, Miss Fitzpatrick."

I yield to her wish with a small nod, and she moves away.

Once she is gone, I head to the terrace, feeling the cool night air hit my skin. The pool reflects the moonlight, and I slip into the water, Muriel's words echoing in my head. Muriel taught me something today. Help is saying, I want to help if I can. Help is doing something concrete, no matter how small. Stroke after stroke, I let the lesson swirl in my mind.

When I am tired, I float on my back and gaze at the stars until I feel a little cold. I swim to the edge of the pool and I see him sitting on a lounge chair, his expression unreadable, a bottle of whiskey in his hand. The sight of him makes my heart race, though I'm not sure if it's relief or something else.

I pull myself out of the water, the cool air hitting my skin as I walk toward him. And for a moment, we just look at each other, the silence stretching between us.

Chapter Forty-Eight

IVAN

I spotted her the moment I stepped out into the cool night air. She was floating lazily in the pool, her skin catching the faint glow of the moon, and something in me shifted. I decided to sit and watch her. Just watching her calms me. The world outside matters no more. They can't take this moment away from me.

I'm not drunk. I'm just a little... smooth. The rough edges are gone.

I walk over slowly, bottle in hand, not wanting to break the spell. Water slides down her skin in shimmering trails. I don't say anything. I just watch her, this woman who's somehow become the only quiet in the middle of the storm.

"I was heading to the office to get the market to dance with me," I say, breaking the silence between us, "but I heard the splash. Figured she'll dance with someone else for a bit. I'd rather be here."

She takes the bottle from me, her fingers brushing mine,

and takes a small sip, her eyes never leaving mine. "Great decision. I... I wanted you here as well."

There's a pause. We're both searching each other's expressions, trying to figure out what to say without saying it. She hands me back the bottle, and I take a long drink.

"You um ... look quite... distant," she notes softly.

I can't help but let out a quiet laugh, though there's no humor in it. "That's one way to put it."

She's waiting. Not pushing, just... waiting for me to trust her enough to share. There's something in her eyes, something that makes me want to let down my guard and stop pretending that I have everything under control.

I shake my head and run a hand through my hair. "Everything's falling apart, and it's happening too fast for me to stop it."

Her brow furrows, concern written all over her face.

I take a deep breath, feeling the words like stones in my throat. "You're already aware that the British and French authorities have frozen the assets I have registered in Europe. The yacht, the properties, the shares... they're all locked away. And now..."

"And now?"

I smile bitterly. "And now... they want more blood. They have got their American brothers coming after everything else —my reputation, my businesses, my assets in this country. If I don't clear this up soon, I'll lose everything that's not in Russia."

She's quiet for a moment, absorbing it all. I half expect her to be overwhelmed, to step away, but instead, she inches closer, her hand resting on mine, grounding me in the moment.

"Is there anything you can do?" she asks, her voice soft, cautious.

"Yes, I can sort it all out. I've got paintings, crypto and assets that I can sell to raise the funds I need, but I need time." The frustration leaks into my tone, and I rub my face, trying to shake it off. "Even if I wanted to ask my brother to help, he can't help, being in debt himself. My sister... well, she's offered, but only in exchange for seventy percent of everything I own once this matter is solved."

Her eyes widen. "Seventy percent? What's her real name, Shylock?"

I shrug and smile softly. "Natalia is a hard-nosed career woman and it is good business to cut the best deal you can especially when you see the other side is weak and with little options. But what choice do I have? She might be my only way out."

Lara doesn't say anything right away. Instead, she moves a little closer, her eyes scanning my face like she's trying to find something, some answer that I can't seem to see.

"You'll figure this out," she says quietly, her hand still resting on mine. "From what I've learned about you so far, you're not the type to let something like this take you down. One way or another you'll solve this."

Her words hit something deep inside me, and for a moment, I feel... lighter. Of course, she's right. I know I will figure this out. And even if I have to give Natalia half, I will be okay. I hate the thought of it, but it's only a couple of billion dollars.

"Thank you. For listening. For being here." I shake my head. "Never in a million years did I ever think I'd be saying this to you."

She smiles, amused. "Neither did I."

For a moment, everything feels still—just the night air thick with something unspoken. I glance at her.

"You know because of all this... I can't buy the house on

the beachfront anymore, right?" I say quietly. The one thing I had promised—the one reason she had agreed to this situation in the first place. The one thing that tied her to me.

Her eyes look deep into mine. "I know that."

"But I'll make sure there's no loss for you. Your father's agency, the commission they were counting on—it won't be affected. I've already settled all his debts and paid off his outstanding loan at his bank as I promised. I won't let you walk away from this with nothing. I just want to tell you that I'll need a bit of time to settle my affairs before you get paid, okay?"

She nods slowly. "I need to wait for my money, huh?" Her voice is quiet, but there's a steadiness to it. "I guess that means I'll have to stay... until my thirty days are up, and if you're still not able to deliver then I guess I'll have to stay even longer."

The twinkle in her eyes tells me she's not just staying for the contract or because of what I can offer her father's business anymore. She's staying for something more—something between us that neither of us dare name yet.

Now I know for sure. They can't take her away from me.

I feel my chest tighten as I look at her. If I stay another moment looking into her limpid eyes, I swear, I'll say something I will never say without half a bottle of whiskey inside me. I peel off my clothes, toss them aside, and dive into the pool. The water wraps around me, cool and refreshing.

When I resurface, I see her watching me from the edge, her expression unreadable. I swim towards her, my pulse quickening as I approach. There's something in her eyes—something that mirrors the way I'm feeling right now.

She slowly kneels by the edge of the pool, her fingers brushing the water. "Ivan... did you hear me? I'm not leaving."

My heart swells at her words. I swim to the edge. Our faces are so close they are almost touching. Her eyes lock onto mine.

"I don't know how this will end," I murmur, my hand brushing her cheek. "But if you're staying, you need to know... you're not just part of a deal anymore."

Her breath hitches as I press my lips to hers, softly at first, but then the need—the desperation—takes over. I deepen the kiss, pulling her into the water with me. She falls in with a quiet splash and wraps her arms around me, and everything else falls away—the house, the deal, the mess I'm in.

After a few moments, she pulls back, breathless, and I feel her hands on my chest. "Ivan," she whispers. "There's something I need to tell you."

I raise an eyebrow, watching her carefully as she hesitates. "What is it?"

She takes a deep breath, her fingers curling against my skin. She looks so vulnerable I want to wrap her in cotton wool and never let the world ever hurt her.

"I want to help," she says. "I'm offering you the deeds to my apartment and my father's house. You can remortgage them and use the proceeds. It's not much compared to what you need, but it's something. Altogether, you should be able to get at least a million from it."

I freeze, stunned by her offer.

My mind races, almost unable to believe what she's just said. Her unexpected offer fills me with shock. I can't believe what she's offering, how far she's willing to go for me. The weight of her gesture leaves me speechless. It's overwhelming and I can feel it breaking something open inside me.

God! I feel like crying.

Before I can make a complete fool of myself, I pull her into a kiss. It is desperate, raw, and filled with everything I can't say. My lips press against hers, hard at first, but when she kisses me back, it softens. I need her closer, need to feel her, as if that closeness will keep me from drowning in the chaos of everything else falling apart.

Without breaking the kiss I yank her into the pool with me and she gasps as the cool water envelops her. Her hands slide up my chest, wet and trembling, but there's nothing uncertain in the way she pulls me closer. She's not just offering me an escape from my world—she's offering everything to me.

I reach for her bikini top, pulling at the straps with a slow intensity. It falls away, revealing her breasts in the moonlight. She shivers and I lower my mouth to her skin, tasting the mix of water and heat. I kiss her breast, sucking hard on her nipple, flicking it with my tongue as she lets out a soft moan, her fingers gripping my hair.

The sound of her breathless gasps fuels something primal inside me. My hands move down her body, pulling her closer, feeling the way her body arches into me. I push her gently against the pool's edge, my fingers sliding lower until they find the thin material of her bikini bottoms. I pull them down with one swift motion, and her legs part as I press against her.

She's slick, warm, and ready. I slide my fingers inside her, curling them deep, and she gasps, her nails digging into my shoulders as her head falls back. The water ripples around us, echoing the raw need building between us. Her hips move against my hand, desperate for more, and I oblige, moving my fingers faster, deeper, feeling her tighten around me.

"Oh, Ivan..." Her voice is ragged, breathless, and her body shudders against me.

I can feel the tension building inside her. She's losing control, and I want nothing more than to push her over the edge.

I bite her bottom lip and suck it into my mouth. Her hands slide down my body, reaching for my underwear, pulling them off in one frantic motion. She wraps her legs around me, pulling me toward her, our bodies slick and throbbing.

Without hesitation, I push into her, burying myself deep inside. She moans as her body stretches to take me in. She clings to me, her fingers digging into my back as I start to move, each thrust harder than the last.

Her breath is hot against my neck. Her moans grow louder with each movement. The pool water sloshes wildly, but all I can hear is the sound of her voice, the feeling of her body gripping mine as I plunge into her again and again.

"Oh, God..." she cries out, her body arching into mine as she nears the edge.

"Come for me," I rasp against her skin, my voice rough with need as I continue to fuck her hard. "I want to feel you."

"Yes, yes," she gasps as her body tenses, and then she goes over, her release hitting her in waves as she cries out, her nails raking down my back. The feeling of her pulsing around me, trembling in my arms, sends me over the edge, and I thrust into her one last time, groaning as my own release crashes through me.

We stay tangled together in the water, breathless and raw, the only sound being the soft sloshing of the pool against the tiles and our ragged breathing. I press my forehead against hers, my hands still holding her close, neither of us willing to let go just yet.

For a moment, everything else fades—the business, the house, the mess I've made of everything. It's just her, grounding me, keeping me from falling apart entirely.

My lips gently brush against hers. "No, I don't need your father's house or your apartment. I'll figure this out."

"We're going to be okay. You wait and see," she whispers back, her eyes filled with some deep emotion that I cannot quite name.

Chapter Forty-Nine

LARA

Today is the day.

The ominous words float in my mind, heavy and inevitable as I sit across from Ivan in the conservatory. Sunlight filters through the large windows, bathing the room in warmth, but it does nothing to ease the tension in the air. The simple breakfast before me—fresh fruit, croissants, and tea—sits untouched. I'm too busy watching him, noting the tight line of his mouth, the way his brow furrows as he scrolls through his phone. He barely looks at his plate, hardly touches his coffee.

I know he's thinking about the $320 million loan that's set to be pulled today. It's like a ticking time bomb, and though he hasn't said it aloud, I can see the strain in every movement. He's been confiding in me more recently, little glimpses into his life and his struggles, but I've been careful not to push. Not to pry. I want to help, but how? What can I possibly do in the face of such a colossal number?

I feel so... useless.

Just then, Muriel enters with a tray, carrying freshly pressed grape juice. She places the glass gently in front of Ivan, her movements quiet and careful. But he doesn't even notice. His focus is entirely on whatever message he's reading on his phone.

Muriel pauses for a second, her eyes meeting mine. There's something in her gaze—a determination. It's one of those looks that says, 'It's time'.

I clear my throat softly, but Ivan doesn't hear me. His mind is somewhere else, wrapped in the chaos of his business falling apart.

I tap the table lightly, trying to break through the fog he's in. "Ivan."

He looks up with a frown as though he's just now realizing I'm here. "Hmm?" His voice is distant.

"I... I want to tell you something." I glance toward Muriel, who nods subtly before stepping out of the room, leaving us alone. "Muriel mentioned earlier that some of your staff... they want to help you."

His brows furrow, confusion flickering in his eyes. "Help me? How?"

"They've been offering their assets," I explain, my voice softer now. "Their homes, their savings. Muriel said she's willing to remortgage the retirement cottage you bought for her. They believe in you, Ivan."

He stares at me for a moment, as though the words aren't registering. I can see the wall he's built around himself, the pride that keeps him from leaning on others. But I know this has to touch him, somewhere deep inside. How could it not? These people are giving everything they have, trusting him with their futures.

"Why would they do that?" His voice is barely a whisper, as though he can't believe it.

"Because of what you've done for them," I say gently. "How you've helped them over the years."

He looks away, his gaze shifting to the window. The light falls across his face, casting shadows on the sharp lines of his cheekbones. For a long time, there's nothing but silence between us. I can feel the clash of his emotions, the battle he's fighting to keep it all in.

Just then, the door opens, and one by one, his staff begin to enter. Muriel steps forward first, holding an envelope in her hands. She's calm, but there's a quiet determination in her expression.

"You secured my future for me when there was no need, no obligation to, Mr. Ivanovich," she says, her voice steady but filled with emotion. "Now, it's only fair that I offer this to you. Please... take this." She places the envelope on the table, her hand lingering for a moment before she steps back.

Ivan's eyes widen slightly, his shock visible. Before he can respond, Brad, one of his longtime drivers, steps forward. "Sir," he begins, his voice carrying a sincerity that makes my heart ache. "You've done so much for us. My apartment... it's yours if you need it."

Another envelope joins the pile.

Then comes the Chefs, the other chauffeur, his bodyguards, the guy who has the cleaning contract. Each one offers their savings, their homes, everything they have. Muriel takes her phone out and other staff from his other houses appear on a Zoom call. They want to help too.

I watch Ivan, his hands trembling, the emotion he's trying so hard to contain finally breaking through. This is a man who's always been in control, always stood on his own, and now... now he's surrounded by people who believe in him so much they are willing to give up everything for him.

The last staff member on the Zoom call finishes and silence falls over the room once again. Ivan stares at the pile of envelopes on the table, his expression unreadable. I can see the tears he's holding back, the way his fingers twitch as though he's not sure what to do with this truly incredible display of loyalty.

I stand slowly, my heart pounding as I walk over to the small cabinet in the corner. My hands tremble as I retrieve the deed to my apartment and my father's house, the same offer I made to him before—the one he rejected.

I place it gently on top of the pile.

"I know this won't make a dent in the $320 million loan," I say quietly, my voice barely steady. "But it's not about the money. It's about showing you that you're not alone. You have people who believe in you."

Ivan looks up at me, his blue eyes filled with something raw, something vulnerable. He's not used to this—this kind of support, this kind of care. For a moment, he just stares, as though he's trying to find the right words. Then, he nods, a small, tight smile tugging at the corner of his mouth.

"Thank you," he murmurs, his voice thick with emotion. And then he looks up at all his staff. "Really, thank you all. I deeply appreciate it." They give to him with sincerity and great affection shining in their eyes and then leave the room, leaving us both alone once again. I return to my seat and watch him stare down in disbelief at the pile of documents and envelopes.

"You're not going to use them, are you?" I ask.

He takes a deep breath, his shoulders slumping.

"No," he somehow works up a smile. "I cannot put their life's savings in danger. What if I am killed in a road accident tomorrow? What will happen then? But I'll keep them and return them at a later date. I... I can see that you all care and that you want to help me. And so, I'll accept that help now. I won't use your properties, but I'll look to them for added strength when I need to remind myself that I'm not alone in this."

My heart swells up and warms at this, but I know it makes me immensely sad.

He continues speaking. "I've decided to accept my sister's help," he admits after a moment, his voice low.

I am stunned by this and quite angry. "What... but..."

"I know," he says. "My sister is a shark, but I have swum with sharks before and survived. Money can always be earned. I'll be okay. The most important thing is to not allow the loan to be cancelled, because that will have a cascading effect on all the other businesses. Once that is secure then I'll dedicate myself to fighting with every ounce of energy to clear my name," he says, determination flickering in his eyes. "And I'll make sure everyone who's helped me is rewarded. Tenfold. At least. I'll never forget this day as long as I live."

Unable to finish his breakfast, Ivan stands. He leans down, pressing a soft kiss to my forehead.

"Thank you," he whispers again before turning and leaving the room.

I sit there in the silence that follows, staring at the uneaten food. There has to be something more I can do. I can't stand the thought of his sister taking advantage of him like this. And since Nikolai is already in debt, he can't help, there's only one other person I can think of.

His father.

The idea feels bold, reckless even. But maybe... just maybe it's the right move. I don't know where his father is—France was the last place I saw him—but I know someone who might.

I pull out my phone and dial Nikolai's number, my heart pounding in my chest as the line rings.

"Lara," Nikolai's voice greets me, teasing as usual. "Fancy you actually using my number and calling me. I would have never expected it in a million years."

I too would have never expected that I would be doing this, but this is my last chance to help, and I will not miss it for anything, even my pride and reluctance.

"So, what can I do for you?" he asks.

"I need your father's phone number," I say, trying to keep my voice steady. "It's... it's personal."

There's a pause, then Nikolai responds, his tone more serious than I've ever heard it. "I will get it. I'll text it to you."

I thank him, feeling a rush of relief when the number comes through. My fingers tremble slightly as I dial. This feels reckless—calling a man I've only met once, and under very different circumstances.

The phone rings once, twice, and then a deep voice answers, a familiar note of authority in the tone.

"Mr Ivanovich," I begin.

"Lara," he says immediately.

I freeze, caught off guard. "You... how do you know it's me?"

"What do you want?" he asks, ignoring my question so I have no choice but to get to the point of why I'm calling him.

"I—I wasn't sure if you'd be in New York," I manage, trying to keep my voice steady. "Can I... can we meet, Mr Ivanovich? You can tell me where you are, and I'll find my way there."

This sounds ridiculous because, of course, I wouldn't be able to find my way there, but then again, I have no interest in dwelling on any problems for the day before they actually exist.

"I'm in New York as it happens," he says. "I'll send a car for you."

I nearly go into shock. It wears off very quickly though when I hear the click of his phone ringing off. Relief washes through me. Instantly, I jump up and do a happy dance. I did it. I called him and made an appointment.

Now all I have to do is ask him to loan his son about three hundred million dollars, give or take a few million.

Chapter Fifty

IVAN

"$250 million?" I repeat, leaping out of my chair in shock and disbelief. "Who is it from?"

My accountant clears his throat before answering, hesitant. "It's a wire transfer from your father's company."

"My father? Are you sure?"

"Absolutely," he confirms. "I was surprised too."

Suddenly I have to sit down, and I crash back down on my chair. Slowly, I swivel and turn around to face the window.

"The funds are clear, and this makes all the difference, Ivan. We'll be able to cover everything—no more scrambling around. You're financially stable again. You can tell your sister to keep her money."

I let out a slow, disbelieving breath. Relief surges through me, mixing with a sense of shame I can't shake. My father, the man I swore to distance myself from, has just saved my empire. For a moment, I can't move. My emotions are tangled—immense gratitude, resentment, and confusion. Why now, of all times? Why would he help after years of coldness, accusations, and mistrust?

The phone call ends, but I remain seated, staring out over the city below. I should feel triumphant—this is a victory, at least for my businesses. But all I feel is hollow, like the price I paid was more than just financial.

I stand up abruptly, grabbing my jacket and going out of the door. "Greta," I call out as I exit, "have the car ready for me downstairs."

I stare out of the window without seeing anything. My heart is beating fast. We drive through the bustling streets and finally arrive at a building tucked discreetly away in the Upper East Side, a fitting choice for a man like him. It's a private, imposing residence, shrouded in luxury and secrecy, just as he always liked it.

The door swings open as soon as I step out, and his British butler greets me.

"So good to see you again, Master Ivanovich."

I was twenty-two years old when he last called me that. "It's good to see you too, Alfred."

He leads us into a dark-paneled study. My father is there, lounging on a leather couch, a glass of cognac in hand. His eyes are as piercing as I remember, but there is something weary about his expression.

"Why?" I ask as I take a seat at the opposite end of the couch, cutting straight to the chase.

He takes a slow sip, his gaze not leaving mine. "Because Lara came to see me. She's a pretty little thing, isn't she?"

The mention of her name sends a jolt through me. I didn't know she'd done that. "She—what?"

"She was desperate," he continues, his tone surprisingly soft. "Shaking like a leaf, but stubborn as hell. She wanted to make sure you'd get the money."

I'm stunned. My throat tightens and I struggle to find words. "Why would it matter to you what she wants?"

He shrugs, setting the glass down. "Because I wanted to. Because she wasn't thinking of herself. I saw sincerity in her eyes, a genuine willingness to sacrifice for you. I've known many people in my life. You can always tell when someone truly cares."

His words crack me open. I feel a mix of anger and gratitude—anger at myself for needing this, for Lara having to step in, and gratitude toward her and, begrudgingly, toward my father too.

"I didn't think you cared," I say, the bitterness leaking through my voice. "About me, or anything I've built."

His expression darkens. "You don't think I care?"

"You proved that in no uncertain terms."

He leans forward, his eyes intense. "Everything you've done, the choices you've made—good or bad—they've been born from the fire I set in you. I may not have been the father you wanted, but I've always been the one you needed."

A silence stretches between us, thick and charged with years of unspoken words.

He puts his glass down. "There is another reason I put the money up. And you're not going to like this. Your troubles run a bit deeper than you imagine, my son," he continues, his voice quieter now. "I've been in contact with high-level officials in Russia. Your problem is coming from within."

I narrow my eyes. "What do you mean?"

"Your siblings," he states bluntly. "One of them is behind this. Feeding incorrect information to the authorities and trying to bring you down from the inside."

The realization hits hard. I never suspected betrayal and definitely not from my family. "You're sure?"

He nods. "I wouldn't have interfered otherwise. Who stands to gain the most from your downfall?"

I run a hand over my face, trying to process everything. "Natalia was going to loan me the money and she wanted seventy percent of all my wealth in return."

He frowns. "I was wrong. You were right to go your own way. I see that now. I was too proud, too angry. Instead of keeping the family together, I split it. I'm sorry. I want things to be different between us."

"Why now?"

"Because despite everything, you're still my son," he says simply. "And whether you admit it or not, you need my help. And because I missed you."

His words are a punch to the gut—truth wrapped in the pain of years of distance. "I don't know what to say."

He takes another sip of his cognac, his gaze softening just a fraction. "You don't have to say anything, Ivan. Just remember who you are—and don't lose that, no matter what they try to take from you."

I feel a strange, unfamiliar warmth—a small crack in the cold armor I've worn for so long. "Thank you," I manage, my voice raw.

He nods as if that's all he needed to hear. "Now, go back to her," he says quietly. "You've found someone worth fighting for. Don't lose her in this mess."

Chapter Fifty-One

LARA

I walk into the house, my mind still buzzing from the meeting with Ivan's father. Relief floods through me—finally, after everything, he has the money. I can't wait to tell Ivan, to see the look on his face when I let him know that the crisis is over. He probably already knows. I imagine his father called him. I wonder, though, how he will react. Is what I did truly a good thing, given their strained relationship?

I am so occupied by my thoughts that I am startled to see Nikolai standing by the window with his back to me. I wasn't expecting him, and the sight of him sends a strange chill down my spine.

"Nikolai?" I call out, feeling a mix of surprise and confusion. "What's wrong? What are you doing here?"

He turns around, a neutral expression on his face. "I heard you met my father," he says calmly. "Just wanted to see how things are going."

I feel a strange knot forming in my stomach. Nikolai's gaze is different—more intense, filled with something I can't quite name. I try to shake off the feeling, reminding myself how supportive and amiable he was in France even though Ivan treated him so dismissively. For god's sake, we laughed and danced together. Sometimes, I'm so foolish, imagining all kinds of terrible things about good people.

"I'm fine," I say with a big happy smile. "Thanks to you I have some good news and I was actually about to call Ivan with it."

"Good news?" he repeats, taking a small step closer. "What kind of good news?"

His tone is deceptively casual, but there's a hint of urgency beneath it.

I hesitate, suddenly unsure of how much to reveal, but he is Ivan's brother. And he's going to find out anyway. Plus, he should be happy. He was instrumental in it. If he had not given me the number, I would never have known how to contact Ivan's father. Maybe now the family can stop the big feud. "Well, after you gave me your father's number, I went to see him and he agreed to help. Ivan has the funds to pay back the bank now."

He blinks with surprise. His eyes flicker with something sharper. "You really did that?" he asks, his voice low. "Went to all that trouble for Ivan?"

His tone catches me off guard. "Of course," I reply, trying to make it sound simple, even though the act itself was anything but. "He needed help, and I care about him."

His jaw tightens at my words. "You care about him," he repeats slowly, as if tasting the bitterness of it. "You've known him for how long? A couple of weeks?"

I frown, confused by the sudden shift. "Why does it matter how long, Nikolai? He needed help, and I did what I could."

He takes another step closer, his gaze intense. "You've seen how cold and business-like he is, Lara," he presses. "You've even seen the way he treats me. But you're here, risking everything for him. Why?"

There's an unexpected vulnerability in his question, a desperate need to understand.

"Because he's worth it," I say softly. "Underneath all the coldness, he's—"

"A broken man," Nikolai interjects, his voice sharp. "One who uses people and then discards them."

My chest tightens at the accusation. "That's not true," I insist. "He's been honest with me."

He laughs, a short, bitter sound. "Honest? You really believe that?" He steps closer again, his presence almost threatening, his eyes searching mine and his voice taunting. "I know Ivan better than you ever could. You think he's changed? You think you've reached him?"

He just crossed a line right there, and he's pissing me off. "Truthfully, Nikolai, I appreciate your concern, but none of this is any of your business."

His expression softens, a hint of something like regret in his eyes. "Lara, I've seen how this goes. I've seen him with other women. He makes you feel special, makes you believe you matter... but it never lasts."

I don't respond.

"He made you sign a contract, didn't he?"

I freeze.

He steps closer, his hand reaching out to touch my arm, the gesture surprisingly gentle. "I knew it. You don't have to be another one of his casualties," he murmurs. "You deserve better."

I pull away, confused and shocked. "Nikolai, stop. I don't need saving."

"Yes, you do," he insists, his voice urgent now. "You don't

see what I see. Ivan will leave you broken, and I don't want that for you."

"Nikolai, you're stressing me out," I say coldly. "None of this is necessary, and frankly, I don't know why you're doing this. What's between me and Ivan is private and not anybody else's business."

"I am in love with you," he confesses, his voice raw. "I've loved you since the moment I saw you."

The words land like a punch to the gut, and I take a step back. "What?"

"Yes, I'm in love with you," he repeats earnestly.

"You don't know me," I manage to say in complete disbelief. "How can you be in love with someone who you don't know?"

"That's why I am here," he says, stepping forward. "So you can give us a chance before it's too late. I'm not denying myself the woman I love because Ivan got there first. I was so happy when you called this morning, you have no idea."

"Nikolai, this is insane," I say, but the fear is rising now. His eyes are dark, almost feverish.

"It's not insane," he insists. "It's real. You and I, we could be happy—far away from Ivan, from all of this."

I shake my head. "I won't leave him."

His face contorts with anger. "Then you leave me no choice," he says coldly. "If you don't come with me, I'll kill him."

The threat sends a wave of terror crashing over me. At first, I am sure he is joking, but when I see the look in his eyes I know that he is not. "What are you talking about?"

His voice is chillingly calm. "I've planted a bomb in his car. If you don't come with me now, he dies."

I try to keep my composure, even as panic rises within me. "You're lying."

"Do you really want to take that chance?" he counters, his voice low and menacing, as he takes a black device out of his pocket. "All I have to do is press this button and... boom! They'll have to scrape him off the tarmac."

I force myself to swallow the terror that's threatening to choke me. "Fine," I say, my voice barely audible, shaky with a mix of fear and desperation. "I'll come with you. Just... let me leave a note for Ivan."

He narrows his eyes, suspicious but seemingly satisfied for now. "Make it quick," he snaps, his tone sharp, but I catch a flicker of something—triumph, maybe? He thinks he's won.

I take a shaky breath and turn toward the dining table, reaching for a notepad and pen, my mind racing. Every fiber of me is screaming for a way out, for something that could save Ivan. My hands tremble as I pick up the pen, but I try to steady them, knowing that any sign of hesitation could tip Nikolai off.

"Lara," he warns, his voice suddenly low and dangerous. "No tricks."

I glance over my shoulder, forcing a hollow smile. "No tricks. You have a bomb," I say, managing to keep my tone flat. I begin writing the note, my hand moving quickly:

> I'm leaving. I can't do this anymore. It's over. Lara

My heart aches with each stroke, and I can feel the panic building, the fear that this might be the last thing Ivan ever reads from me. But even as I write my eyes dart around the room, searching for something, anything I can use. My gaze lands on the small silver salt shaker on the sideboard, and an idea strikes me—one that's risky, but it's the only chance I have.

Nikolai's attention wavers, his eyes flicking toward the

window, as if he's making sure everything outside is clear. His momentary distraction gives me the opening I need. As I set down the pen, I reach for the salt shaker with my other hand, trying to keep my movements slow and unsuspicious. I twist the top off, my heart pounding in my chest, and spill a thin line of salt on the dark wood of the dining table.

My fingers shake as I carefully trace the words into the spilt salt:

It's Niko

Each letter is a desperate plea for Ivan to understand. My pulse thunders in my ears, and I glance back at Nikolai, who's pacing now and speaking furiously in Russian to someone on his phone., his back turned to me.

"Lara!" he barks suddenly, making me jump. "Let's go."

The sound of his voice snaps me back, and I hastily place the salt shaker back on the sideboard, trying to look calm. "I'm ready," I say, my voice firmer than before, despite the fear still clawing at me.

"Show me the note," he orders.

I hold it out to him.

His eyes flick over the words, then puts it on the dining table. For a couple of heart-stopping seconds, he watches me, suspicion lurking in his gaze. I hold my breath, terrified he might notice the salt on the sideboard. Muriel keeps the place so spotless it sticks out like a sore thumb, but he nods, his expression cold, and gestures toward the door.

We head out to the car, and I force myself to keep walking, each step feeling like a betrayal. I glance back at the house, hoping, praying that Ivan sees the message in time.

As soon as we reach the car, Nikolai yanks open the door

and gestures for me to get inside. "Take off your jewelry," he orders, his voice harsh. "All of it."

I fumble with my necklace, hands shaking. The pendant Ivan gave me—the one with the tracker—hangs heavily in my grasp. I remember his warning: If you're ever in danger, swallow it. The words echo in my mind as I look at Nikolai, his eyes cold, unyielding.

"Do it," he insists, growing impatient.

I bring the pendant to my lips, feigning difficulty in unclasping it. I steal one last look at Nikolai's distracted gaze, then take a deep breath and swallow it, feeling the cold metal slide down my throat. It's the most desperate thing I've ever done, but it's the only hope I have left.

He glares at me, noticing my slow movements. "Hurry up," he barks. "We don't have all day."

I quickly remove my earrings and bracelet, tossing them out of the window as he demands. He doesn't seem to notice anything unusual, too focused on navigating the traffic.

As the car starts moving, I fight to keep my composure, knowing that this could be my only chance to signal Ivan. The feeling of the pendant still lingers in my throat, uncomfortable but also strangely reassuring. I cling to that small bit of hope, praying that he's already searching for me, that he's following the tracker.

"Relax," Nikolai says suddenly, his voice low and deceptively gentle. "This is for the best."

I turn my head to face him, my voice barely a whisper as I respond. "You're insane."

He just smirks, his eyes glinting with cold certainty. "One day, you'll thank me."

But I don't believe him—not for a second.

Chapter Fifty-Two

IVAN

I feel an unusual sense of lightness as I drive back home. Lara's courage with my father impresses and touches me—she went beyond anything I could have expected, risking her pride, maybe even her safety, to help me. There's an urgency in my chest, a desperate need to get back to her, hold her and thank her properly for what she did. I can't remember the last time I felt this... grateful, or this all-encompassing love for another human being.

She's changed everything.

The thought of seeing her lovely face brings a rare smile to my own, one that lingers even as I reach the front door. I step inside, expecting to hear her soft footsteps or maybe find her waiting for me in the living room. Instead, the house is unsettlingly quiet.

"Lara?" I call out, my voice echoing through the empty rooms.

I head to the living room, glancing around. Everything looks normal, but there's a gnawing feeling in my gut. That's when I see the note on the coffee table with my name written hastily across the front. I snatch it up, and as my eyes skim over the words, my chest tightens:

I'm leaving. I can't do this anymore. It's over. Lara.

Instantly, I know this is not her. My grip on the paper tightens. My Lara would never leave like this. This is the work of a coward or someone being held against her will. Panic flares as I scan the room again, desperately searching for something —anything—that could explain what's going on.

That's when I see it. The salt spilt on the dining table. I run to it. A message is scrawled in the salt on the dining table. *It's Niko.* The air leaves my lungs in a rush. What the hell has he done?

My hands are trembling as I pull up the tracker app, my heart pounding erratically as the signal blinks—she's moving north. My father owns a derelict warehouse in that area. He was hoping to get planning permission to develop it but it was turned down by the city officials, so he decided to keep it empty until there was a change of administration. I feel sure that is where he is heading. There's no time to think. No time to lose. I sprint toward the door, dialing my head of security on the way.

"Get every available man to my location," I bark into the phone, already running toward the car. "We're tracking Lara's signal. Go now. I think she's being taken to the old cotton mill warehouse. Be careful. He might be armed."

He doesn't ask questions. He simply responds, "On it."

I jump into the driver's seat, slamming the door shut. Engine roaring and tires screeching, I tear out of the garage. Adrenaline courses through me, propelling me forward. I weave through traffic recklessly, swerving between cars, my knuckles white on the steering wheel. I press the gas harder, pushing past the speed limit, past the point of reason. I have to get to her. I have to save her.

My breaths come in sharp bursts, each one shallow and ragged. My chest tightens with every second that passes, and the thought of what Nikolai could be doing to Lara makes my blood run cold.

I hit the car's Bluetooth. "I want visuals. Keep her tracker active," I order, hearing the click of radios on the other end as my security team coordinates.

"ETA in three minutes," one of them confirms, the calm professionalism comforting me, but three minutes feels like an eternity.

The signal from Lara's tracker finally stops moving, settling on a location. As I guessed, at my father's abandoned warehouse. I slam my foot on the brake as I reach the address, skidding to a stop just outside the looming structure. I can hear the hum of other engines pulling up behind me—my guards arriving, the sound of doors slamming shut as they jump out.

"Cover all exits," I shout, leaping out of my car. "But leave Nikolai to me."

My heart is hammering as I charge toward the entrance, fury searing through my veins. I don't wait for backup, don't hesitate—I kick open the door and storm inside. The cold air hits me like a slap, but I barely feel it.

"Lara!" I shout, my voice reverberating through the hollow building. There's no response. My steps echo against the concrete floors, the dark, empty space amplifying the urgency in my chest.

Suddenly, I hear a muffled cry, faint but distinct. Lara. I sprint toward the sound, every fiber of me focused on finding her. I crash through a rusted metal door, and that's when I see them.

Nikolai has her pinned against a wall, his hands rough and ugly, and Lara's face is contorted with terror. The sight sends a surge of rage through me, a blinding, murderous rage.

"Get the fuck off her!" I roar, charging toward him like a man possessed.

Nikolai spins around, his face contorting with surprise.

I don't give him a second to recover. I slam into him, ripping him away from Lara with virulent vindictiveness. He stumbles back, and I seize the opening, landing a vicious punch straight to his face. His head snaps to the side, and I watch his blood spray from his nose and satisfaction courses through me.

"Ivan!" Lara's voice is hoarse and desperate, but I can't tear my eyes away from Nikolai.

"You fucking piece of shit," I snarl, shoving him against the wall. I grab him by the throat, squeezing hard. "You dare touch her?" My words are barely coherent, each syllable seething with rage.

He wheezes, trying to claw at my hand, but I tighten my grip, feeling his skin slick with sweat. He throws a wild punch, but it's weak, a pathetic attempt to defend himself. I slam him against the wall again, the impact shaking the metal wall.

"You fucking coward," I hiss, my face inches from his. "You think you can just take what you want?" I ram my knee into his stomach, feeling the air rush out of him.

Nikolai crumples to the ground, gasping for breath, but I'm not finished. I kick him in the ribs, hard, relishing the way he groans in pain. "This is just the beginning," I promise, my voice low and menacing. "You're going to pay for every lie, every betrayal."

"Fuck you," he spits, blood dripping from his mouth. He

tries to stand, but I punch him again, harder, feeling the satisfying crack of bone beneath my knuckles.

"Ivan, stop!" Lara cries, her voice desperate, but I barely hear her. All I can see is Nikolai's face, twisted with fear and defiance. I grab him by the collar, pulling him close.

"You're going to confess," I growl, my voice shaking with fury. I want to finish him off right here, but that would be stupid. I have too much to lose. "To everything. Or I swear I'll make your death slow and agonizing."

His eyes flicker with fear for the first time, and I know he believes me. He knows I'm capable of every promise I make.

"Get him out of here," I order, shoving him toward my security detail. "And don't let him out of your sight."

They grab him and restrain him quickly, and I turn back to Lara. She's collapsed on the floor, her body shaking with sobs. My heart wrenches at the sight of her in a heap. I kneel beside her, my voice breaking.

"It's okay," I whisper, pulling her into my arms. "It's over. You're safe now."

She clings to me, her fingers digging into my skin as if afraid I'll disappear. I hold her tighter, pressing my lips to her forehead, desperate to reassure her.

"I'm sorry," I say, my voice raw and filled with regret. "I'm so fucking sorry."

We don't waste any more time. I carry her out of the warehouse, cradling her against my chest, and load her into my car. I drive with one hand, the other gripping hers tightly, feeling her trembling lessen as we speed away.

When we reach home, I don't say a word as I lead her inside. Her body is covered in dirt and the remnants of Nikolai's violation, and I can see the disgust in her eyes. I take her to the bathroom and turn on the shower, the sound of the water somehow comforting.

"Come here," I say softly, helping her step inside.

The warm spray cascades over us, steam filling the small space. Lara's body is tense at first, but I wrap my arms around her, holding her close. I can feel her start to relax, the water washing away the grime, the fear.

"Ivan," she whispers, her voice barely audible. Her eyes are wide, haunted.

"I love you," I say, the words coming out rough and desperate. "I fucking love you, Lara. When I thought I lost you. When I thought—"

Her lips cut me off, crashing against mine with a frantic need. I respond instantly, the kiss deepening, becoming something raw and fierce. We shed the soaked clothes between kisses, our hands frantic, searching. Her skin is warm under my touch, slick with water, and I feel an overwhelming desire to reclaim every part of her that Nikolai tried to take.

Our kisses grow slower, more tender, as the urgency fades into something deeper. I trace my hands along her body, exploring every curve, every tiny little scar. She shudders under my touch, and I feel her press closer, her need mirroring mine.

We sink down under the spray, the warm water cocooning us as we move together, our bodies finding a rhythm that is slow, intense, and filled with a desperate kind of love. I kiss every inch of her skin, each touch a silent promise.

Lara's eyes meet mine. "Did you always have contracts for all the other women you wanted to... sleep with?"

I frown. "Never. You are the first. Why do you ask?"

She shakes her head. "Nothing. Just something Nikolai said."

My jaw tightens. "If he knew about our contract then he must have got the information from Greta."

"She hates me."

"Then she has no place in my organization. She will get her marching orders first thing in the morning."

For the first time, I see the fear in her eyes completely fade. There's trust there too, a fragile but undeniable connection that's survived the chaos.

"I won't let anyone hurt you again," I whisper, my voice thick with emotion. "Not ever. I love you, Lara Fitzpatrick. With all my heart."

She nods, her fingers threading through my hair, pulling me closer. "And I love you, Ivan Ivanovich."

And everything is perfect in my world.

Epilogue

IVAN

The priest begins the ceremony, his words a gentle hum in the background. I can barely focus on anything other than the woman beside me, her hand warm and steady in mine. We exchange vows, our voices low and filled with raw emotion.

"Ivan," Lara says, her voice breaking slightly, "I promise to stand by you, through every battle, every storm. You've shown me a love I never thought possible."

My chest tightens. I reach for her hand, squeezing it gently. "Lara," I murmur, my voice rough with sincerity, "you brought me back from the edge. You taught me what it means to truly care for someone, to trust, to hope. I vow to protect you, always, and to love you with everything I have."

The ceremony feels too short, each moment a blur of love and anticipation. When the priest finally announces us as husband and wife, I waste no time. I pull her close, our lips meeting in a kiss that's as passionate as it is tender, sealing our promise in front of everyone who matters. My father, my mother, Lara's father, my sister, my loyal staff who have become rich beyond their wildest dreams, and some friends. No Nikolai though.

He has absconded to Russia. He can never come back to the States as there is a warrant out for his arrest. One phone call and he would be in custody, but I'm not revengeful. I have everything and he has nothing. I know now that it was jealousy that made him try to destroy me. He hated that my father loved me more and I had become a billionaire on my own merit.

As we walk back down the aisle, hand in hand, there's an unexpected lightness in my step. The faces around us blur into a sea of smiles and tears, and I can only focus on Lara—my wife.

We step out of the church, the bright sun warming our faces. The guests cheer, showering us with rose petals and rice, their voices filled with joy. I turn to Lara and my heart is so full it feels as if it might burst.

"You did it," I whisper, my hand resting on her cheek. "You saved me."

She laughs softly, her eyes shining with unshed tears. "We saved each other."

We make our way to the beribboned vintage Rolls waiting to whisk us away, but before I open the door, Lara pauses, her expression shifting. There's a nervousness in her eyes, something unspoken lingering between us.

"What is it?" I ask, concerned.

She takes a deep breath, her hand finding mine. "Ivan... there's something I need to tell you."

I frown. "What is it? Are you okay?"

She looks up at me, her eyes bright and filled with a mix of fear and excitement. "I'm pregnant."

Time stops. The words hang in the air, heavy with meaning. I stare at her, disbelief and joy colliding inside me. "You... you're pregnant?" I manage to say, my voice hoarse.

She nods, a small smile breaking through her nervousness. "Yes. I found out a few days ago, but I wanted to be sure before I told you."

A wave of pure, unfiltered joy washes over me. I can't contain it. With a laugh, I lift her off the ground, spinning her around as she laughs with me. "We're having a baby," I say, my voice choking with emotion. "We're going to be parents, Lara."

She laughs through her tears, holding onto me tightly. "Yes, we are. And you're going to be an amazing father."

I set her down gently, cupping her face with both hands. "I can't believe this," I say, pressing my forehead to hers. "I never thought I could be this happy."

Lara smiles, her eyes filled with love. "We deserve this, Ivan. After everything... we deserve to be happy."

I kiss her again, slowly and deeply, pouring every ounce of love and gratitude into that moment. It's not just a kiss of passion; it's a promise, a vow to be the man she needs, the father our child deserves.

As we climb into the car, ready to drive toward the future ahead, I steal one last glance at the church behind us. I think of everything that's brought us here—the betrayals, the battles, the love that refused to break, no matter how hard the world tried to tear it apart.

I take Lara's hand, intertwining our fingers, and she leans her head on my shoulder. "Are you ready for this?" I ask, my voice soft.

She looks up at me, her eyes clear and certain. "With you, Ivan? Always."

And as we drive away, leaving the past behind, I know one thing for certain: This is just the beginning.

. . .

That's all Folks!

Coming Soon...

TWISTED LOVE
Chapter 1

Earl

The lilies reek.

I fucking hate lilies.

I learned to hate them because of her.

Their strong sweet cloying perfume used to suffocate her and make her feel faint. The church looks like a glamorous winter woodland, but it doesn't fool me. Not for one second. Nothing about this charade does.

Clearly the bride had no say in her own wedding arrangements.

But I know who did. Her new mother-in-law, the high and mighty Mrs. Evelyn Bellafonte, sitting in the front pew in her Chanel two-piece cream suit, her back ramrod straight, absolutely furious that her beloved son is marrying beneath him. Well, I might be able to help there...

COMING SOON...

I'm sitting in the last pew of that cold, perfectly beautiful Church, farthest from the altar and I can't take my eyes off the blushing bride.

Raven Moore stands with her head bowed under a delicate veil, the soft lace spilling over her shoulders. Her dress fits her perfectly. It is elegant and understated, exactly what she dreamed about when we were dirt poor kids living in a caravan park. When she used to talk about this day like it was some kind of magical fairytale ending. Back then, fool that I was, I pictured it too.

Only in my version, I was the one standing beside her. Because I believed her. I believed we were one. No one and nothing could separate us. No even Death. Our love would last even beyond the grave.

'If I should die first, I will haunt you until you join me,' I vowed.

'I wouldn't have any other way,' she whispered fiercely.

I stare at her now and my fists clench into blocks of hate. He lifts her veil and I want to rush forward and knock his hand away. I hate her, but she is mine. Not yet, I remind myself as I watch her get ready to say her vows to a man, I'm sure she has no feelings for. Why? Because she is a gold digger. A beautiful liar. She can always be counted on to sell herself to the highest bidder. That is her downfall and perhaps it will be mine too. But I'm already dead inside. All that is left is my need for revenge. It eats at me, sharp and unrelenting, day and night. Follows me into my nightmares.

My gaze shifts to Charles Bellafonte, the proud groom.

He stands tall, too smug for his own good, a handmade suit clinging to his shoulders like armor. His hand hovers close to hers, brushing against her fingers like he already owns her. His mouth is curved in that signature smirk, the one that used to make me want to wipe it off his face with a fucking baseball bat.

He hasn't changed.

I haven't changed either. I still want to rip that smug look off his face and crush it beneath my heel until there's nothing left.

My jaw clenches so hard it aches.

And Raven... she just stands there. Her head is still bowed as if she can't bear to look at him. Or maybe she's trying to hide her misery. Good, I hope she feels miserable. She deserves to.

Why shouldn't she feel as hollow and broken as I've done since the day I stood behind her door and heard her say the words I will forget as long as I live?

Sure, he's a good kisser, but he has no prospects. A loser. A grease monkey. I'm only with him temporarily. As soon as I find someone with money—real money—I'm ditching him.

The words slam into me like they did back then, cutting deeper than they have any right to after all these years.

Real money. I turn my attention back to Charles. That won't be you, Charles, my boy. His wealth, his status—it's all gone. He's living a big fat lie. He's nothing but a fraud, senselessly blowing up even the last scraps of what his father left behind.

This wedding is lavish, sure, but it's all smoke and mirrors, an illusion created on borrowed dime. Charles pulled every string, cut every corner, scraped the bottom of the barrel to make this happen. All for her. To keep her. To fool her into thinking he's still the man she thinks he is. Ha, ha, Raven is about to experience the biggest disappointment of her life.

I should allow her to walk right into this with her eyes shut. Marry a man who can't give her the life he promised, who will disappoint her every day for the rest of her life. But no. That's not enough pain for her. No, that is not enough. Raven Moore must suffer at my hands.

Watching her realize she traded me for a pampered poodle won't fill the void. I am here to wreak havoc. For Charles, it'll be the humiliation of everyone knowing he's nothing but a fraud. For Raven, it'll be longer, slower, and I'll have the front-row seat to every moment of it.

The priest's voice echoes through the church.

"If anyone has an objection to this union, speak now or forever hold your peace."

My chest tightens. It's time.

The priest smiles and then clears his throat, the small sound amplified by the silence of the room. His voice is steady as he speaks, ready to move them one step closer to saying their vows.

"Since no one has an objection to this union...

The words hang in the air, thick and heavy, settling over the crowd.

My heart pounds, steady and deliberate. My breath slows.

This is it.

I push to my feet, the pew beneath me creaking softly. All at once, the air shifts. A collective gasp ripples through the congregation. Every head swivels toward me.

The tall, dark man in black. That's what they'll whisper later, the stranger who stood at the back of the church and shattered their perfect illusion.

My voice is calm, clear, and deliberate as I speak. "I object."

Raven's head snaps up, her hazel eyes rush towards me. How long I've waited for this moment. They widen in shock as her lips part in a gasp of dismay.

And in that moment, for the first time in years, she sees the monster she has created.

Enjoyed the sample? :)
Pre-order the book here:
TWISTED LOVE

About the Author

If you wish to leave a review for this book
please do so here:
Devil In A Suit

Please click on this link to receive news of my latest releases
and great giveaways.
Georgia's Newsletter

and remember
I **LOVE** hearing from readers so by all means come and say
hello here:

Also by Georgia Le Carre

Owned

42 Days

Besotted

Seduce Me

Love's Sacrifice

Masquerade

Pretty Wicked (novella)

Disfigured Love

Hypnotized

Crystal Jake 1,2&3

Sexy Beast

Wounded Beast

Beautiful Beast

Dirty Aristocrat

You Don't Own Me 1 & 2

You Don't Know Me

Blind Reader Wanted

Redemption

The Heir

Blackmailed By The Beast

Submitting To The Billionaire

The Bad Boy Wants Me

Nanny & The Beast

His Frozen Heart
The Man In The Mirror
A Kiss Stolen
Can't Let Her Go
Highest Bidder
Saving Della Ray
Nice Day For A White Wedding
With This Ring
With This Secret
Saint & Sinner
Bodyguard Beast
Beauty & The Beast
The Other Side of Midnight
The Russian Billionaire
CEO's Revenge
Mine To Possess
Heat Of The Moment
Boss From Hell
Sweet Poison
The Guardian
Fight Me, Little Pearl

Printed in Great Britain
by Amazon